ONE DAY AND FOREVER

SHARI LOW

Boldwood

First published in Great Britain in 2025 by Boldwood Books Ltd.

Cover Design by Alice Moore Design

Cover Images: Shutterstock and iStock

A CIP catalogue record for this book is available from the British Library.

Paperback ISBN 978-1-83518-470-7

Large Print ISBN 978-1-83518-471-4

Hardback ISBN 978-1-83518-469-1

Ebook ISBN 978-1-83518-472-1

Kindle ISBN 978-1-83518-473-8

Audio CD ISBN 978-1-83518-464-6

MP3 CD ISBN 978-1-83518-465-3

Digital audio download ISBN 978-1-83518-468-4

This book is printed on certified sustainable paper. Boldwood Books is dedicated to putting sustainability at the heart of our business. For more information please visit https://www.boldwoodbooks.com/about-us/sustainability/

Boldwood Books Ltd, 23 Bowerdean Street, London, SW6 3TN

www.boldwoodbooks.com

This book is dedicated to every single member of the spectacular Boldwood Books team... working with you all is truly the highlight of my career.

Special thanks to Caroline Ridding, Amanda Ridout, Nia Beynon and Claire Fenby-Warren, who are the best support and inspiration a writer could have. And to Jade Craddock and Rose Fox for making sure the words make sense.

And a huge, heartfelt thanks to the wonderful readers who have made this, my 25th year as a writer, the most special one yet. I am so grateful to you all.

Love, Shari x

A NOTE FROM SHARI...

Dear you,

Thank you so much for choosing this book. I hope that you'll love meeting Alice, Zac, Kara and Ollie on a day that changed all of their lives.

This is a standalone story, and can be read completely on its own, but some of my characters do like to pop up in more than one book. In *One Day and Forever*, those characters are Alice and Val. If you've read *One Long Weekend*, you'll already know the story of how they became friends, but if not, and you're curious to read their backstory, that's where you'll find it.

There are also little cameo appearances by the lovely Tress, from *One Day With You* and *One Year After You*, and the wonderful Bernadette, from One Last Day of Summer.

And the scandalous world of the original movie franchise that inspired Ollie's role as an actor on the spin-off TV show about sixteenth-century Scots called *The Clansman*, can be found in *The Rise*, *The Catch* and *The Fall*, the gritty, glam Hollywood thrillers I wrote with my pal, TV presenter Ross King.

In the meantime, thanks again for choosing *One Day and*

Forever. It's the first of three books that will be released in 2025, so if you'd like to hear all about what's coming next, please look me up on Facebook or Instagram, or sign up to my newsletter at www.sharilow.com.

Much love,

Shari x

ON THIS DAY WE MEET…

Kara McIntyre – In the last week she has quit her job as costume designer at the Clydeside TV Studio, called off her wedding and moved out of the flat she shared with her fiancé, Josh. 2025 isn't starting off well.

Drea McIntyre – Kara's older sister. Owner of upmarket travel concierge service, just days away from her dream destination wedding to Seb Canning, the love of her life.

Josh Jackson – Kara's now ex-fiancé. Director of the PR company that represents the Clydeside TV Studio.

Jacinta McIntyre – Kara and Drea's mother, free spirit, former actress, afficionado of floaty chiffon outerwear and all things luvvie.

Corbin Jacobs – Lead actor on the soap, *The Clydeside*, lecherous arse and root of all Kara's professional woes.

Ollie Chiles – Kara's best friend, born and bred in Glasgow, now lives in LA after shooting to stardom when he landed a major role in *The Clansman*, an American TV spin-off of the movie franchise of the same name, watched by millions across the globe.

Sienna Montgomery – Ollie's wife (she kept her maiden name when they married), born in LA, actress and former Disney teen star, now navigating the bumpy world of the New York stage.

Moira Chiles – Ollie's mum, a former pub and club crooner, now a cabaret singer on cruise ships. Been known to declare that she has the best set of pipes ever to come out of Glasgow. Although, she'll concede under pressure that Lulu comes close.

Calvin Fraser – Semi-retired entertainment manager, prides himself on his grooming standards, his patience, and his ability to survive almost forty years in the shark-infested waters of the film and TV industry.

Alice Brookes – Recently reverted to her maiden name after finally escaping almost thirty years of marriage to notorious corrupt politician Larry McLenn. Currently living in her friend Val's spare room.

Val Murray – Widow, mum, gran, force of nature, friend and nucleus of a group of kick-ass women who lift each other up with love, support and an ever-present biscuit tin.

Zac Corlan – Family law solicitor specialising in divorce, only child, born in Dublin to Scottish mum, Morag, and Irish dad, Cillian.

Cillian Corlan – Zac's father, owner of a construction company, still mourning the loss of his wife, Morag, who passed away almost a year ago.

PROLOGUE

KARA

Glasgow Airport – 2 January 2019

Kara squinted at the departures board on the far wall of the bar and wondered why the weather gods had decided to mess with her route, while the rest of the world was bang on schedule. Iceland was preparing to board. As was Palma. If she was going for a jolly to Helsinki, she'd be taxiing towards the runway. Everywhere else was peachy, except her forty-five-minute jaunt to Dublin that had already been delayed for over an hour. Bloody fog at Dublin airport, apparently. According to the nice lady at the check-in desk, nothing had been able to land there all afternoon. There was no word on when it would clear, but Kara feared if they didn't get called soon, she was going to miss her onward flight to New York. She'd booked that route because there was an American immigration service in Dublin airport that allowed travellers to clear US passport control there and avoid the massive queues at JFK, but now it was backfiring like her clapped-out Mini.

Karma. That's what this was. The gods of pissed-off

boyfriends were trying to teach her a lesson. Josh had told her repeatedly that going to New York for three days for her best friend, Ollie's wedding was a ridiculously stupid idea, but she'd been adamant that she was going, and it had blown up into a huge fight which had ended with her storming out. Which would have been a really dramatic exit, if she hadn't then had to mooch back into their Glasgow city-centre flat to collect her bag and her carry-on luggage. Even so, she'd been proud of herself for sticking to her plan, but look where it had got her. Delayed. Stuck. Panicking that she might not make it.

'Another drink?' the waiter asked as he passed her, clutching a tray laden with pints of lager for a nearby table of ten whose T-shirts advertised that they were going on SHUGGIES STAG – CARBS ALL THE WAY TO MARBS.

Okay, one more drink while she contemplated the misfortune of the situation. 'You read my mind.'

It was barely out of her mouth when a rousing cheer went up from Shuggie and his fellow revellers at the arrival of more liquid joviality. She wished she could share in their merriment, but right now the only high spirits she could muster were being served by the waiter.

The departures board flickered, and she watched as the numbers on the screen changed. Dublin. Now delayed until 20.15. Bloody hell. It was only four o'clock. There was no chance she was getting out from Dublin to New York tonight unless there was a really late flight to JFK that they could bump her to. Maybe she should just call it a day now, give up, go home, admit to Josh that he was right and then call Ollie in the Manhattan apartment he shared with his fiancée, Sienna, to tell him that she wouldn't make the nuptials, and he was going to have to find another Best Person. Yeah, that's what she should do. Concede defeat. Take the hit.

Only... nope, she couldn't. Because Ollie Chiles had been her best mate since she was three years old, and she wasn't going to miss his wedding if she could help it. Even though this flight had fired her credit card up to the limit, even though her feet would barely touch the NYC sidewalks because she had to be back at work on Monday, even though her boyfriend thoroughly disapproved of the whole trip and even if the prospect of meeting his world-famous fiancée, actress Sienna Montgomery, was more than a little terrifying. It was still bizarre to her that Ollie was marrying someone they used to see on TV when they were in high school and would watch American teen shows while they pretended to do their homework.

'Excuse me, do you mind if I sit here? The only other free seat is with that group over there,' he pointed to Shuggie's crew, 'and I don't have the T-shirt.'

The Irish accent cut right through her thoughts, making her raise her gaze from the pits of frustration, up denim-clad legs, to a black T-shirt and a thick Columbia padded jacket, then on up to the embarrassed expression of a guy who was drop dead... ordinary. Attractive, kind of. If this was a romcom, he would look like Channing Tatum or Zac Efron, but instead, it was just a tall, perfectly pleasing dark-haired, blue-eyed bloke with an embarrassed but hopeful expression.

Kara glanced around and saw that every other table was indeed occupied – probably due to the flight delay and the hectic post-holiday period. There was always a huge influx of tourists to Scotland for the New Year celebrations and it felt like most of them were now crammed into this bar as they headed for home.

'Of course. Sure. I'm a bit gutted I don't have one of those T-shirts myself. Although, if my flight gets delayed any longer, I'm going with them and I'll drown my sorrows in Marbs.'

She was aware that a simple, 'No, I don't mind,' would have

sufficed, but oversharing was her biggest vice. If a taxi driver, waitress in a café, or a little old lady on a bus struck up a conversation with her, she was immediately locked in, and they were best friends by the time they parted ways.

Credit to him, her unmistakably weary mutterings didn't seem to faze him. Nor did the fact that she was now being given a large glass of wine by the waiter, whose expression remained completely non-judgemental as he removed the two empty wine glasses that were already loitering on the table. Before she'd even taken a sip, Kara felt her cheeks flush at the prospect of a third large wine in two hours. That would normally be the halfway point to a family-size packet of cheesy crisps and a heartfelt rendition of Robbie Williams' 'Angels', so she should probably call it a day after this one. In the meantime, she ran an internal monologue, ordering her gob to stay closed. *Do not strike up conversation with unsuspecting stranger. Do not invade his peace and quiet. Do not talk nonsense.*

As her new table companion ordered a bottle of beer, she picked up her phone, and acted like she was intently studying something important, while actually scrolling through her Instagram feed, which was peppered with adverts plugging various strategies for self-improvement, countless 'revolutionary' new diet plans, the top ten New Year's resolutions for 2019, must-see NYC tourist attractions, the beginner's guide to tantric sex, training on how to nail a job interview and tips on improving communication in relationships. Even her algorithms had decided that every area of her life needed work.

The new arrival shrugged his jacket off and onto the back of the chair. 'Dublin?'

Okay, so maybe he was the chatty type. Or maybe just being polite.

Kara put her phone face down on the table. 'How did you

guess? Oh. Obvious. I said I was delayed and it's the only one not going out on time. You too?' It wasn't exactly a stab in the dark. The accent – her favourite, thanks to her movie history convincing her that if she were ever trafficked, Liam Neeson would somehow find her.

'Yep. Going home.'

Actually, when he smiled, he climbed many notches up the attractive scale.

Kara pushed the thought from her mind as she picked her phone back up, feeling a surge of dread as she wondered if she should text Ollie and let him know about the delay? There was still time for him to choose another Best Person for his wedding just in case she didn't make it on time. And if he went for the bog-standard Best Man approach, it would probably save him a headache, because Ollie had already let slip that Sienna, his wife-to-be, had already made it perfectly clear she wasn't thrilled about the whole 'female best pal' thing. It was like Julia Roberts and Cameron Diaz in *My Best Friend's Wedding*, but without the Hollywood dental standards. Sienna just didn't understand that she and Ollie had been like brother and sister since they were kids. Their mums were best mates, so they'd pretty much been brought up together, and yes, it was love – just not the kind that involved nudity.

'What about you? What takes you to Ireland?' he asked, then immediately back-pedalled. 'Sorry, I don't want to be that guy who intrudes on your evening, then forces you to make conversation. Feel free to tell me to mind my own business.'

Her shoulders dropped an inch or so, as her 'sod it' gene kicked in. What was her sister, Drea, always saying? Only worry about the things you can control. She was a bit like a walking catalogue of one-line wellbeing quotes, but she had a point.

'I'm just passing through, on the way to New York for my

friend's wedding. My best friend, actually. At least, I was. That might change if I don't get there in time for the "I do" bits.'

'Ouch. I guess she'll be gutted if you don't get there.'

'*He*. It's a bloke. We grew up together. I used to steal his snacks in nursery. His mum made great rice crispie cakes, so it was totally worth it.'

Mr Not Zac Efron gave a sheepish shrug. 'Apologies for the assumption. I bet *he'll* be gutted.'

Kara felt another surge of dread at the prospect of explaining her travel fiasco to Ollie, then changed the subject so she didn't have to dwell on it. 'What about you? Were you in Glasgow for New Year?'

'Did the bloodshot eyes and the obvious dehydration caused by a three-day celebration give it away?'

'I couldn't possibly confirm or deny,' Kara teased him, thinking this was the first time all day she'd smiled and meant it.

'Guilty as charged. I come here every year with my mum. She's originally from Glasgow and visits her family every New Year. She's staying a few more days, but I have to get back to work.'

'Demanding job?' She tried to work out his age and guessed he was somewhere around the same age as her, about twenty-four.

'Lawyer. Almost. Still training but I'll be fully qualified this year.'

That got her attention. 'Serial killers and horrible Netflix crimes that would make me hide behind the couch?'

'Worse. Family law. This is the busiest month of the year for divorces. Sorry – I know that makes me sound cynical, but I promise I'm not. Divorce is a last resort – we try to mediate and solve the problems before anyone signs on the dotted line. I'm

Zac. Pleased to meet you.' That made her smile. So he did have something in common with Mr Efron after all.

'Kara. Same.'

At least the gods of pissed-off boyfriends were now giving her something to take her mind off the pissed-off boyfriend at home, the inevitably pissed-off best friend in New York and her pissed-off self. And then they snatched it away again with an abrupt announcement.

'Attention, all passengers travelling on Flight 2342 to Dublin. Please contact the nearest passenger services desk.'

Kara's shoulders slumped. 'That doesn't sound good.'

'Nope, it doesn't.'

'There's a passenger services desk just across the waiting area there. We should probably...' Kara began, then her words drifted away as a nod out to the main departures area made the point for her. She briefly wondered when they'd become a 'we'. Two and a bit glasses of wine and she was already thinking too deeply about every little thing. That usually happened after at least four.

'Yeah, we should,' he agreed.

They made small talk about the weather, their New Year activities and the inconvenience of the delay while they made their way to the passenger services desk. It wasn't hard to spot. A queue of dissatisfied customers was already forming in front of it.

They slotted in behind two bespectacled blokes who bore an uncanny resemblance to the Proclaimers, which immediately set off a chorus of 'I Would Walk 500 Miles' in Kara's head. Which might be the only journey she was taking tonight, because by the looks of things, she clearly wouldn't be flying.

A groan broke out at the front of the queue and reverberated back towards them, in a relay of passed-on information. The gents in front of them got the info, then turned to them to repeat it. 'Apparently the flight has been cancelled and they're putting us all on another flight tomorrow morning,' one of the almost-Proclaimers told them.

Her first thought? Well, that made the decision for her. There was no way she'd make the wedding now. Bugger. Damn. She'd be as well just giving up on the whole trip.

'So the airline is putting us all up in an airport hotel for the night,' said his look-alike companion.

Her second thought? That wouldn't be necessary for her. She had a perfectly good home to go to only twenty minutes away.

'Just one of those things, I guess,' Zac said, with a shrug. 'Only thing we can do is make the best of it.'

Her third thought? Josh was at home. And he'd be so smug if the gods of pissed-off boyfriends sent her back there tonight. She honestly didn't think she could give him the satisfaction of the win.

'What are you going to do, Kara?' Zac asked.

Her next thought? She liked the way he said her name.

'I guess I'll stay over at the hotel and decide in the morning.'

SIX YEARS LATER...

3 JANUARY 2025

8 A.M. – 10 A.M.

1

KARA MCINTYRE

'If I promise I'll give you all my worldly goods, including my signed Lenny Kravitz poster and a kidney, will you let me out of this? Let me stay in bed for the next two weeks. Please don't make me go to your wedding,' Kara pleaded, but her words were muffled because her head was under one of the pillows on her sister's double bed.

Luckily, her older sibling, Drea's very nice fiancé, Seb, had flown ahead to Hawaii on New Year's Day with his two brothers, to have a mini-stag celebration before they tied the knot, otherwise Kara would have been on the couch for the last two and a half nights. The last two and a half awful, terrible nights, since Kara had quit her job, left her home, and called off her half of what was supposed to be the sisters' beach-front double wedding of their dreams in Honolulu. In their picture of that day, the two sisters would stand side-by-side, both glowing as they promised their futures to the men they'd chosen to spend their lives with. That vision had been shattered in the early hours of the first day of the year, when Kara had made the decision to renege on the forever stuff. Although, in the moment, she hadn't quite thought through the reality that she would still have to attend her sister's nuptials, rubbing salt in the wounds of her newly shattered heart. Today, she and Josh should be flying off to their own 'happily ever after'. Instead, she was under a duvet and would give her Vera Wang white silk gown, her Jimmy Choo bridal shoes, and her diamanté hairband to anyone who would let her stay there.

Kara lifted her head up and squinted open one eye to check that her sister was paying attention. Over at the entrance to her custom walk-in-wardrobe, Drea was carefully slipping a beautiful cream satin dress into a garment protector as she shook her head. 'No. Unlike someone else in this room, I won't call my wedding off, and I can't marry Seb without you there. Even if... you know... You're not doing it too.' She padded across the room in her white furry slippers and sat down on the edge of the bed, taking Kara's hand. 'I promise, you'll thank me later. Babe, I love you. I'm gutted about everything that's happened to you this week and you know I'm here for you...'

The pause made Kara eye her sister suspiciously. She had no doubt that Drea meant those words, but saying them out loud and making touchy-feely demonstrations of affection were definitely not in Drea's playbook, unless they were a warm-up for some frank outpouring of harsh realities. Kara braced herself for the incoming storm.

'But in the meantime,' Drea whipped up the aforementioned storm, 'I don't want to be a total cow, but you need to get your big woman pants on and try not to do anything that'll screw up my wedding even more. So I'm asking you, please, go along with this even though I know it must hurt. And when we come home, I'll dedicate my whole life to making you feel better about what happened. Oh, and Josh is an arse who was never right for you anyway. The man who caused you to quit your job is also an arse.

And it's not fair that your whole life has gone so spectacularly tits up, but I'm proud of you. In case I haven't mentioned that in the last hour.'

Kara didn't have the strength to argue, and besides, Drea did make several valid points, the most pertinent of which was that right now Drea's wedding took precedence over Kara's non-wedding. Especially as Drea had been the one to organise every single detail and turn their dream marital aspirations into a reality. The combination of teenage Drea's Saturday job on the reception of a travel agency and a fondness for *Baywatch* had inspired their mutual, lifelong desire to have a joint beach wedding somewhere exotic. They'd got lucky with the timing, with Drea getting engaged to Seb two years ago, then Kara and Josh following suit not long after. Now Drea ran her own, very successful travel concierge service and she'd immediately kicked into gear, researching, planning, booking, and the result was to be a spectacular joint wedding at sunset on a breathtaking beach in Hawaii.

It had all been perfect. A dream that was coming true, right up until... Kara tried to block the thought. The fact was that three days ago, she was gainfully employed at the Clydeside TV studio, home of *The Clydeside*, Scotland's longest-running, twice weekly soap, managing their costume department, doing a job she adored. Now she was not. And a few minutes past midnight on the first of January, while the rest of the world was celebrating the dawn of the New Year, she'd decided that she could no longer marry Josh Jackson. She'd called off their dream wedding. Called off their future. Moved out of the flat they'd shared, breaking her own heart in the process. The only things that had been keeping her together ever since were the conviction that she'd done the right thing and the contents of Drea's very flash, state-of-the-art wine fridge.

'Now get up and start packing. The taxi will be here to take us to the airport at four o'clock, and it'll take that long to get rid of the bags under your eyes, so let's get cracking.' And there was the sister she knew and adored – all soppy stuff gone, and back to her pragmatic, but brutally honest self.

Kara groaned and rolled over, aware that resistance was futile. Pushing herself up on her elbows, she squinted both eyes open this time. Drea's bedroom was like something out of an Instagram blogger's dreams. The plush white carpet that your toes sank into when you walked – or at least, they would if you were allowed to step on it without spotlessly clean indoor slippers. The cream panelled walls. The arched entrance to the dressing area and the walk-in wardrobe. True, she'd done most of it herself using YouTube videos of IKEA hacks, but still, that took planning, dedication and action, as well as a focus on organisation and aesthetics that Kara just didn't possess. Everything she'd grabbed from home before she left was currently residing in a black bin bag and a battered suitcase that she'd bought for a trip to Ibiza when she graduated from college eight years ago.

'Oh shit, shit, shit. You have got to be joking me.'

Kara sat up properly, immediately latching on to the panic in Drea's voice. 'What's up?'

Drea dragged her gaze from her phone, then marched over to the window and threw her snow-white chenille curtains wide open. Kara had no idea what was happening that would incite the horror on Drea's face. A riot in the streets? A tornado? Aliens landing?

Drea peered up at the sky. 'I just got an alert from the airline – apparently there's reports of adverse weather headed our way. It's saying to make our way to the airport at the normal time, but that there may be delays.'

Kara's mind fleetingly drifted back to a long-buried memory.

Six years ago. A storm. A delay at the airport. It hadn't turned out to be a terrible thing back then. Maybe it wouldn't be so bad now. It would at least give her a bit longer to come to terms with the crap show of her life before she was stuck in a metal tube with hundreds of other people.

Drea wasn't handling the news in the same accepting fashion. 'Buggering bugger. Why can't the world just let me fly to the other side of the globe to marry the man I'm madly in love with?'

Fully awake now, Kara picked up her phone from the bedside table. It had been on silent for two days now and the screen was just a long list of missed calls and texts that had come in over the last forty-eight hours – most of them from Josh, a few from her mother, a couple from her best mate, Ollie. Probably time to think about rejoining the outside world.

She flicked on to her emails for the first time since she'd left the studio on the 31st of December, expecting there to be nothing much more than notifications of January sales from every company she'd bought something from over the last decade. 'Oh bugger. Buggering bugger,' she repeated Drea's words, but for an entirely different reason.

'What?' Drea asked. She'd now resumed packing and was organising her skincare routine into a white beauty box with built-in light that cost more than Kara spent on moisturiser in a year.

'An email came in yesterday from work and I didn't see it until now. I mean, former work.' She checked the name of the sender at the bottom of the communication.

John Stoker
Head of Legal Services

'It's from the legal department at the studio.'

She began reading it aloud.

'Dear Miss McIntyre,

'We have been informed that you resigned your position at the Clydeside Studio, effective 31.12.24. As per company policy, we would request that you attend an exit interview so that we may clarify the circumstances surrounding your decision to resign. We would be grateful if you would meet with myself and Abigail Dunlop, Director of Human Resources, on 3 January at 10.30 a.m. at The Clydeside Studio. Please respond to this email in order to confirm attendance. During this meeting...'

Drea cut her off, defiant. 'Tell them to shove it. You're no longer employed by them, and even if you were, you're on holiday. This time off has been booked for a year.'

'Yes, but... Sod it – I want to hear what they have to say.' In a flurry of flying fingers, Kara shot off a succinct reply.

I will be there.
    Regards,
    Kara McIntyre.

Not exactly *War and Peace*, but it made the point.

Galvanised by something between fear and blind fury, she pushed back the duvet and climbed out of bed.

'The thing is, I know it's too late because I've already burnt that bridge and told them to shove their job, but I want it all done officially and in black and white. They'll only have heard *his* side of the story. I want everyone who wasn't there, including Abigail Scary Knickers Dunlop, to hear mine.'

The 'his' in question was Corbin Jacobs, the lead actor on

The Clydeside and the man who, at The Clydeside New Year's Eve party, had put her in a position that gave her no option but to quit. If anyone listened to the crap he espoused daily, they'd believe he was the next Anthony Hopkins. The reality was he'd been brought in as eye candy replacement for Rex Marino, the previous hot, thirty-something star of the show, who'd fled to the USA after being ridiculed in a tabloid scandal on this side of the pond. Kara never thought she'd ever say it aloud, but she'd take two of that slimeball, Rex Marino, over Corbin Jacobs. At least Rex could keep his hands to himself.

'Scary Knickers?' Drea asked, amused.

'It's what we call the HR boss. Anyway, that's not what we're concentrating on right now. We're focusing on me making it official that Corbin Jacobs is a vile tosser.'

'Babe, you know I'm with you all the way on this, but meeting them won't make a difference. He's the star. We both know how it works. His word against yours. It's pointless.'

Kara began peeling off the old Westlife T-shirt that acted as her comfort sleepwear, noticing for the first time that there were stains down the front from last night's midnight consolation snack of Doritos and salsa. Another moment of class and dignity.

'You're right. I know this. But I need to stop by the flat anyway, to pick up a few things I left behind – stuff I'll need for this trip to be the sad spare part at your wedding – and the studio is on the way, so screw it, I'm going.' When she'd left in a hurry in the middle of the night, she'd remembered the basics, but forgot to bring anything from her holiday drawer – including swimwear, sarongs, summer dresses and, most crucially of all, the small matter of her passport. Not that she was going to tell Drea that, because it would cause her sister's anxiety to escalate to a gale force that could rival any incoming storm.

'Wait a minute. You never mentioned going back home. What

if Josh is there? He's been blowing up our phones for the last two days, so he clearly wants to speak to you. Just leave your stuff, Kara. We can buy replacements for anything you've left behind.'

The sweatpants Kara slept in now joined the T-shirt on the top of her growing washing pile at the end of the bed. Drea was so allergic to untidiness, no doubt she'd have it washed, dried and folded before Kara was out the door.

'No. I don't want replacements; I want my own stuff. I'm unemployed now, remember? No splashing out on needless purchases. And if Josh is there, then... well, I'll just have to face him. I'm not going to change my mind.'

'Are you sure about that?' Drea didn't even try to hide the cynicism in every freshly tinted hair of her raised eyebrows.

'Yes!' Kara replied assertively, before buckling with a weaker, 'I mean, almost definitely.' Then a reinforced, 'I mean, yes!'

'Oh dear God, you're a nightmare. This is like a really bad play. Kara and the Coat of Many Indecisions. I can't keep up with the drama.'

Kara was now raking in the bin bag for clean underwear to go with the black jeans and semi-crushed sweater she'd just pulled out of her suitcase.

'How can I stay with him after what he did, Drea? How could I marry a guy who didn't defend me when I needed him? The truth is, Josh hasn't put me first in a really long time. It just took what happened the other night for me to see that.'

Kara felt her throat begin to tighten again and had to push down yet another urge to go back under the duvet. She had loved Josh Jackson for nearly eight years now. It had taken him almost six to propose, but she had been happy to go with the flow, to just live each day as it came. No demands. No ultimatums. No pressure. None of those things were in her nature. Now, she could see that was the problem. For the last few years, since he'd launched his PR company, work had been his number-one priority and she'd been relegated to second place. Maybe third, after his workout schedule. The worst thing was, it hadn't even occurred to her to mind.

The last forty-eight hours in bed had given her time to think. Time to reflect. Time to decide that there was no going back. Even if that thought chipped a huge piece right off her heart.

'You know, he didn't even want to take the time off to get married. That's why we were only coming for a week and not staying for a fortnight like you guys. He wasn't even giving me fourteen days. Why didn't I see that was a problem? Why did I put up with that? Why has it taken the huge bomb to go off in our lives before I noticed all the other things that were wrong?'

'Because you loved him,' Drea answered simply. 'And because you're way too nice and a bit of a pushover, but I don't want to kick you when you're down, so we'll just brush right over that.'

'I wasn't a pushover the other night,' Kara retorted, stating the obvious. She had replayed what had happened at the Hogmanay party in her mind so many times, she couldn't even bear to think of it now. The bottom line was that she'd had an altercation with Corbin Jacobs and she'd expected Josh to take her side, but he didn't. She'd hoped her bosses would take her side, but they didn't either. So she had – in not too polite terms – said goodbye to them all. 'And look where that's got me.'

Drea was now picking up her washing pile. 'You did the right thing, Kara.'

'I know I did and I'm not backing down. I need to draw a line under everything, instead of avoiding it or running away from it all. So today I'm going to go make my resignation official and tell my side of the story...'

'I can see why telling your boss to shove his job in the middle of a posh nightclub might not be considered official,' Drea agreed.

Kara nodded, then barrelled on, 'And if I see Josh at home, that's probably a good thing because we have stuff to discuss. I was going to leave it until we came back, but if he's there, then I'm just going to bite the bullet. I need to arrange to get all my stuff out of the flat. We need to disentangle our lives. Fight over custody of our book collection. Get my life sorted out.'

Her sister clearly realised that resistance was futile. 'I have no idea where this new assertive you came from, but I like her. But just promise you'll be back here in loads of time for the car to the airport. Leaving here at 4 p.m. Repeat after me: 4 p.m.'

'Four p.m. I'll be here.'

The front door slammed and Kara and Drea automatically locked eyes, both of them dreading what was about to come.

Dressed in a full length, pink fake fur coat, Jacinta McIntyre swept into the room with more impact than the average tornado. 'Dear God, it's colder than a serial killer's freezer out there.' She paused, her gaze sweeping from Kara's bare feet to her bed-head coiffure. 'You know, darling, I love you dearly, but heartbreak doesn't look great on you. Could you try to be a bit more Julia Roberts about it? I always think she's a fabulous crier. And you've already got the hair. Although a good brush wouldn't go amiss.'

As Jacinta kissed her on the cheek, Kara's hand automatically went to her wild red curls in a futile bid to tame them. Jacinta wasn't one of those mums who gave sympathy and comfort in times of distress. An actress to her very core, she viewed every drama, disaster or upset as a plot twist, necessary to get to the bit where the heroine triumphed, and all was happy ever after. Once upon a time, she'd worked fairly consistently in small but interesting roles in Scottish television and theatre, supplementing her income by teaching drama one or two days a week for local authorities. Nowadays, she told everyone she was semi-retired, which was her way of dealing with the reality that she hadn't been offered a single role since she'd turned sixty the year before.

'It's only a flying visit – I'm getting my hair done across the road in five minutes. Drea, darling, are you organised for the trip?' She immediately answered her own question. 'Of course you are. Sometimes I don't know where I got you from. Neither me nor your father had a logical bone in our bodies.'

Kara watched as Drea rolled her eyes, refusing to bite. Kara was usually viewed as chronically uninteresting by her mother, but apparently her current situation was worthy of Jacinta's rapt attention, as she focused back on her.

'Right then, darling, what have I missed?' she asked. 'Do you need me to help to hide evidence or bury a body?'

Much as Jacinta's breezy delivery irked her, Kara appreciated the sentiment. Sometimes she wondered if their mother's over the top, flighty, dramatic flair was the reason that she and Drea had developed very different personalities. Drea's core traits were that she was driven, logical, practical and cynical, while Kara preferred to be low key, non-confrontational and to go with the flow.

'Not today, Mum. But I do need to dash.'

'Just tell me you're not going to take that man back. Urgh, I never liked him. You deserve so much better.'

Even if that were a possibility, she wouldn't admit it because it would set her mum off on a rant that would cause her to miss her shampoo and blow dry. Jacinta had never approved of Josh, because she'd always said he wanted everything to be on his terms. In hindsight, she wasn't wrong.

'I won't take him back, Mum. I'm rushing because I've got a

meeting at the studio. They want to speak to me about what happened.'

Jacinta gasped. 'What? Don't dare back down with that buffoon, Corbin Jacobs. All smarm and no talent, that man. If the universe hadn't blessed him with that face, he'd be doing adverts for stairlifts.'

Again, Kara didn't disagree, but she wasn't going to get into that right now, because she had to be at The Clydeside in half an hour and the clock was ticking.

'I won't back down, Mum. But right now, I'll let Drea give you a run-down on everything…'

Over behind their mother, Drea's eyes widened in outrage as she mimicked stabbing Kara.

'…because I need to run. And you're going to be proud of me. I might not be Julia Roberts, but today I'm going to speak to the bosses at the studio and maybe Josh too, and I'm going to stand my ground with them all.'

She was pretty sure none of them, including her, was completely confident about that statement. But there was only one way to find out.

2

OLLIE CHILES

Ollie stepped out of the shower to grab the phone that was ringing on the stone top of his vanity area. Calacatta Gold Marble. Just one of the ludicrously expensive stone accents in his townhouse in the beautiful Park Circus area of Glasgow. If the kid that had grown up just a few miles away from here on the South Side, in a tiny, terraced council house with one bathroom between four of them, could see him now, he'd punch the fricking air and then nip down to the corner shop and blow his entire pound pocket money on a can of Irn-Bru and a packet of football cards.

And yet... Weirdly, he still felt more at home back then in that terrace than he did here, in his seven-figure, majestic Georgian townhouse. Although, that was probably because he'd spent a grand total of about twelve nights here in the year since he'd bought it and had it decorated by one of the hot new interior designers in the city. The concept of getting other people to carry out his wishes was still so new to him. Little more than six years ago, he'd been a jobbing actor, mostly in theatre, and he was staying in a cupboard-size studio in New York, because the

London play he'd worked on for six months had moved stateside and taken most of the cast with it. When the run came to an end, he still had a few months on his work visa, so he'd landed the part of a chorus member and understudy to the leading man in a short-lived but weighty Broadway play, starring Sienna Montgomery, former Disney teen star turned serious theatre actor. He'd respectfully punched the air when the show's leading man went down with appendicitis and Ollie had stepped into the role, garnering praise and attention from both the critics and Sienna. They'd married three months later, after a whirlwind romance, with his best mate, Kara, by his side, four weeks before his visa was about to expire.

That had been just the start of his meteoric life transformation. A few weeks later, he'd got a call to replace an A-lister who'd pulled out of a new TV show, the first series of *The Clansman*. It was a TV spin off of a major Hollywood movie franchise about sixteenth-century Scottish warriors, written and directed by Hollywood royalty, Mirren McLean. To his eternal gratitude, Mirren had remembered him because years before, when he was just starting out, he'd had a small part in the eighth movie in *The Clansman* film series, and she'd decided he'd be the perfect person to replace the big-shot dropout on the new show. Before he could catch a breath, he was on a plane, meeting Mirren again, and signing contracts. He'd shot the eight episodes in just over three months in various locations including LA, Vancouver and Croatia, where, by the miracles of television, some of the exterior scenes mimicking sixteenth-century Scotland were filmed. It was the kind of big-budget global TV show that every actor dreamed of working on. It became an international sensation, catapulting him to a level of fame that would see him mobbed in ALDI. That year, he did what felt like a million online interviews, racked up a gazillion fans and was soon on a plane back to LA to shoot the next series. First class. And he tried not to be starstruck that Harry Styles was in the seat behind him.

Five seasons later, he got recognised in every country he travelled to, was being offered serious movie roles, was rumoured to be the next Bond, earned millions per series, and had been voted Hottest Hollywood Male three years in a row. He was also overworked, exhausted and lived between so many time zones, he rarely remembered what day of the week it was. Just in the last fortnight, he'd done about twenty-five thousand airmiles and he'd only managed to spend Christmas with Sienna because he'd flown from LA to New York to meet her there. He'd spent a couple of nights in the apartment she was renting while she was working on a mediocre off-Broadway show that met its unexpected demise on Christmas Eve. He'd consoled his wife as much as he could, before he'd had to hop on a flight to Croatia, to shoot some extra scenes. One week there, including New Year's Eve and New Year's Day, and then yesterday, he'd flown into Glasgow for a whistlestop overnight stay that would allow him to pick up fresh clothes and re-pack his case, before heading to Hawaii later today for Kara's wedding. The one that was apparently now cancelled. And he already knew that the person whose name was currently flashing on his phone probably wasn't mustering up much sympathy for his friend's heartbreak.

Sienna.

'Hey, babe, I was just thinking about you,' he opened the FaceTime call. 'I miss you.' He tried to pull out his best smile and sound as sexy as possible, in the ever-present hope that it would remind her why she fell in love with him. Tomorrow would be their sixth wedding anniversary, and that all-consuming joy and the bliss of their first couple of years was a dim and distant memory for them both. Not that he blamed her after the latest knock to her career. When they met, she'd been the more successful one, the star who was rumoured to be under consideration for a Tony nomination. But that was then. There had been a slump in the parts she'd been offered after that, and the last two or three years had been tough for her, culminating in the premature closure of her latest show. Now that the run had jack-knifed, she was benching her love of the theatre and heading back to LA for the TV pilot season auditions that came around at the beginning of every year, and was clearly not thrilled about it.

'Back at you,' she said, with an unmistakable edge of weariness that made it depressingly clear that she didn't.

He heard the bing-bong of an announcement in the background noise. 'You still at the airport? I thought you'd have been halfway to LA by now.' He did a quick calculation of the time – 3 a.m. in New York. Her red-eye flight should have left a few minutes before midnight.

'Me too, but the flight was delayed because of the snow. I've been in the airline lounge for the last four hours, but they're just about to start boarding now.'

Ah, that made sense – there was a slight slur to her words that definitely said four or five vodka martinis.

'Nightmare. I'm sorry, babe.'

She shrugged. 'The joys of flying commercial. What about you? Did you speak to Kara?' His wife was a wonderful actress, but she couldn't mask her disdain when she said his friend's name. It was nothing new, so he rolled right over it.

'I haven't been able to get hold of her yet, so we haven't spoken since the text.'

It had come in the early hours of the morning two days ago.

Wedding off. My choice. Still going to Hawaii or
Drea will never forgive me. Best man no longer
needed but please still come and be my
emotional support human.

He'd picked the message up ten hours later, when he'd
woken from a jet-lagged deep sleep, and immediately tried to call
her. No answer. He'd sent a text.

Shit! You okay? What can I do?

A few hours later, the reply came back.

Nothing. Licking my wounds. Long story. See
you at Glasgow Airport day after tomorrow,
same plans as before. Will explain everything
then. Now only love you, Drea, Stevie Nicks and
Lenny Kravitz. xx

That was it. There had been several missed calls and a couple
of texts back and forth since then, but he still had no clue what
had happened. All he knew was that it must be bad, because
Kara wasn't one for unnecessary drama. Speaking of which...
Sienna had now pulled off a huge pair of sunglasses (yep, even in
New York in January in the middle of the night), and she looked
stunning as always, even with no make-up and a baseball cap
pulled low down on her forehead. Although, she must need her
Botox topped up because for the first time in years he could see
the grooves of a frown between her eyes.

'But you're still going to Hawaii? And you'll be there on our
wedding anniversary. Have you even considered cancelling and
coming back to LA instead? With the time difference, you could
be there tonight and we could do dinner at the Sunset Tower.' It
was one of his favourite restaurants, but the last thing he felt like

right now was getting dressed up for a night on the town. 'I thought we were going to try to make this work, Ollie?'

Ah, there was the guilt trip, right on time.

A couple of months ago, they'd squeezed in a couple of sessions with Sienna's therapist to discuss their marriage. Years of working in different time zones, on schedules that rarely matched up, had caused a drift that they could no longer ignore. After talking it through, they'd both agreed that they'd stopped prioritising each other and committed to making an effort to breathe new life into their relationship. If he were honest, it was still dangerously close to flatlining, but he wasn't prepared to give up yet. As soon as he got back from Hawaii, he was going to spend a month in LA and they'd both promised to try to rekindle what they'd once had.

When he'd got the text to say the wedding was cancelled, he had thought about skipping Hawaii, but only for a split second. Kara never asked him for anything, and she was clearly going through it, so he couldn't bring himself to desert her. Not now.

'Babe, I'll only be there for two days and then I'll be home. Or you could change your mind and come to the wedding. My mum will be there too and—'

'How can you ask me to do that? Ollie, my career is in crisis! I'm not doing a fucking hula dance when I should be back in LA, talking to my agent, setting up meetings and auditions. I don't have time to go swanning off with your friend who isn't even getting fricking married now...'

There were so many things about that outburst that pissed him off, he didn't know where to start. Kara was so much more than a friend, she was family. As were Drea and their mum, Jacinta. His dad had been a passing ship, a fleeting holiday romance that was over the moment his mum and Jacinta had got on the plane back from Tenerife. Three months later, his mum had found out she was pregnant. Nine and a half months later, he was born into a world that consisted of his mum, his lovely grandparents, Jacinta, Drea, Kara and him. It had stayed that way until his lovely mum, a well-known pub and club singer who had been known to claim that she possessed 'the mightiest set of pipes in Glasgow', landed a gig as a cabaret singer on cruise ships and sailed off when he was sixteen. Not for one second had he felt abandoned or neglected though. She'd done it to support him while he was studying and trying to break into acting, and when it came to day-to-day mothering, Jacinta had stepped right into the void that his mum had left. The two lifelong friends were like a tag team, but without the wrestling ring and the overblown dramatics. Actually... maybe just without the wrestling ring.

'Sienna, I'm not doing this. You make it sound like Kara is just some random mate, but come on, you know she's like a sister to me...'

He was about to launch into his usual defence, but she cut him off as she slipped her shades back onto her face. Even the sight of his naked six-pack wasn't softening her attitude. 'Oh, spare me, Ollie. I've been hearing it for years, and I'm over it. The only reason we're not celebrating our anniversary today, on the day we were supposed to get married, is because of your oldest fricking friend.' The disdain had ramped up now to 'very obviously pissed off.'

'Come on, that wasn't her fault...'

'No, it was yours. You were so desperate to marry me, you put it off for twenty-four hours until she could get to us. My mother has still never forgiven you.'

He had no defence to that one. Six years ago, he'd been madly in love with this beautiful star he'd been seeing for three months, and feeling like the luckiest guy in the world because he'd blurted out a proposal on Christmas Day and she'd stunned him by saying yes. Caught up in the moment, they'd decided to have a tiny wedding as soon as they could get the paperwork sorted out. That's why, a week and a half later, he was waiting for Kara to fly in to be his Best Person at a City Hall wedding that consisted of his bride, her parents, and... Actually, that was it. His mum was in the middle of an ocean and couldn't leave the ship for three more months, so they'd zoomed her in. His grandparents had long passed by that time. And Jacinta and Drea couldn't make it at such short notice because they both had commitments they couldn't change. When Kara's flight had been delayed for a full twenty-four hours, he'd implored Sienna to postpone the ceremony for a day and back then she'd been so in love with him that she'd willingly agreed.

He wasn't sure she'd make the same decision now.

'So you're not changing your plans, even though I'm asking you to do that for me,' she demanded, and Ollie watched as her chin jutted forward, a challenge from someone who had got her own way her whole life.

'Babe, I couldn't, even if I wanted to. Which I do!' White lie. He was getting desperate not to come off as an asshole and trying to make her feel better. 'Calvin is picking me up in half an hour because I've got a few promos to shoot here for the show.' That wasn't strictly true, and he hated to fudge the truth with her, but he wasn't ready to tell her what was really going on.

Calvin Fraser had been his first ever manager, back in his early acting days in Scotland, before Ollie had headed off to pastures new across the pond. He'd semi-retired now that the biggest star on his roster, soap queen Odette Devine, had hung up her crown, but they still caught up whenever Ollie was in town and Calvin occasionally brokered endorsement deals with Scottish brands. Ollie felt his face flush at the knowledge he was lying by omission, but he just hoped Sienna was too distracted by her anger to notice. Calvin was joining him today for something far more important than a promo shoot, but sharing that information could wait until later. Right now, he still had a situation to defuse.

'Look, I'll make all this up to you, I promise.'

'I remember you saying that six years ago.'

Situation escalated. Shots fired. Right in the jugular. Man down. He'd seen this play out too many times. The only smart move was an emergency evacuation. Thankfully, American Airlines intervened to facilitate that.

Another bing-bong in the background. A call for the last remaining passengers for the flight to LA.

'I need to go. Talk later. If you can fit me in.' And with that, she pouted the lips that were injected at a shockingly expensive Beverly Hills clinic every six months, and hung up.

How was this his life? Knackered, wet, naked, standing in a cold bathroom in Glasgow, getting bollocked by his wife. Not exactly the high life. And now the doorbell was ringing. He pulled a towel around his waist and made his way down to the ground floor, where he checked the security monitor at the front door. One of his favourite faces filled the screen, so he immediately opened the door, but stood behind it just in case there were any paps out in the wild. The last thing he needed was a half-naked pic of him opening the door. It would be all over the internet before he'd had a chance to get his jeans on.

Only when Calvin had cleared the doorway did Ollie close the door and reveal himself.

'Hang on, hang on!' Calvin ordered, taking in the sight in front of him. 'I just need to take a minute to remind myself that political correctness is a thing, and I'm no longer allowed to comment on the fact that you've got abs that resemble the peaks of the Andes. What was left of my self-esteem has just been crushed to dust.'

Ollie laughed. 'Good to see you, pal. Two minutes, I'll be right back. You know where the coffee is.'

He took the stairs two at a time to his bedroom, where he threw on a pair of jeans, a chunky black jumper and ran some styling powder through his hair. Shaving could wait until later. Maybe tomorrow.

He was back down in the kitchen in less than ten minutes. This time, he gave Calvin a proper hug and was rewarded with a black coffee in a travel mug.

Calvin gestured to the door. 'Ready to go, my friend? We're seeing it at 11 a.m. but we're stopping for breakfast in a little spot nearby.'

'So it's still available?' A property. The kind of place he'd dreamt about his whole life. One that Calvin had been talking to him about for the last month. One that could change so many things in his world.

'It is.'

Ollie stood back to let the older man go first. He'd have to tell Sienna about this viewing, but not yet – she was furious enough without sending her into orbit.

Lately he'd been feeling that their marriage had been a contractual obligation and neither he nor Sienna had been living up to their ends of the bargain. And he had a sinking feeling that today was the day he might be about to throw in a deal-breaker.

3

ALICE BROOKES

In a well-practised move, Alice scooped the teabag out of her mug, waved it at the automatic bin, waited until the steel lid lifted, then dropped the bag of camomile leaves inside. Most mornings she shared a pot of normal tea with her friend and housemate, Val Murray, but today she'd been in the mood for what Val called, 'that fancy posh nonsense'. Judging by the roll of Val's eyes, she wouldn't be changing her mind about that any time soon.

'You're not allowed to roll your eyes at me on my last day here. You have to play nice and treat me like your very favourite person in the world so that I'll come back to visit you,' Alice teased, but even as she said it, she had to swallow the lump that kept rising in her throat.

As always, Val wasn't slow with the smart counter points. 'Aye, you'll be back. They always come back,' she said dramatically. 'Except our Dee's dodgy pen pal who slept on the couch for six months when he first moved to Scotland at the end of the nineties. He's in jail now for running one of those Ponzi schemes. Don't ask.'

Alice didn't, but she couldn't help laughing. It was common knowledge that thanks to Val and her huge heart, her home had accommodated many waifs and strays over the years and Alice was the latest one. She'd been here since last May, after meeting Val on the day Alice finally made the break and left her bad bastard of a husband. It was only a few weeks after Alzheimer's disease had taken Val's husband, Don, but still she had offered up her spare room without question or judgement, and Alice had been grateful for the roof and the safe harbour. As the weeks and months had passed, it had become so much more than that.

As someone who had been isolated from any friends for the entirety of her marriage to former politician-turned-corrupt-crook, Larry McLenn, Val had become the first pal she'd had in decades. Someone to chat to every day when she came in from her cleaning jobs. Someone to mull over life with. Someone to laugh with, every single day, because Val refused to let the world drag her down.

And that wasn't even taking into account the other women of all ages in Val's life who regularly stopped by her terraced house on an estate in the village of Weirbridge, about twenty minutes from Glasgow. There was her chum, Nancy, a widow who lived only a few streets away and who'd also had tough times but was having a second lease of life after meeting an old classmate at a school reunion and falling in love with him. There was Tress, who dropped her toddler, Buddy, here two days a week because Val and Nancy were his beloved childminders. Sometimes Buddy was collected by Keli, a nurse at Glasgow Central hospital and Tress's soon-to-be sister-in-law. And Carly and Carole, Val's nieces, two women not much younger than Alice, but miles apart in lifestyle, because they led very glam lives in London. They visited every month for at least a weekend and absolutely livened things up. Then there were the old friends of Val's daughter, Dee, who'd been tragically killed by a drugged-up driver a decade ago. They still popped in every couple of weeks for a blether and a glass of vino or a cup of tea with a biscuit from the tin that had permanent residence in the middle of the kitchen table. Alice was sure it had some kind of miracle self-replenishing properties because it hadn't been empty since the day she'd got here.

And at the centre of it all was Val. This woman had truly put her back together again. Alice had gone from having no one in her life other than her adult son, Rory, to having what felt like a sisterhood, all of them rooting for her to get back on her feet and build an incredible new future. Damn, there was that lump in her throat again.

This, right here, was probably the thing that she'd miss most. Both of them, sitting at Val's well-worn oak kitchen table in their dressing gowns at the start of the day, Alice usually fresh from her shower because she'd already done the 5 a.m. cleaning shift at the local school. Val, just out of bed, her voice still husky, with her white blonde bob tucked into a terry towelling turban. They'd drink their tea, eat their toast and contemplate what things they could come up with to add just a bit of sunshine into the day. A mid-afternoon coffee in one of the cafés in the village centre. Zumba class in the evening – even though they got the steps mixed up and always seemed to be going the wrong way. A visit to one of the elderly folk in the village, armed with a packet of caramel wafers and an hour of chat.

Not today, though. Today was her last day in Glasgow, before she moved south to start a new chapter of her life with Rory and his girlfriend, Sophie, in Reading. The couple had met when Sophie was on a weekend break in Glasgow seven months before, and they'd known almost instantly that they were for keeps. Now Rory had made his life down in Reading, and when the couple had asked Alice to join them, there had only been one possible answer. She'd lost so much time with Rory over the last few horrific years with Larry, and for a time had cut her son out of her life to protect him from the worst of his father's cruelty. Larry had used a toxic combination of manipulation, blackmail and threats against their son to stop her leaving, so she'd stayed because it was the only way to protect Rory. It had cost her years of pain, humiliation and abuse, but now she was free and both she and Rory wanted to make up for those lost years. Moving closer to him would help, but she'd declined their offer to live permanently in their home, keen to let them have their own space. The plan was to stay with them for a couple of weeks until she found her own place, somewhere nearby, so that they could all be in each other's daily lives.

Now the day had come to leave, Alice was feeling every emotion: happy, sad, scared, excited, just for starters. She hadn't gone to work before dawn this morning because yesterday had been her last day on the mops. She'd completed her early shift at the school, a deep cleaning session they always did when the kids were on their Christmas and New Year break, then her late shift at the Town Hall, then she'd pulled off her Marigolds for the last time. Val had stood beside her as they'd tried to give them a ceremonial burning in a steel mop bucket in the back garden last night, but the rain kept putting the flames out. Probably just as well – it was a rash gesture because the Marigolds still had a bit of life left in them.

Val reached for the slab of butter that sat between them, sliced off a hearty knob and began buttering her toast. 'So tell me then, what's the plan for today? Just so I know when to fit in sulking and sobbing uncontrollably because you're leaving me,' she asked breezily.

Alice followed suit with the butter. 'Enjoy this little interlude of sunshine with you...' she said, with a grin. 'And then head over to Burnbank for that funeral. It's at 11 o'clock. After that, I'll treat you to lunch somewhere lovely, then back here to finish getting organised. I'm already packed, but I've still got a few odds and ends to do. My flight is at seven, so I'll leave for the airport around four o'clock.'

Val swallowed her first bite of the day. 'Tell me again whose funeral it is.'

'The sister of the girl who was my best friend when I was in my teens and early twenties.'

'And we're going because...?'

Alice wasn't sure she had a good answer to that. She'd spotted the death notice in the local paper and immediately recognised the name. Audrey Benning (Née McTay). Back in the eighties and nineties, Audrey's younger sister, Morag McTay, had been the pal who'd worn a matching puffball skirt when they'd gone to the old Apollo concert hall or the Barrowlands, to see Big Country or Simple Minds or a dozen other bands they'd loved. She'd been the one who'd carried their shoes, because Alice was holding the kebabs after a night of dancing at a long-gone nightclub in Glasgow's Sauchiehall Street. For over a decade, since they had met in their first year of high school, Morag was the one who'd shared all her secrets, and plotted to land her dreams. And then one day, when they were both in their twenties, she'd left, moved to Ireland, and Alice had never seen her again.

'I'd like to pay my respects. Nostalgia, I suppose. Audrey was always good to me, even though she was probably sick of her wee sister and her pal always raiding her wardrobe and borrowing her make-up. Optimism, too, if I'm honest. I'm really hoping Morag will be there. It would be great to see her after all these years.'

'She's the pal who moved to London?'

'Dublin,' Alice corrected her, with a smile. Val had a

formidable memory for information or gossip, but sometimes the details got slightly confused. 'She'd met a lovely Irish guy who was working over here for a couple of months, and the next thing she announced she was going back there with him and off she went, never to return.'

'And you never heard from her again?'

Alice put the crusts of her toast down on her plate, and as always, Val reached over and took them, with a mutter of, 'This is why I'm two stones heavier than you.'

'A couple of postcards at first, then nothing. You know how it was back then. Phone calls were expensive and there was no internet or texts. When people moved away, that was it, unless they came back to visit, and as far as I know, Morag never did. I guess she just got consumed by her new life. I was already with Larry at that point, completely wrapped up in him and madly in love...'

An involuntary shudder punctuated that comment. Even now, she felt for her twenty-five-year-old self, who couldn't possibly have imagined that the suave, successful bar owner she'd met back then would become a cruel, controlling nightmare of a man, a notoriously corrupt politician who would trap her in an unhappy marriage until his very public downfall three decades later. It wasn't even a year since she'd escaped him and she still felt a moment of anxiety when she woke up every morning, until she remembered that he was out of her life.

'Anyway, I've always regretted losing touch with her, so I'd love to catch up with her now, and it feels like there's something significant in the timing, with it being my last day in Glasgow. If Audrey had passed away next week, I wouldn't have seen the notice or been able to go to the funeral. Almost feels like I was meant to be there. Does that sound mad?'

'Absolutely. But I'd probably do the same, so I'm not judging.'

'You don't have to come with me, though.'

Val let her last gulp of tea go down. 'I know, but I don't want you going off on your own, in case there's no one you know there. Besides, I've been to so many funerals in the last few years, I know the words to all the hymns, so I'm great with the singing.'

The twinkle in Val's eye made it obvious she was joking. Alice had learned pretty quickly that dark humour got this woman through everything.

'And anyway,' Val went on. 'It's your last day, and I've told my people to clear my hectic, highbrow schedule so I can spend it with you. And let me tell you, Alice Brookes...' Alice had dropped Larry's surname the day she left him and hearing her maiden name still gave her a thrill. 'You'd better not vanish off the face of the earth or I'll be on the first flight to London to track you down. Rory and Sophie will have to barricade the front door to stop me.'

'I'm sure Rory and Sophie would put the welcome mat out for you,' Alice countered. 'They both adore you.'

'Aye, that goes both ways. I'll miss you though, pal.' Val reached over and took her hand and gave it a squeeze.

'I'll miss you too. More than I can say. But you know it's the best thing. A fresh start, far from the stigma of being Larry McLenn's ex-wife. I'll never be able to escape that in Glasgow.'

'I know, ma love, and you're right.' Val sniffed, then took her hand away to dry her eyes with the sleeve of her dressing gown. 'Agh, no bloody wonder I've got wrinkles,' she said, with another loud sniff, before pushing herself up and reaching for both their plates. 'Right, well, let's get a start on then. It's going to take time to turn this dried-up husk of a face into a thing of beauty this morning.'

Emotional moment passed, Alice nodded gratefully. She'd

miss this woman beyond words, but it was time for a new chapter.

Today was the day she would finally cut ties with the past and embrace her new future. For almost thirty years, her life had been held hostage by Larry McLenn. But there was nothing that he could do to hurt her now.

4

ZAC CORLAN

This was the first time all week that the kitchen had been empty of people and Zac knew it wouldn't last long, so, coffee in hand, he opened his Aunt Audrey's back door and let the freezing-cold air shock him awake. His *late* aunt. He kept forgetting that bit. She was still in every inch of this house, from the large ceramic chicken that sat on the counter storing fresh eggs, to the giant sunburst clock that hung on the far wall. Aunt Audrey had been a character. One who, if she were still here, would have been yelling at him to get the door closed because 'the cold out there would make your bits fall off.'

At 8 a.m. on any other weekday, he'd be in his office in Dublin, contemplating the pile of broken promises that came with the caseload of files in his in-tray. Being a lawyer who specialised in divorce definitely wasn't a job for the faint-hearted and January was always his busiest month. But instead of being at work, he was in a house in Glasgow, preparing to bury the aunt that he'd visited with his mum and dad at least twice a year for his entire life.

Aunt Audrey had passed away suddenly, suffering a heart

attack on Christmas Eve, almost a year after his mum, Morag, had succumbed to the cancer she'd lived with for years. Mum had died on the first weekend in January. The two women in his life, both gone in the space of twelve months.

'Christ, would you shut that door? The cold out there would make your bits fall off.'

That came from his cousin, Jill, Audrey's daughter and her absolute double, right down to the freckles, the ginger hair, her raucous laugh and her favourite sayings. Jill and her twin, Hamish, were a few years older than Zac, the elder brother and sister that he'd never had.

'You sound just like Aunt Audrey,' he told her, with an affectionate smile, that was returned, despite the pale mask of exhaustion and grief that Jill had been wearing since he got here last week. The irony was, that his and his dad's flights to Glasgow had already been booked for Boxing Day, because even though his mum was no longer with him, he'd still felt the need to come here for the New Year celebrations as he'd always done. Back in November, when he'd organised the trip, it hadn't been a popular decision with Camilla, his colleague and girlfriend of the previous six months. She'd been thinking more along the lines of St Lucia. Maybe Barbados.

When he'd dug his heels in and insisted that this year, the first without his mum, it was even more important than ever that he came with his dad to spend New Year with his aunt and family in Glasgow, she had lost all patience, especially when he broke it to her that she wasn't invited. He wasn't being difficult, but he figured the last thing Aunt Audrey needed was a stranger in her home at what was sure to be a tough time for her.

Camilla had called off their relationship and cleared out the drawer where she used to keep some essentials when she slept over. Last he heard, she'd consoled herself by taking three girl-friends on that Christmas and New Year trip to Barbados.

He hadn't admitted it to a soul, but the truth was that he'd been relieved, glad that he was free to spend Christmas with his dad in his childhood home in Dublin, then fly here with Dad to spend New Year with Aunt Audrey and the rest of the family. His mum had grown up in this house, and Audrey had moved back in to take care of their ailing parents many years ago. There was something special about it. It felt like his mum was in every room. In every picture. In every memory they had here. There was nowhere else he'd wanted to spend New Year. But, of course, they'd all been blindsided when, instead of coming here to share the turn of the year with Aunt Audrey, it turned out that they were actually coming for her funeral. He'd been stunned when he'd received the phone call late on Christmas Eve to say she was gone and even now, it still didn't seem real.

'Your dad still sleeping?' Jill asked him. She was holding a shoebox, which she put down on the kitchen table as she took the coffee he'd just poured her from the pot he'd already made. The coffee machine had been his Christmas gift to Aunt Audrey a few years back and she'd been chuffed to bits. Audrey and his mum would fire it up every morning they were here, and then the two of them would chat for the next hour while sipping their caffeine hits.

'Yeah. He's taken this pretty hard, especially with it being so soon after losing Mum. You know he adored Aunt Audrey too.'

Jill nodded, a sad smile crossing her lips. 'And it went both ways. They were legends, all of them, weren't they?'

She didn't have to explain what she meant. His mum, his dad and his Aunt Audrey were a formidable team. Audrey had divorced her husband back in the nineties, and since then the three of them had stuck together, even though they were sepa-

rated by a few hundred miles and a small stretch of sea. The
Corlans would come here for New Year, and then Zac and his
mum would come back for a month in the summer too. The
Bennings would come to Ireland for Easter and then the second
half of the school summer holidays. And the three adults would
make sure the kids enjoyed every second of it.

Zac returned the smile. 'They were.' He pulled out a chair
and sat opposite Jill, still savouring the peace. Since he'd got
here, the house had been full of visitors paying respects, neighbours handing in more food than they could eat, and officials
planning the ins and outs of today's funeral. Neither his mum
nor Aunt Audrey had been religious, so the service was going to
be at the crematorium, with a Humanist celebrant, who also
happened to be one of Aunt Audrey's lifelong friends, so she
could speak from a place of true affection and personal experience. Afterwards, there would be tea and sandwiches at the only
hotel in the village, The Georgian House, up on the Main Street.
That had been the venue for every celebration and Hogmanay
party in his memory, and they all knew it was Aunt Audrey's
choice because it had been written into her letter of wishes, the
one they'd found after she died. Apparently, she'd written it after
his mum had passed, and the loss had given her a sense of her
own mortality.

Zac hadn't read all of it, just the parts that Jill had recounted
to him detailing her plan for today: the ceremony, the venue,
even the music – Blondie's 'Call Me', 'Love Is All Around' by Wet
Wet Wet, and 'My Heart Will Go On' by Celine Dion – all chosen
because they were, in rotation, her favourite songs to belt out
after a few Proseccos in a karaoke bar.

Jill's gaze went to the sunburst clock on the wall. 'The cars are
coming at 10.30, so we've got a couple of hours of the calm before

the storm. Are you sure you don't mind that we're deserting you and your dad this afternoon?'

Zac shook his head. 'Of course not. I'd choose a week in Center Parcs over another day with me too,' he teased. It had been Aunt Audrey's Christmas gift to Jill and her husband, Archie, and Hamish and his wife, Mandy – a long weekend for both their families in Center Parcs, leaving today. Audrey could never have known that it would coincide with the day of her funeral. Jill and Hamish had considered cancelling, but she'd been so happy to treat them and their children that they'd decided it was the perfect way to honour her. Besides, their kids had just experienced their first heartbreak, losing the gran they adored, and a sad Christmas, so Jill knew her mum would have wanted to cheer them up before they went back to school next week. The cars were packed, and the plan was for them to set off after the wake. Zac and his dad were already booked on a flight back to Dublin tonight too.

'Listen, there's no good time to do this and I don't know if we'll get a chance after the service, so I just wanted to give you this now.' She slid the shoe box across the table towards him.

'What is it?' he asked, leaning forward to take it.

'I think it's a box of your mum's things from when she was younger. It was in her old bedroom, and it's probably been there since the eighties. We found it when we were looking for something of Aunt Morag's to put in the coffin with Mum today. That was in Mum's wishes too.'

Jill's eyes filled when she said that, and he forgot about the box as he went round to her side of the table to give her a hug. She let him hold her for a few moments, then pulled her shoulders back and, forcing a smile, waved him away.

'Argh, don't let me start. We've still got the service to get through and she'd want me to hold it together. You know what she was like. She'll be sitting on a cloud somewhere with your mum, looking down on me right now and telling everyone who'll listen that I've always had a touch of the theatrics. Anyway, here you go. I think it's just full of photos and cards, but I'm sure it'll make you smile. I'm going to go and start getting ready and hunt down some waterproof mascara.'

When she got up from her chair, Zac gave her another hug before she went, then sat down in her seat, reaching over to pull his mug of coffee towards him. He thought about leaving the box until later, but curiosity got the better of him, and he'd already showered and shaved, so he still had well over an hour before he had to get his suit on.

The top of the shoe box had the letters C&A written across it, and Zac had a vague memory of that being a big store in the centre of Glasgow when he was a kid. He lifted the lid off, and saw immediately that Jill was right – inside was a pile of envelopes, letters, photos, cards, concert tickets... all of which looked decades old. He flicked through them and some dates jumped out at him. Postmarks from 1988. Scribbled dates on the back of photos of his mum and Aunt Audrey going back to childhood ones from the seventies. Pics of his parents, looking younger than he'd ever seen them. His job had long since trained him to keep it together in times of sadness, but Jill's dose of the 'theatrics' had suddenly become contagious. He blinked until his eyes unblurred, and then carried on flicking through each gem of a gift from a bygone time. There were birthday cards to his mum from his grandparents. A letter offering his mum what he knew was her first job, as a typist at a legal firm in the city centre. She'd loved that job, and he'd always wondered if that was why she'd so fervently encouraged his interest in the law and been so incredibly proud when he'd qualified.

He pulled out another card, this time one with flowers on the front, but no greeting. Strange. His mother had never struck him as someone who would go for the floral vibe. Intrigued, he opened the card and received a full blow to the windpipe as he saw the loops and curves of his mum's handwriting. Even now, he didn't quite understand why some things hit harder than others, but these were the same shapes he'd seen on every card and letter he'd ever received from his parents. The words were completely different though...

> *Dear Alice,*
>
> *I've been trying to write this note to you for the longest time, but never seem to manage it. I don't know where to start, so I'll just begin by saying I'm so, so sorry. When I explain what happened, I'll understand if you never forgive me. I didn't mean—*

That was it. It stopped right there. No full stop. No other information, other than the obvious – it had never been sent.

Zac read it over a couple more times, his puzzlement increasing with every read. His mum wasn't the kind of person who would ever deliberately hurt someone, so this must have been some kind of misunderstanding. Or an accident. Or... Nope, that was all he could come up with.

And who was Alice? He put it to one side, deciding to ask his dad about it later. He knew that after they met, his mum and dad had spent a couple of months here together before they'd moved back to Ireland, so his dad might have known this 'Alice' too.

Mystery parked for now, he went back to the box and continued to flick, until he reached a strip of photo booth pics of his mum and dad, both of them pulling faces into the camera. The frown of puzzlement was replaced by a beaming grin as he stared at the image, taking in every young, unlined, gleeful curve of their faces.

When every detail was imprinted on his mind, he turned the strip over, and there was that handwriting again:

9 March 1995 – Our first date!

That was one he'd treasure forever, he thought as he slipped it back in the box. One to frame. One he'd show his kids one day when he was telling them about their grandparents. One...

The thought was barrelled right out of the way by another one, a niggle that he couldn't quite put his finger on. He took the photo strip back out of the box. Stared at their faces. Then turned it over again.

9 March 1995 – Our first date!

The realisation of the problem came to him quickly, but it was so preposterous, so utterly baffling, that his legal brain questioned it a dozen times before even considering admitting it as evidence.

9 March 1995.

He'd been born on the 24th of October the same year.

Just over seven months after his parents' first date in March. That couldn't be right. He knew from photos and his mum's stories about his birth that he'd been a strapping ten pound full-term baby. If that was the case... he did the calculations... he must have been conceived in January.

None of this made a shred of sense.

He jumped as the door opened behind him and his dad came in, yawning as he made a beeline for the coffee. 'Morning, son.

Jeez-oh, I slept like a log. How's you? What's that you've got there?'

Zac had no idea why he did what he did next. While his dad reached into the cupboard for a mug, he slipped the strip of photos and the card into the front pouch of his hoodie.

'Och, just old photos and cards that Mum must have kept. Some pretty handsome ones of you in there, Dad. No wonder she couldn't resist you.'

'Aye, it was a curse being as handsome as me,' his dad fired back, with typical Cillian Corlan humour. It was only when the coffee was poured and his dad joined him at the table that Zac could see the exhaustion and grief in every line of his face.

He wasn't in the habit of keeping secrets from his old man – in fact, Cillian was as much of a mate as he was a father. But this discovery? No. And the questions that were now in his mind? Another no. This wasn't the time.

Whatever secrets he'd just stumbled over were going to have to stay buried… at least for today.

10 A.M. – NOON

5

KARA

At 10.15 a.m., Kara climbed out of her fifteen-year-old, custom-painted Tiffany blue, battered old Mini and ignored the slush on the ground that seeped into her suede boots as she stared at the Clydeside Studio building in front of her. Okay. She could do this. She brushed away the snowflakes that were now falling thick and fast on her shoulders, straightened her jacket, adopted her very best determined expression and began striding towards the door.

'I am a strong, badass woman. I am a strong, badass woman. I am a strong...'

'Kara!'

The yell was immediately followed by a scurry of feet and then two arms being thrown around her.

'Tress!' Kara exclaimed, thinking that if the circumstances were different, she'd be overjoyed to see one of her favourite people right now.

Tress was the set designer for the studio, and one of the loveliest, kindest people you could ever meet – a miracle considering the blows life had thrown at her. A couple of years before, on the day her son was born, her husband had died in a car crash, and Tress had been devastated to discover that the passenger in the car that day had been his mistress. It was the worst kind of tragedy, but somehow Tress had picked herself back up, and she was now in a relationship with a hot doctor, and they were bringing her son up together. If Tress could get through that, then Kara could get through a HR meeting to discuss the ins and outs of why she was no longer employed.

'Oh honey,' Tress blurted, 'I heard what happened at the Hogmanay party. Are you okay? What's going on? You know if I'd been there, I'd have totally had your back.'

Kara didn't doubt that for a second. Tress was a true woman's woman – as was she, and some could argue that's what had got her into this mess in the first place.

'I know and thank you. I wish you had been there too. Honestly, it was a shit show. I still can't quite believe it all.'

Tress pulled open the huge glass door to the studio and let Kara go through first, then followed behind her. 'So tell me exactly what happened.'

Before Kara could respond, she was interrupted by a gentleman in a security uniform – not someone she recognised from the normal security team – and one of the assistants in the HR department. Kara grappled to pinpoint her name. It wasn't someone she knew well, but she'd once asked Kara to run her up a Scooby Doo costume for Halloween and Kara had grafted on for four hours after the end of her working day to make it happen. Although, her and Scooby might as well be strangers given the way the woman was looking at her now.

'Miss McIntyre,' the security guard stated, and it wasn't a question. 'Could you come with us please?'

Kara exchanged eye contact with Tress, and she knew what they were both thinking – this was like every spy movie where the FBI showed up, and ten minutes later the good guy was having to crawl out of a bathroom window and slide down a fifty-storey-tall drainpipe, before disguising his identity, lifting false passports from under a floorboard and then stealing a Grubhub delivery moped to escape.

Actually, Tress probably wasn't thinking that, but Kara definitely was.

'Erm, sure,' she answered, thinking how ridiculous this was. She'd worked here for ten years, it had been home to her, her dream job, and now she was getting treated like a suspicious stranger.

'Did you bring a witness?' the HR assistant asked, deadpan. Clearly Scooby took her job very seriously.

'A witness?'

'It was in the email we sent you. In cases of a personnel dispute, you're entitled to bring a witness.'

Damn, she hadn't got past the bit in the email where they told her they wanted to meet her this morning. She could have dragged Drea away from her premarital packing and brought her. Or called Ollie and asked him to come – she was pretty sure he'd landed in Glasgow last night.

'Yes, I'm her witness,' Tress jumped in, obviously reading the panic on her face. If Kara hadn't been so intimidated by the whole situation, she'd have hugged her again.

'Follow us please,' Scooby demanded.

This was so unnecessary. She knew exactly where the HR office was and would have been perfectly capable of making her own way there. What did they think she was going to do – spray paint 'Corbin Jacobs is a sleazy tosser' along the corridor on the way there?

'I am a strong, badass woman. I am a strong, badass woman. I am

a strong...' She repeated it in her head, all the way to their destination.

'Wait here please,' Scooby Doo announced, pointing to two chairs in reception at the HR department. Kara and Tress did as they were told, while security took a step back and stood at the door.

Tress leaned in. 'I have no idea what I'm doing,' she whispered, 'but I'm here for you. Just try not to get me fired too. Small child to feed.'

Kara responded with a smile, but said nothing else, hyper-aware of the security guard a few feet away and the HR assistant who had now taken a seat at the desk in front of them. The door to the HR director's office was closed, but Kara was pretty sure she could hear rumblings of voices behind it.

Almost half an hour later, they were still sitting there, and in that time, Kara had googled 'how to handle an exit interview', 'employee rights' and declined three calls from Josh, then swiped two texts away without reading them. She had no interest in anything the man she was supposed to marry this week had to say. After that, she'd scrolled through Twitter to see if anyone had posted footage of Ollie arriving in Glasgow last night. It was a weird life when that was the easiest way to track your best friend. Meanwhile, she could see that beside her, Tress had caught up with all her emails and booked a ten-day Easter holiday to Paphos.

That was the point at which Kara's patience ran out. She'd seen this power play. Keeping someone waiting was straight out of countless spy movies. Or maybe it was Chicago PD, she couldn't quite remember.

She stood up. Time to test out that strong, badass woman mantra.

'Look, I've waited long enough. When I got the email, I

thought I could come here and be treated with courtesy and respect...' She was making this up as she went along, but that sounded pretty good. 'But clearly that isn't the case. I'm leaving, and you'll be hearing from my lawyer.' She didn't even have a lawyer, but again, Chicago PD.

'Miss McIntyre,' came a voice from the doorway that led to the inner sanctum of Human Resources management. 'Apologies for our tardiness. We were waiting for a couple more people to join us, but it appears they've been held up.'

Kara didn't believe a word of it, especially as it was coming from the mouth of Abigail Scary Knickers Dunlop, the notoriously ruthless head of HR. Behind Abigail, Kara could see John Stoker, the studio's top legal guy who'd sent the email to summon her. She suddenly got the feeling that a costume designer and a set designer who'd just booked a jolly to Paphos were going to be no match for these two.

'Please come on through and we'll get started without them.'

Kara met Tress's gaze again, and got an encouraging nod.

Sod it. Nothing to lose.

They followed Abigail into the office, where John introduced himself, then gestured to two seats on the opposite side of the small boardroom table.

'Thank you for coming in to meet with us. I must start by apologising.' For a split second Kara got the wrong end of the apology stick and thought they were repenting for the behaviour of their star and the studio heads. He soon set her straight. 'I believe you had actually booked a holiday period beginning today. I wasn't aware of that when I sent you the email suggesting we meet this morning.'

Holiday. For her wedding. The one that was no longer happening.

'That's okay,' she said, trying to keep her chin high and her voice strong. 'I don't actually leave until tonight, so I was happy to fit you into my schedule.'

Two could play at the posturing game. They didn't need to know that until she read that email, her entire schedule today had been, 'Wallow for as long as possible. Cry. Eat high-sugar foods. Wallow some more. Go to airport.'

'Excellent. Well, I'll get right to it,' he went on, with an air of impatient irritation. 'I've been told that you resigned your position at the studio's Hogmanay party, and we'd just like to establish what exactly happened leading up to that event.'

'I'm pretty sure you already have that information,' Kara said boldly, refusing to appear intimidated, although she absolutely, most definitely, totally was intimidated.

John didn't confirm or deny. Oh, he was good. 'We'd like to hear it from your perspective. I'd also like to record this meeting, with your permission.'

'No. You're not recording me. I don't have legal representation, so that puts me at an unfair disadvantage.'

Those twenty minutes reading up on employment interviews hadn't been wasted. Beside her, Tress was nodding in solemn agreement, although Kara was fairly sure she had no idea whether that was a good move or not.

She could tell that answer had displeased them, but she remained defiant. If anything had become clear to her this week, it was that she'd had enough of people trying to tell her what she should do.

'Okay, then,' Abigail said, with a heavy, disdainful sigh, 'Perhaps you could just give me the details of the incident from your perspective.'

Kara wanted to point out that 'her perspective' was the only one that mattered, because it was the truth. She had absolutely no doubt whatsoever that Corbin Jacobs' side of the story would require more dramatic acting than the double-episode, Sunday omnibus of the show.

'Certainly. I'm just going to be honest and lay it all out there. Take from it what you will.' She could do this. She could. Do not show fear. She took a deep breath, exhaled, and began. 'As you said, we were at the studio's Hogmanay bash at the Halcyon Club in the city centre. Many of the studio management, staff and cast of the show were there too, including Corbin Jacobs. It's important to mention that he has a reputation in the studio for being sleazy, inappropriate and way too touchy-feely with the women. He's hit on just about every female in the eighteen to fifty age bracket, and the only reason he stops there is because he's also ageist.' She paused, backtracked. 'Actually, that last comment might not be true, as it's a personal opinion, not an ascertained fact.' Hopefully that would convince them that she was trying to be honest and fair.

'Anyway, at the Hogmanay party, I was dancing with one of the girls...' She cleared her throat. 'I mean, *women*, on the show. An actress.'

Abigail interrupted her, with the sharpness of a trained interrogator. 'You're referring to Casey Lowen?'

'Yes.' Casey was a relatively new addition to the cast – in her twenties, pretty, sweet, and she played the long-lost granddaughter of the character who'd been made famous by Odette Devine, the former matriarch of the show who'd retired about six months ago. And Kara really hoped they didn't ask her opinion on that because she'd be far too willing to tell them that Odette had been treated terribly – the TV soap equivalent of put out to pasture. More blatant ageism at work there.

'Anyway, I was dancing with Casey and then she went off to the loo. She'd been a bit upset all night because Corbin was repeatedly hitting on her. He'd clearly had a few drinks and he was trying to dance with her, trying to persuade her to leave with him, or to go up to the roof terrace with him. I'd just like to point out that it was minus four degrees, which says something about his state of mind. Anyway, a few moments after Casey went to the loo, I decided to go too, and that's when I saw her with Corbin in the corridor outside the toilets.'

'They were talking?'

'*He* was talking. She was trying to walk away, but he kept pulling her back. He was laughing as if that was amusing him.'

'Pulling her back? How?'

Kara could still picture every detail. 'She was wearing a chiffon shrug. He had a hold of the back of it and wouldn't let go. And then when she did manage to pull free of him, he grabbed her wrist.'

Abigail Dunlop was writing all this down, while John Stoker just listened intently, wearing his very best poker face. Beside her, Tress was wide-eyed and engrossed.

'And that's when you stepped in?'

'No. I stepped in when she told him to let go and he wouldn't.'

'Are you aware that Corbin Jacobs and Casey Lowden previously had a relationship?'

She should have expected that comment to come – as if it was some kind of excuse for his behaviour. Irritated, she went straight back with, 'The whole world is aware. They did a six-page spread in *OK! Magazine*. But since he's old enough to be her dad, it's not too surprising that it was over very quickly.' She knew she was straying into personal opinion again, but her friends, her sister, and 80 per cent of TikTok felt the same way. She got back to the facts. 'But that still doesn't give him a right to touch her, to grab her against her will, or to harass her.'

'And what happened next?' Abigail wasn't letting up for a second.

Okay, she was just going to have to blurt this out because there was no way to sugarcoat it.

'I told him to let her go. He told me to fuck off and mind my own business. Casey asked him again to take his hand off her wrist and she was getting really upset at this point. He didn't. I told him he was a lecherous prick and he leaned right into my face and screamed at me, calling me a word I won't repeat but it starts with a C and it came with so much venom that some of his spittle landed on my face. He still hadn't let Casey go and I could see she was getting more and more upset. So I stamped on his foot while wearing the stilettoes I'd borrowed from my sister – who still doesn't know about that detail, incidentally – then I heard his toes crunch and he screamed. But he also released her, so mission accomplished.'

'So you attacked him?' John Stoker clarified.

Kara shook her head. 'No. I acted in self-defence in order to make him stop behaving in an aggressive way to both my friend and myself.' She tried to say that with as much confidence as possible, but if this ever saw the inside of a courtroom, she wasn't sure a jury would see it that way. That was a problem for another day.

'At that point, Jeremy Hill appeared.' He was the head of production on the show. 'Corbin was demanding medical attention by this time, and ranting and raving… He told Mr Hill what I'd done, and we then had a very tense conversation, that boiled down to Mr Hill telling me that physical violence was a sackable offence.'

'To which you replied?' Abigail's tone remained scarily blunt.

Kara's face began to burn. 'To which I replied…' She stopped again, this time to raise a question. 'Do you want me to use the

actual words? I was highly infuriated at this point and my professionalism may have wavered.'

Beside her, Kara could see that Tress was biting her bottom
lip, her expression a combination of dread and horror.

'Yes. Exact words please.'

Oh, sweet Jesus. Kara took a deep breath.

'I said that I wouldn't want to work for a company that would
employ a sleazy twat like Corbin Jacobs anyway, so I quit and he
could shove his job. Effective immediately.'

There was a silence as they all processed the facts of that
exchange. Kara wasn't sure if she felt better or worse for retelling
it. John Stoker was now whispering something to Abigail, his
hand strategically placed so Kara couldn't even get a sense of
what he was saying.

Tress took advantage of the pause in proceedings to lean into
her ear. 'You're a fricking rock star. You should have broken his
other foot too.'

That made Kara feel slightly better until Abigail chimed in
with, 'Obviously we still have other people to speak to as part of
our investigation, including Mr Jacobs, Mr Hill and Miss
Lowden. But I do have one more question. Do you still stand by
the position that you're resigning your employment here, no
matter the findings and consequences of our investigation?'

'No!' her internal voice screamed. 'I'm skint, homeless, and living
out of a suitcase and a bin bag!'

'Yes,' she said, holding her chin high again. She had integrity.
Morals. Values. And a loan she'd taken out to go to LA to visit
Ollie last summer, but she wasn't going to worry about that right
now. What mattered was that she wasn't going to give them the
satisfaction of firing her. 'I won't work here if Corbin Jacobs
remains part of this studio.'

Another long pause and she knew what they were thinking. She was dispensable. The star of the show was not.

'Then I thank you for your time this morning. We'll be in touch to let you know the outcome of our investigation.' Abigail didn't even crack a smile to accompany her dismissive nod.

Taking the hint, Kara and Tress got up and made for the door. So that was that, then. Her career, her job that she loved, one that she was bloody good at, all gone because of one misogynistic, aggressive twat.

Tress was closest to the door, so she left the room first, partially blocking Kara's view of the reception area. Which was probably why it took her several seconds to register that Corbin Jacobs was standing there. Or rather, leaning there, on a set of crutches, with one foot in a plaster cast that went up to his knee, wearing a smug grin she'd pay money to wipe off.

And standing next to him was the head of Public Relations for the studio, a suave operator who had also been hired as Corbin's personal PR guru. He had been there at the party too, had caught the tail end of the altercation. He'd watched Corbin scream in her face and call her a C.U... She couldn't even process the rest of that thought. He was the man who'd quickly gone into damage control mode, automatically doing what was best for his clients, Corbin and Jeremy. He was the man who'd told her she'd been wrong, that she had to forget it ever happened, and that she should basically beg Corbin and Jeremy for forgiveness. He was the man who'd watched both her and Casey suffer the abuse Corbin had doled out that night, and who still, *still*, chose to represent him, instead of being on the right side of this. Even when she'd begged him.

Oh, and he was supposed to be on holiday today too, yet here he was, still standing by that scumbag's side.

Yep, there, staring straight at her with an expression she couldn't quite decipher, was her now-ex-fiancé, Josh Jackson.

6

OLLIE

It didn't matter how sunny it was in LA, or how bustling the New York sidewalks were, Ollie always got more of a kick driving through the streets of Glasgow, especially on a day like today, when the Christmas lights were still up, and the pavements were already busy with folk on their way to work, and shoppers headed to bag a bargain in the January sales.

When he was a kid, his mum and Jacinta would bring them all into the city centre on a Saturday afternoon, to go to a matinee at the cinema or – if they'd just been paid and had a bit of extra cash – the theatre. Years later, when they were in high school, Kara would drag him into town every Christmas for the switch-on of the lights at George Square. In the summer, they'd all lie on the grass in Victoria Park or over in Kelvingrove Park in the West End. And when they were in college, they would pub crawl their way around half the bars in the city centre. Glasgow was part of him – and the more he was away, the more he missed it.

Sienna had never felt the same way about his home city. Born and raised in Santa Monica, she'd grown up in the warm

sunshine at the beach and in the swish opulence of the stores on
Rodeo Drive in Beverly Hills, so the grey, rainy streets of Glasgow
had no appeal. That had been part of the whole 'opposites
attract' thing when they'd met – him, a working-class lad from
Scotland, with a mother who was a legend in pubs and karaoke
bars across Glasgow, and her, a wealthy California beach chick
from a famous acting family that stretched back three genera-
tions. Even her considerable acting skills hadn't been able to pull
off any kind of enjoyment of the life here in Glasgow. She'd come
back with him three or four times since they married, but every
time, he could see after a week or so that she was craving her
own world.

All of that made what he was about to do today even crazier.
They'd already driven from the Park Circus area of the West End,
across the city to the South Side, where they'd stopped for bacon
rolls and mugs of builder's tea in a greasy spoon that had been
there since Ollie was a kid. He'd pulled a beanie down over his
hair, shoved on a pair of fake specs, and neither of the two other
people in the place had batted an eyelid at the strangers. No-one
would expect a world-famous super star to be sitting in the
corner munching crispy bacon. Although, the waitress had
raised an eyebrow when Calvin had pulled a napkin out of the
table dispenser with a flourish and tucked it into the neck of his
cashmere sweater.

Now, they were about five minutes away from their destination, and the whole point of the trip.

'How's your mum doing?' Calvin chatted away while he
drove. 'Ah, I miss that woman. In another life, if I hadn't... you
know... been irrevocably attracted to handsome but flawed chaps
with a touch of arrogance and a nifty line in chat, then I would
have swept that fine woman right off her furry slippers.'

Despite the unease that had been seeping through his bones

as he pondered his incompatibility with his wife, Ollie grinned. 'She's doing great. She docks in Miami tomorrow and then she's flying to Hawaii for a family friend's wedding. I'm meeting her there. She always asks for you too. You know she loves you.' Calvin had been his mum's manager for many years, and he always said...

'You know, I've said it a million times, but it was one of the great injustices of my career that Moira Chiles didn't make it in theatre. I wholeheartedly believe she could have been one of the great musical stars of her generation.'

They both knew why that hadn't happened. She'd simply refused to live in London because she was a single mum to a small child and she wouldn't leave him. She also had elderly parents and she wouldn't even consider leaving them in anyone else's care. 'I do just fine and I'm perfectly happy up here in the pubs and clubs,' she said, so often that he truly believed that until he was well into his teens and developed enough emotional intelligence to understand that she'd had to convince herself of that because the reality was that despite her gargantuan talent, she'd sacrificed her dreams so that she could be his mother.

'I'll tell her you said that again. It'll make her day. She's still convinced that she'll get her name in lights one day and I wouldn't bet against her.'

Before Calvin could say any more, he let out a yelp and a couple of expletives as the car skidded in the slush when they turned a sharp corner. The windscreen wipers had been on full pelt to clear the snow that had been falling since they left his house, and it was laying thick as they turned into a side street lined with tenements that had seen better days. There were a couple of empty shops. Some boarded-up windows on the bottom-floor flats. A few teenagers hanging out by a chip shop at the end of the road, its shutters already up and the lights already on. They drove about halfway down before Calvin pulled in and stopped the car, in front of a building that Ollie knew only too well, but it looked a lot different now than it did in his childhood, when he would be brought here every Sunday by his grand-parents.

'Majestic, so it is,' Calvin quipped, with a grin. 'I tell you now, if this church collapses to rubble when we're in there, and wipes us both out, I'll be having a word with the big man about his real estate when I get upstairs.'

Ollie didn't reply, too busy taking in every inch of the building as he climbed out of the car.

There was a gent in a suit, with a parka over the top, huddled under the porch at the entrance, who stepped towards him now, hand outstretched. He introduced himself as the estate agent handling the sale of the property and then held open the huge, wooden door for them to enter, launching straight into his sales spiel.

Ollie tuned in and out of what he was saying.

'It hasn't been a house of worship for over twenty years.'

'Used as a community centre for a decade, then bought by a developer.'

'For the last ten years, the developer has been sitting on it, waiting for the area to undergo some kind of regeneration.'

'Developer has decided to cut losses and sell.'

It was pretty much all information that he knew already, because Calvin had done the research and briefed him on it.

The idea was simple – a theatre school for kids with a passion for acting or singing, who couldn't afford private lessons, one that would be a safe haven and somewhere that they could come to learn, to socialise and to develop their talents. It was Calvin's retirement project, something that would leave a real lasting legacy. He already had a group of talented actors on board, grants lined up, and plans for fundraising, but he needed a big name to partner with him and provide a substantial cash injection to buy the building and share the cost of the renovation. Calvin also wanted someone who would be more than just a name, someone who would not just make a financial commitment, but a time commitment too.

When Calvin had first brought this to him, Ollie knew his old friend was hoping he'd throw his heart into the ring and be that main partner.

Ollie wanted to be that guy. He just didn't know if he could get Sienna on board and if he couldn't, it was a deal-breaker.

They spent the next hour walking the premises, talking through plans, options, costings. By the time they got back in the car, he was sold. This could be awesome. The chance to do something that mattered. Make a difference to the community.

Calvin hadn't even put his seatbelt on before his enthusiasm got the better of him. 'So what do you think? Shall I steal your wallet right now or just hack into your bank account and Venmo the cash over to my offshore account?'

Ollie sighed, picking his words. 'I love it. I can see potential, and I think we could create something really special.'

'I sense a "but" coming. Will I need my morning cocktail before I hear it?'

'Sienna. Give me a few days because I'm going to have to speak to her and try to get her agreement, but it's going to take some work.' He didn't add that she was already pissed off with him, so that might make it a tad more challenging. 'It's not even the financial investment. She's on my case to spend less time here, so I'm really going to have to graft to get her to buy into this.'

Calvin started up the engine. 'And what about you? How do you see the future mapping out?'

Ollie shrugged. 'I'm committed to the show for seven years, and it's mostly filmed in Europe and Vancouver. To be honest, I'd rather move my base back here. LA life is great, but it's not home.'

Calvin pulled out of the parking space and as they passed the group of youths on the corner, eight teenagers gave them the finger and one threw an Irn-Bru can that bounced off the back window.

Calvin remained totally deadpan. 'Totally understand. I mean, Malibu is a hovel compared to this little slice of paradise. Home or lunch?'

'Sorry, mate, raincheck on the lunch. I need to get home and packed. I've got a flight out of here later today. Talking of which, just need to make a quick call.'

He pulled his phone out of his pocket and tried Kara again. He'd originally planned to ask her to come here with him today, because she had a brilliant eye for all things theatrical. They were definitely products of their childhood. Kara's mum, Jacinta, had been an aspiring actress at the same time as his mum was taking as many singing gigs as she could get to pay the bills, so both women had dreams of stardom. When fame didn't come to them, they'd both turned into rampant stage mums, and put all their kids in drama classes. As they hit their teens, Ollie was the only one who stuck with it. Kara's older sister, Drea, got a boyfriend and decided watching him play football on a Saturday was a far more enjoyable way to spend the day. Kara kept going but only to keep Ollie company and because she could sew, so she was a brilliant help with the costumes.

Kara's phone didn't even ring, just went straight to voicemail. Dammit. It was easier for him to get a hold of Hugh Bloody Jackman than it was to track down his lifelong friend. He tried

Drea, who picked up, with, 'Kara McIntyre's secretary here. Fielding calls for my sister since 2006.'

'Hey, it's me.'

'Who?'

He shook his head, but couldn't help laughing. He would never get big-headed or carried away with his own ego as long as he had friends like these. 'You're hilarious, you know that?'

'I do. I also know that you're probably looking for my sister, because she hasn't answered her phone for two days.'

'I am. Is she okay? How bad is it?'

'Not okay and pretty bad. I'd like to do all kinds of illegal things to Josh Jackson right now. Life would have been much simpler if you'd just married her when she asked you.'

'I was eight, and she only asked me because she wanted my bike.'

'Also true,' Drea chuckled. 'Look, I'll let her tell you what's going on because she'll want to explain it all in detail and I've got a to-do list the length of a toilet roll to get done before we leave for the airport. She's at the studios for a meeting right now because she told them to stick their job—'

'What?' he exclaimed, making Calvin swerve. She loved her job. This didn't make any sense at all. What the hell was going on?

'Another long story. Look, we can spill all the sordid details at the airport. Tell me you're still coming.'

'I'm still coming.'

'Okay, see you there, 4 p.m. I need to go now because I've got a wedding to pack for and my time is far too important to waste on idle chit-chat with TV stars. Love you and bye.'

Click.

Calvin kept his eyes on the road, but was clearly intrigued. 'Everything okay?'

'Yeah, just one of my mates having a hard...' His words faded away as a ping on his phone interrupted him. Then another. Then another. Then Calvin's phone, attached to the dashboard by some magnetic device, started popping off too. It was like the scene in so many movies where there's a press conference and all the journalists' phones start ringing at the same time to alert them to some unrelated travesty.

Frowning, Ollie scanned his phone screen. Notifications from Instagram. X. Facebook. Texts. WhatsApp messages. Either he'd been nominated for something amazing, or he'd been cancelled, or the press had got hold of some false rumour and it was firing around the cyber-verse.

He opened the first one and got the answer straight away. A salacious headline on a celebrity blog:

Sleepless In Sienna? Actress spotted in mid-flight clinch with co-star.

Yet another false story. Alert over. He felt his shoulders drop down a few inches. These fricking people were just scumballs, making up shit like that for clicks. It was nonsense. Probably some fake photo of a woman who looked remotely like his wife. He'd been doing this long enough to know that it didn't warrant another moment of his time.

Ping. Ping. Ping. Bloody hell, the internet was really going for this one. At least three journalists he knew on a personal basis had just texted him. He was about to click off the article and read the texts when curiosity got the better of him.

He scrolled down, until the photo became clearer and his shoulders rose right back up again. The inside of an airplane cabin. A guy that Ollie immediately recognised as Van Weeks, Sienna's co-star in the play that had just closed. Although, you couldn't see every detail of his face because it was being partially blocked by the woman who was joined to him at the lips. Black baseball cap. Long dark hair.

If this was a fake photo of his wife, it was the best one he'd ever seen.

Just as the car turned into his street, his gaze dropped down to the line below.

CLICK HERE TO SEE FULL SHOCKING VIDEO OF SIENNA MONTGOMERY IN ILLICIT ENCOUNTER WITH VAN WEEKS!

His finger hovered over the button. This might be a made-up story for clicks, but he was about to take the bait.

7

ALICE

Alice slipped a solitary pearl earring on each ear, then stood back to survey herself in the mirror. Even now, more than six months after she'd left Larry, she still hadn't become accustomed to being happy with the person she saw reflected in the glass. For the entirety of their marriage, she had lived a lie – to the public, she was married to the successful entrepreneur who'd started his career in the bar and nightclub industry, before entering the political field and rising to become a Member of Parliament. In reality, she was trapped in a marriage hell with a man she despised, but who kept her with him using threats and manipulation, because it suited his political image.

It was only two years ago, when a newspaper exposed him as a corrupt, drug-using, disgrace to his government office that his downfall began, and his allies had scattered like rats off Larry's sinking ship. And Alice had silently applauded every indignity and humiliation that had come his way, even if she was well and truly dragged down with him. She didn't care. She was happy to take the fall, guilty by association.

It had taken her over a year after that to finally escape him, more than twelve months of living in poverty, ruined, desolate, destroyed – and yet every day was bearable because she knew it was one day closer to leaving him. They'd lived in a hovel, but she'd taken cleaning jobs, squirrelled money away, plotted, schemed, waited. Finally, after Larry was involved in an accident while driving a taxi when he was drunk and high behind the wheel, she had her chance and she took it. Somewhere in the midst of that time, she'd also discovered that Larry was having an affair with a work colleague called Sandra, and she'd tried to warn her what he was truly like, but Sandra had fired back with scorn and malice. Alice often wondered if she'd found out for herself yet.

Meanwhile, Alice knew that the survivor inside her own mind, that woman who'd lived for that final year in isolation, shunned by the friends she'd made in her gilded public life, only spending money on the very basics, would be over the moon to see her today. Sure, when she was out in public, some people still recognised her, judged her, assumed the worst of her, but the people that mattered knew the truth. Now, she recognised herself again. She could hold her head up and she could breathe. When she joined Rory and Sophie in Reading tomorrow, no one would have a clue who she was, and the transition to her new, anonymous life, lived on her own terms, would be complete. She'd have a family again. Privacy. Peace. And eventually, she'd have her own home too. She couldn't wait.

'Alice! My heels are on and my feet are already killing me, so could you get a shoogle on!' came the holler from the bottom of the stairs.

Smiling, Alice straightened her jacket, patted the bun of hair that was its natural grey, but with subtle blonde highlights to soften it, slipped her feet into low black pumps and grabbed her bag from the knob on the front of the wardrobe. The room was small, and the navy walls and grey carpet hadn't been changed since Val's son, Michael, had left home a decade ago, but it was clean, comfortable and to Alice it was a haven of safety and relaxation. Apart from the occasional harassment when she was late, and Val was waiting at the bottom of the stairs in three-inch heeled boots.

By the time Alice joined her, Val already had her car keys in one hand and her handbag in the other, as she announced, 'My wee Jeep can fairly pick up speed, but it's not a helicopter, doll, so we need to get cracking.' Before catching sight of Alice and adding, 'Och, you don't scrub up too bad, you know. Although you could always do with a bit of blue eyeliner.' It was a standing joke, with Alice and everyone else in Val's life having given up trying to sway her from the same Princess Diana make-up she'd been wearing for decades.

Everyone also knew that Val cared not a jot what they thought, so it gave them all free rein to dish the snippy comments right back at her.

'But it's no longer 1986, so I'll pass,' Alice fired back, grinning.

God, she'd miss this. It had taken a period of adjustment to get back into the way of amusing conversations and barbed banter and finding hilarity in the simplest conversations with genuine friends, but now, in Val's home, it had become a way of life.

It only took a gaze to her right, where her suitcases were sitting packed and ready to go to the airport later in the afternoon, to remind her that it would soon be over, so she covered up the pit that caused in her stomach with a jokey, 'Right, let's go then. Can't stand around here all day chatting.'

Her sarcasm was rewarded with a loud 'Pfft,' from Val, followed by the clicking of her chum's heels all the way down the hall.

'Urgh, my hair and my good suede boots will be ruined in this,' Val muttered as they made their way down the slushy path towards the parked car, brushing snow off their shoulders when they finally got into the Jeep. The traffic was relatively quiet, because the schools hadn't returned and many people took the rest of this week off to recover from the Christmas and New Year break, so despite the weather, it didn't take long to get out of Weirbridge and onto the road to the crematorium, which was only about ten miles away on the outskirts of the nearby town of Burnbank.

'How are you feeling? Nervous?' Val asked her. 'It's a long time since you've seen your old friend.'

Alice watched the snow fall on the leafless trees that lined the road as they passed by. 'Not nervous. Sad, for Audrey and the family she leaves behind. And a little regretful. I'm sure Morag and I drove Audrey crazy when we were younger and it would have been lovely to have connected with Audrey again before she passed. It seems like the thirty years since I saw them last have gone by so quickly. And also, if I'm honest, I'm a little bit hopeful about seeing Morag again, although it's in such a sad setting. Even if we could just reconnect, then meet up again properly some other time, that would be wonderful. I know we can't turn back time, but maybe we can just have a different time. One where we get to be in each other's lives again.'

Val sighed, shook her head. 'Not even out the door yet and you're replacing me. You're lucky I'm good-natured and thick-skinned.'

Alice played along. 'Val, we both know you're irreplaceable, but in some ways Morag wasn't too different from you.'

'A demon at the Slosh and fond of Duran Duran?'

The Slosh was a legendary Scottish version of line dancing, usually performed to a seventies track called 'Beautiful Sunday' by Daniel Boone. The minute the opening bars rang out at a Scottish party, the dance floor would fill, and Val had made it her speciality. Alice bowed down to her ability to do the Slosh in three-inch mules, while sipping a vodka and coke and carrying out a conversation with the six people nearest to her.

'That too. But she was good at reading people. You know, she once tried to warn me about Larry. In fact, it was the last thing she ever said to me. Something about him not being who I thought he was. At the time, twenty-five, fearless, naïve, I was swept off my feet by the promise of a wonderful life with him, so I just thought...' She paused, realising this didn't reflect well on her, before carrying on in the knowledge that Val was the kind of pal you could bare your soul to without judgement. 'Urgh, I hate to admit it. I just thought she was maybe a bit jealous. How stupid could I have been? How could she see it and I didn't?'

'Because you were in love. Young. Optimistic. And, to be brutally honest, that odious horror of a man spent his whole career convincing people he was one of the good guys. Every single person who voted for him fell for it.'

That was true, and something she'd watched time and time again as Larry climbed up the political pole, but it didn't make Alice feel any better.

Val indicated before turning into the grounds of the crematorium, then parked in the first available space. 'Okay, pal, you're ready?' she said, with a supportive smile.

'I'm ready,' Alice said calmly, before taking a deep breath and opening the Jeep door.

It was only a few minutes before the service was due to start, so a large group of mourners were already waiting outside, under the roof canopy, adhering to the tradition that they shouldn't go inside before the coffin and the immediate family. They didn't have long to wait. Moments after Alice and Val joined them, a hearse, followed by two long black limos snaked up the drive towards them.

The family alighted from the cars first, and Alice scanned them for sight of Morag, but she couldn't see her. In fact, she didn't recognise anyone at all. Had they come to the wrong service?

Or maybe not. The older man, the one who was now making his way from one of the family cars to the hearse, could that be Cillian? She wasn't at all convinced. It was difficult to tell from thirty yards and thirty years away.

Alice bowed her head respectfully as the coffin was taken out of the hearse and raised onto the shoulders of the pallbearers, who then, slowly, steadily, entered the building, with the rest of the mourners following behind them, to the sound of Westlife singing 'You Raise Me Up' coming from the speakers. Alice didn't have to look at Val to know what she'd be thinking – that whoever chose that song had the kind of sense of humour she'd have liked to get to know. Instead, she kept her head down as they slipped into the back row.

The celebrant introduced herself, explained that this would be a humanist service and then went on to welcome everyone.

'Thank you all, on behalf of Audrey's family, for being here today to celebrate her life.'

Audrey. That confirmed they were at the right service. So where was…?

'Audrey was dearly loved by her children, her grandchildren, by her beloved late sister, Morag, who passed away just a year ago…'

Alice didn't hear the rest, drowned out by the noise of the wind being punched out of her chest. Morag was dead? Perhaps she'd been naïve, but she hadn't even considered that could be the case. Morag was the same age as her, barely fifty-five. No age at all, really. Alice felt a crushing wave of sadness, of heartbreak for her old friend, and of sorrow that they would never have a chance to meet up again, to reminisce, to share stories about the time in their lives when they thought anything was possible and the world was at their feet. She'd completely messed her own life up, but she sent up a silent prayer that Morag's had been much happier, that she was loved and that she'd woken up every day glad of the choices that she'd made.

Val's hand slipped into hers, and Alice was grateful, yet again, that she'd found this woman, and sad that Morag didn't get to meet her too. They'd have enjoyed each other. Now that page had turned.

She listened to the rest of the ceremony, to the funny stories that Audrey's son, Hamish, told about his mum, to the heart-breaking eulogy from her daughter, Jill, and to the beautiful words from the celebrant about life, about death and about touching the hearts of others.

Poor Morag. Poor Audrey. Alice's heart broke for them both. But that grief came with something else – even more determination to live the years she had in front of her on her own terms.

When the final words had been said, the platform that Audrey's coffin rested on lowered into a void in the pedestal and then the top closed on it. The heart-crushing sobs of a few of the congregation were the only sounds to be heard, until the opening bars of the final song came from the speakers.

Val leaned in close to her ear. 'Do you still want to go to the hotel? I'm happy to do whatever you feel you need to.'

Alice gave a small shake of her head. No. She'd hoped that it would be a bittersweet reunion with an old friend. Now that wouldn't happen, going back to spend time with a group of mourners she didn't know just felt like an intrusion on their pain.

I'm sorry, Morag, she sent up a silent message to her pal. *I wish I'd listened. I wish I'd stopped you leaving. I wish I'd come with you. I wish I'd been a better friend. I wish that I'd had the sense to keep in touch, to track you down, to find out why we drifted apart and to bring us together again.*

But now it was time to go, because all she'd wanted was to see Morag again. To share the stories of their lives. And yes, maybe to ask her old friend why she'd warned her about Larry and why she'd broken off all contact. However, Morag was gone, so Alice was going to have to come to terms with the fact that there was no-one left who could give her the answers to those questions.

8

ZAC

As the ceremony ended, the opening bars of 'My Heart Will Go On' filled the room, proving that no one could say Aunt Audrey didn't have a wry sense of humour. Everyone remained in their seats, some of them joining in, others just patiently waiting to be directed. The crematorium ushers appeared at the end of the front pew and beckoned the immediate family out, before moving down the aisle, making sure everyone filed out row by row. Zac placed his hand on his dad's crestfallen shoulder, then walked slowly behind him, the last of the family line to exit the row.

As commanded by the end-of-life wishes of his wonderfully prepared Aunt Audrey, as soon as they got outside, he waited at the double doors of the crematorium, Jill and her husband, Archie, on one side of him, Hamish and his wife, Mandy, on the other, to shake the hands of the mourners who'd been good enough to come and pay their respects. Aunt Audrey was big on manners and traditions like that. Hopefully, if she was indeed watching from above, she'd understand that his dad had decided that he wouldn't participate in the line-up, in contradiction of

Audrey's request. Zac hadn't been surprised when his dad came over to whisper that he was going to head straight to the hotel, to make sure the tea and sandwiches (specification number eight on Audrey's plan for the day) were ready and waiting for the mourners to arrive, because he had a feeling that his dad was just struggling with the emotion of it all, and the memories it was bringing up of the day, less than twelve months ago, when they'd buried his mum. Zac felt a comfort in being beside his cousins in this moment, but his dad had always been one to stay strong and stoic and deal with his pain on his own.

Every single person who came out of the building worked their way along the family line, some hugging, some shaking hands, the ones he hadn't met usually introducing themselves before they expressed their condolences. Some even shared a little anecdote about Audrey and he reacted to them all with gratitude, touched that, just like his mum, she'd left her mark on so many people's lives.

Zac had just shaken the hand of one of his aunt's neighbours – *'wonderful woman – she was the only one on the street who knew what colour bin went out every week; when she went on holiday it was chaos out there'* – when he turned to see that there were only two people left. Must have been the ones who'd sat in the back row.

Both were women, the first, a striking vision, in a black furry jacket, which was the opposite end of the colour spectrum from her pale blonde hair, cut in a razor-sharp edge around her neck, but weirdly wide like a motorcycle helmet.

'My condolences to you all,' she said when she reached him. 'I'm sorry to say I never had the pleasure of knowing Audrey, but I wish I had. She sounds like some wumman. I'm actually here to support a friend who was close to Audrey's sister, Morag, back in the day.'

It was so unexpected, it almost winded him.

'That was my mum,' he said.

'Och, son, I'm so sorry. I heard the celebrant mention that she passed away last year. What a time you've had. My heart is sore for your whole family. You take good care of yourself. I'm sure your mum and your aunt would want that for you.'

'They would. Thank you.'

He gave her hand a grateful squeeze before letting it go.

The very last mourner wrapped up her conversation with Jill, and moved along the line so that she was standing in front of him. He had no idea if this was the friend the other woman had been referring to, but she was a very elegant lady in a dark navy suit, her hair pulled back into a small bun at the nape of her neck.

He forced a tight smile as he reached out to shake her hand. One more mourner. Just one more. The cars were already lined up next to them, ready to take them to the hotel.

'I'm so sorry for your loss,' she said in a very soft, polite voice, that was nothing like the gravelly brogue of the woman who'd gone before her.

'Thank you. It was very kind of you to come today. I'm Zac. Audrey was my aunt.' He must have made that introduction twenty times in the last half an hour.

'So I guess from the accent that you must be Morag's son,' the woman said. 'I was so sorry to hear that she'd passed away. I came here today to pay my respects to Audrey, because she was always very kind to me, but I was actually Morag's friend when we were growing up. To be honest, I was hoping that she'd be here and I'm so sorry that she isn't. Your mum was a very special lady. I was sad to lose touch with her when she moved to Ireland.'

He lost interest in the fact that the cars were waiting, or that the other family members had now headed in that direction. This woman had known his mum before she went to Ireland. All he wanted to do now was speak to her, ask her a million questions about the young Morag Corlan. Or Morag McTay, as she'd have been then.

'So you knew her before she left Glasgow, before she had me?' It was out before he'd thought it through, but if she thought it was a strange question, she didn't show it.

'Yes. We met when we started high school. And then, later, we worked together at the same legal firm. I was the receptionist, and she was one of the secretaries. We were best friends for many years. She was great fun and we had some wonderful times.'

This was totally intriguing. If they were such good friends, why had they lost touch? Why hadn't his mum gone to see her when they came back on any of the twice-yearly visits to Glasgow that they'd made every year of his life? It didn't make sense. He'd always known his mum to be a faithful friend who hung on to the people she loved. Her own funeral had been absolutely packed with pals that she'd met and kept close in her thirty years in Ireland. Now that he came to think about it, though, when they were in Glasgow, the only people she spent time with were family members. Why had he never questioned why she had no friends from here? And why was he only realising that now? Or was it just that his brain was so blown away by the questions raised by the strip of photos of his mum and dad on their first date, that he was questioning everything and nothing was making sense anymore?

The note of apology to someone he'd never heard of, and the photo booth snapshots were now burning a hole in the inside pocket of his jacket. He wasn't sure why he'd brought them – it just felt right to keep something his mum had touched close to his heart, and he hadn't wanted to leave them back at Aunt Audrey's house in case his dad spotted them. His father had enough to deal with and Zac didn't want to force him to have a tough conversation on a day like this – or on any other day.

'Excuse me, Zac, but the cars are waiting for you.' That came from Hamish, who'd come back to get him.

Zac felt his pulse quicken, realising that it was time to wrap up a conversation that he didn't want to end. Maybe this woman was one of those people who exaggerated relationships and tried to make herself feel important by inserting herself into other folk's dramas and heartache, but, truthfully, he was pretty good at reading people and didn't get that vibe from her.

That thought gave way to another one. Maybe she'd be able to shed some light on the timescale of events, perhaps answer his question about the date on the back of the photographs. 'I don't want to put you on the spot, but are you coming back to the hotel for tea? I'd really like to talk to you a little more.'

'I wasn't planning to, but...' The woman's gaze went to her friend, the lady with the blonde hair, who was patiently waiting a few feet away, and he watched as they appeared to have a silent conversation that consisted of eyebrows raised in question, then very subtle nods, leading to, 'Yes, okay. I'd be very happy to come back to speak with you. I think Morag would have liked that.'

Zac's shoulders dropped in relief. 'Thank you so much. I'll see you there.'

He shook her hand again, then watched as she took a few steps towards her waiting friend. He turned around, ready to make his way to the large black vehicle only a few feet away, when he had a thought.

'Excuse me,' he called after her, keeping his voice as low as possible, so as not to be disrespectful to his surroundings. 'I didn't catch your name.'

The older woman turned, gave him an apologetic smile. 'I'm so sorry. I should have introduced myself. I'm Alice.'

9

ALICE

Glasgow Airport – May 1995

Alice rolled down the window of Larry's Mercedes and tried not to panic because he was doing 95 mph on the motorway. The legal firm she worked for had already made three of his speeding fines disappear and she wasn't sure they could swing a fourth.

That was actually how she'd met him. He was a frequent flyer at her office, and always stopped at her desk for some chat, which she was happy to reciprocate. All in the name of customer service of course. Nothing to do with him being six foot three, and so good-looking he could easily be one of those male models on the aftershave adverts. Not that he was in need of a job. Everyone knew that Larry McLenn owned several of the coolest, trendiest wine bars in the city, and he was photographed almost as much as the celebrities who partied in them. Alice had seen him a few times when she'd been in his bars with her ex-boyfriend – a Premier League football player who'd transferred down to an English club a few months before. Alice hadn't cared that he'd moved away. She was twenty-five, free, single, had a great job, and was loving life in her tiny but gorgeous city-centre flat. In fact, she was the one who often got mistaken for a model, which she always thought was hilarious because last time she checked, Cindy Crawford and Naomi Campbell weren't nipping into C&A for their Saturday night outfits. Not that it mattered. Her best friend, Morag, always said that she could throw on a bin bag and make it look good.

When Larry had asked her out, she hadn't hesitated. Who would? Sure, he was a bit older than her, in his early thirties already, but that just meant he already had his life sorted and knew what he wanted – and as he'd been telling her since the first time they got together, what he wanted now was her.

It went both ways. They'd been dating for six months, and she loved everything about him: his charm, his intelligence, his drive, the way he got things done. Sure, some people – her parents included – thought he was arrogant and a bit boastful and flash, but she knew that was just confidence. They just didn't know him as well as she did, didn't see how much he loved her, how well he treated her, always spoiling her with little gifts and treating her to amazing nights out and weekends away. He made her absolutely giddy and not just because he drove too fast.

Today was just another example of his good heart. Morag was going to Ireland with her boyfriend, Cillian, and Larry had offered to drive them to Glasgow Airport for their flight. How kind was that?

Morag had insisted they could get a taxi, but Larry wouldn't hear of it. That's how sweet he was, giving up his night to do something lovely for one of her friends. Just as she was thinking that, he took one hand off the wheel, and reached over to the passenger seat to squeeze her hand. Her anxiety over his Formula One driving slid up a notch, but she knew he was just trying to console her because she was sad about Morag leaving.

And Morag must be feeling the same way because neither she nor her boyfriend, Cillian, had said a word since they'd got in the car.

Larry took his hand back, and put it on the wheel as he steered the car off the motorway, down the slip road and round to the car park in front of the terminal building. They got lucky when a Cortina pulled out of a space in the front row and Larry nipped straight in there.

There was no queue at the desks, so they were checked in and upstairs at the café in no time. Weirdly, this was one of Alice's favourite places. There were only a couple of cafés in Glasgow that were open twenty-four hours, so ever since she'd bought her very first Fiat Panda at eighteen, her and Morag would jump in the car and come here for a late-night hot chocolate and a pile of snacks. They'd watch the people milling around, arriving too late for night flights or too early for the first flights of the day. And they'd talk for hours, until it was time to go home and get ready for college, or later, for work. There would be plenty of time to sleep when they were old, that was their motto.

Strangely, though, Morag still wasn't her usual chatty self tonight. Cillian and Larry went off to the counter, with instructions to bring back two coffees, four packets of pickled onion crisps – Larry hated it when she ate those, but it was her and Morag's favourite flavour – and two walnut whips.

'Nervous about meeting Cillian's family? Is that why you've been so quiet today?' Alice asked, as soon as the guys were out of sight. 'They'll love you; I know they will.'

Morag had only started dating Cillian a couple of months ago, so no one was more shocked than Alice that her pal had quit her job at the firm and decided to go back to Ireland with him. He'd been in Glasgow working on a construction project for his

Irish employers, so he had a good job that could support them until Morag found work, but still it was a bit out of character. Morag had always been the more sensible one of the two, the level-headed one that didn't get carried away or swept up in her emotions. At least, until now…

'No, I'm not worried,' Morag answered, pulling the cuffs of her sleeves down over her hands. That was what she always did when she was worried. 'I just… I'll miss you.'

'Oh, Mo,' Alice wailed, as she stretched over and wrapped her arms around her friend. 'I'll miss you so much too. You know it's not too late to change your mind.'

Pulling back, Morag fanned her face, trying to dry the tears. 'No, I can't. It's the right thing to do. I know it's quick, but I really like Cillian. And it's time for a change of scene. I want to see different places. I can't go through life only having lived in Glasgow.'

This was the same story she'd been telling since she first broke the news and Alice still didn't get it.

'That's not true, we've been to Benidorm. And Magaluf. I've still got the scars from when I fell over the sea wall.' Alice hoped bringing up one of their favourite memories would cheer them up, but it actually did the opposite. She had to pull a napkin from the silver container in the middle of the table to dab her cheeks.

'I am happy for you, though, I promise. Cillian is so lovely. Look at us, all grown up and somehow we both managed to land really great guys.'

Bloody hell, Alice watched her friend's face crumble and realised cheery stuff wasn't working either. Morag was getting more upset by the minute.

'Did I hear something about "great guys"? That has to be us, Cillian,' Larry interrupted with a cheeky wink, as he put down a tray with the coffees and four packets of plain crisps. 'They didn't have pickled onion, so I got these instead.'

Alice frowned as she cast a glance over at the counter. She was sure she could see what she'd asked for in a basket behind the tills. Larry must not have noticed.

'And I didn't get the chocolate because you told me you were on a diet. Don't want to lead you astray.'

Okay, so sometimes he took things a little too literally, but he was only looking out for her and he was right. She did want to lose a couple of pounds so that she could squeeze her size-twelve body into the two new dresses he'd bought her for their holiday next month to Marbella. Both the dresses and the holiday were his birthday gifts to her, but he'd somehow managed to buy size tens. He'd told her they were non-returnable because they were designer, so she was just going to have to make it work. Walnut whip deprivation was a small price to pay.

Morag didn't seem to be quite as understanding about it and didn't even thank Larry for the coffees. Alice would never in a million years say anything, and she felt terrible for even thinking it, but sometimes she wondered if Morag was a little bit jealous of her relationship with Larry. All the girls in the office used to talk about how gorgeous he was and maybe Morag had fancied her chances with him a little bit. It would definitely explain how weird she'd been acting towards her lately.

Hopefully some time away in Ireland would sort it all out, and when Morag was ready to come back, whether that was in a few months or a year or whenever, she'd be her old self again.

Cillian sat down on the same side of the table as Morag and spotted her red-rimmed eyes. 'You okay?'

Morag nodded. 'Yep. I was just telling Alice how much I'm going to miss her.'

Alice handed out the coffees from the tray. 'I'm going to visit you as soon as you're settled though. Just let me know when I can come. I'll be over so often you'll be sick of me.'

Beside her, Larry coughed and she felt his knee nudge hers, so she changed the subject. Not that he would mind her going to visit Morag, but he did like her to be with him at the weekends, even if it was just waiting at his flat for him to come home from one of his bars.

'We'd like that, Alice,' Cillian said, and she thought again what a nice guy he seemed to be. Not that she knew him well yet. When Alice had been seeing the footballer, Morag was dating a guy who did something in finance, and they would all hang out together most weekends. There had been no double dates lately though, so Alice had never really got to know Cillian. She'd change that when she visited, or when they came back to Glasgow for weekends.

'Tell me about your home over there, Cillian,' she asked, taking the pressure off the situation by changing the subject of her best friend leaving.

For the next ten minutes, while they drank their coffees, they chatted about Ireland and Cillian's family and all the things he had planned for Morag when they got back to his hometown on the outskirts of Dublin.

'His friends sound so nice,' Morag chipped in. 'All really good, decent men. Not like some of the ones here.'

Alice wasn't sure where that was coming from, but she didn't dwell on it. It was only right that Morag was viewing her new life through rose-coloured glasses. 'Then you'll have to bring some of them over when you come back. A couple of the girls in the office are still single,' she joked.

Their laughter was cut short by the scraping of Larry's chair as he pushed it back. 'Right, Alice, we'd better be going. I don't know what the traffic will be like on the way home and I need to stop in to speak to a couple of my managers.'

'But their flight doesn't leave for another—'

'I know, and I'm so sorry, but it's work,' he said, and Alice could see from his apologetic smile that he felt bad dragging her away.

Reluctantly, she got up, and Morag and Cillian did the same.

Morag pulled her handbag off the back of her chair. 'It's okay. We should probably go on through security anyway.'

'We'll walk you there,' Alice told her, ignoring Larry's quiet sigh. Okay, so they were in a hurry, but this was her best friend, so he could give her another five minutes.

Bags picked up, they left the café and made their way across to the glass wall of the terminal, where the entrance to the security section was located.

When they got there, Alice pulled a little camera out of her bag, just one of the gifts Larry had bought her since they met. 'Larry, can you take a picture of us?' She turned back to Morag. 'I need proof you existed, just in case you run off into the sunset and forget all about me.' She was teasing, but Morag wasn't laughing, and Larry didn't look too pleased about yet another delay to them getting out of here. He snapped a couple of quick pics of the girls, and a couple with Cillian in them too then tossed the camera back to her.

Alice turned and hugged Cillian. 'Take care of my girl. She's special, you know?'

'I do,' he agreed, and Alice warmed to him even more.

Larry had given Morag a peck on the cheek, and now the two men were shaking hands and saying goodbye, which gave the girls a moment together. They wrapped their arms around each other, all the swallowed tears coming right back up again.

'I'll miss you so much. Take care and have an amazing time,'

Alice said in Morag's ear, inhaling the scent of her daily squirt of Rive Gauche.

'I will. I love you, but Alice...' Morag whispered, holding on tight. 'Be careful with Larry. I don't think he's who you think he is.'

Before Alice could fully absorb what had just been said, Morag McTay spun around and walked out of her life.

NOON – 2 P.M.

10

KARA

As Kara opened the door to her flat, she noticed that her hands were still trembling. She didn't know if it was from adrenaline, devastation or sheer bloody fury. Josh. Her erstwhile fiancé. Still siding with Corbin Jacobs. Even after everything that had happened. And somehow – some-*fricking*-how – he obviously expected her to understand that decision.

As soon as they'd locked eyes in the HR reception, she'd frozen, her brain shutting down the ability to move, think or speak for a couple of seconds, until he'd stepped forward, 'Kara, can I talk to you?'

The sound of his voice had been enough to snap her out of her comatose state. 'No.'

Her gaze had shifted to Corbin Jacobs, who, despite looking like a casualty from the alien invasion dream scene they'd done on the show a couple of months ago, was eyeing her with an expression that sat somewhere between smugness and disgust. Before Kara could act on her urge to take Tress's advice and stand on his other foot, Abigail Dunlop had emerged from her office. 'Corbin, Josh – we're ready for you.'

That had been the moment of truth – would Josh go in there with them or continue trying to speak to her? She hadn't waited to find out. Her racing heart had been about to explode, so instead, she'd charged right past them and then bolted down the corridor, out of the door and into her car.

Now that she was back at the home she'd shared with Josh, she fired a quick text off to Tress.

> Sorry I ran out on you. Thanks so much for being my wing-woman today. Xx

The reply was immediate.

> No worries. I'm 100% on your side. If I can do anything to help, please holler. Xx PS: Josh was with Corbin? I'm so sorry. I hope you're okay.

Everyone in the studio would be talking about this by now. Kara has a stand-up fight with Corbin, and her fiancé was still all chummy with him, business as normal. Tress, a work friend who had only just learned the details of the story, was supporting her, yet her boyfriend of eight years couldn't do the same thing? Her hands began to shake a little more. Fury. Definitely sheer bloody fury.

And sadness too, as she scanned the flat that had been her home for the last seven years. Josh had already owned this place when they'd met and Kara was sharing a different flat with Drea, so it had made sense that she moved in here after a year or so of dating. At the start, there had been vague plans to look for something else that would be a joint investment, but somehow they'd never got round to it, because Josh hadn't wanted to leave here. Not that she'd minded, because she'd loved this place. She just wished she'd considered that after paying half of everything for all this time she was going to walk away with nothing except a broken heart and a whole pile of sorrow.

A huge sob of grief began to rise up in her throat and she swallowed it back. No. She wasn't going to fall apart here. Right now, she was going to gather her stuff together while Josh was at the studio, get out of here, and then schedule falling apart for when she was surrounded by people she loved and wine.

She crossed the deep walnut floor towards their bedroom, stopping at the doorway because it was right next to the sideboard in the living room that held pictures of all the special moments in their lives. The two of them on a beach in Kos, when he told her he was in love with her for the first time. The night they got engaged, sitting on the end of a pier, their feet dangling over the waters of Loch Lomond. And there were family pics too. Josh's clan, at his thirtieth birthday, when they'd rented log cabins in the Highlands and partied for the whole weekend. They'd thought about getting married the same way, but she hadn't wanted to withdraw from the joint wedding pact with Drea. Josh's mother hated to fly, so his family had been totally accepting of their decision to do a private destination wedding by themselves, on the promise that they'd have a huge celebration in the next couple of months back here. Hopefully no one had splashed out on their party frocks yet.

Her gaze landed on another picture, right at the back – Kara, Drea and Jacinta, with Ollie and his mum, Moira, all posing outside the Shaftesbury Theatre in London, brimming with excitement to see *Flashdance*. She must have been about sixteen, but she remembered every detail of it, because it was Moira's last trip with them before she'd gone to work on the cruise ships. Ollie had grown about six inches that year and somehow his baby face had morphed into a level of handsomeness that shouldn't be allowed. They'd had the best time, laughed all

weekend, and for about five seconds, as Ollie slung his arm
around her coming out of the theatre, Kara had experienced a
flutter of attraction to him, that she'd rapidly brushed off and
refused to consider ever again, which was just as well, because
only a few months later, he'd gone to London, the first of many
trips away that would eventually, years later, lead him to New
York and Sienna.

Snatching the picture up, she carried it into her bedroom.
Her *former* bedroom. None of this was hers now. Nothing. Their
bedroom had always been her happy place, the one room in the
home that she'd decorated. The rest of the flat was all dark wood
floors and white walls, with tasteful art and neutral furniture, but
not in here. The walls were a calming ivory, and the bed linen
was her favourite shade of yellow, with mint-coloured cushions
and a matching throw draped across the bottom. The floors were
a light oak, and the windows were dressed in voile that let the
sun stream through on the occasions it actually shone in the city.
Luckily, there were no neighbouring windows with an eyeline to
the room, or they'd have had the pleasure of watching her
wrangle into her Spanx every morning.

Under the window was her favourite thing of all – her old
desk, the one that had got her through art school and that she'd
used almost every day since. It was a kaleidoscope of colour
charts, fabric swatches and sketches. At night, she would sit
there, designing, drawing, planning out her concepts for
upcoming shows. With a soap like *The Clydeside*, set in a fictional
Scottish town in the present day, there hadn't been much of an
opportunity to use the more theatrical side of her imagination –
other than that one alien invasion scene, but the less said about
that the better – but she'd loved her job, nonetheless. Creating a
character's wardrobe was like shaping a part of their personality
and she'd relished it and taken huge pride in her attention to

detail. Yet, now she was out of the role she'd adored for a decade, all for sticking up for what she thought was right and trying to fight back against the misogynistic attitudes and gargantuan egos that still bubbled under the surface of the industry.

Would she do it again? Absolutely. Although, it might make her feel more reassured that it was worth it if Casey Lowden had been in touch. Not that Kara needed any kind of thank you, but it would be good to know that Casey had her back, just as Kara had hers at the party.

She shrugged that off. No point getting bogged down in what had happened. It was done. All she could do was move forward, get a new job, find somewhere to live, build a whole new life. Starting now.

She grabbed one of Josh's holdalls from the bottom of his wardrobe and began filling it up with things she'd missed when she'd hastily packed in the early hours of the New Year. The photo she'd taken from the sideboard in the living room went in first, then her jewellery, minus the engagement ring that she'd left on Josh's bedside table right before she'd walked out. If she sold it, there would be enough for a deposit on a rental flat, but she didn't want that money, because it would always be a reminder of how the man she was supposed to be able to depend on more than anyone else in the world had let her down.

That night, she'd needed him to do the right thing, but instead, he'd done the wrong thing, because that was the job he was paid to do. He'd gone straight into Mr PR mode, minimising the whole event, then immediately attending to Corbin, trying to calm him down as he was wailing about the damage she'd done to his foot. Josh had got him out of there, asking one of his staff to take him to the ED at Glasgow Central Hospital, and then he'd gone into a huddle with the studio head, Jeremy, discussing the situation and strategising over the next move. They'd even had the absolute mind-blowing audacity to suggest *she* apologise. That's when Kara had left. Sad. Hurt. Disgusted. When he'd eventually come home, several hours later, she was already in bed. Fool that she was, she'd expected him to come in and be concerned for her, but no. He was in full-scale PR mode and he'd told her she had to make sure everything was swept under the carpet.

'No. He's a horrible perv and I'm not doing it. Josh, I don't think you understand – he had a hold of her and wouldn't let go. He was totally harassing her. You know as well as I do that he's pulled shit like that with other women in the building. And you saw the way he was screaming at me too. What else was I to do?'

The vein in his cheek that always popped up when he was angry had been in full view. 'Make a complaint. Speak to him in private back at the studio. I don't know, Kara. But now you've caused a public scene that I'm going to have to manage in the media, and they're going to have to write in a limp for the lead character.'

'So tell me, since you don't seem to think that a grown-ass man verbally abusing your fiancée in public is a deal-breaker, what would you have done if it was me that he'd got physical with?'

'It wasn't you, though.'

Eyes blazing, she'd refused to back down. 'Just go with me here. If it were me, the woman you're marrying next week, and the mighty Corbin bloody Jacobs had a hold of me, despite my objections, would you have wanted me to put up with that or would you have wanted a pal to do whatever she could to get me away from him, even if it caused a bit of a scene?'

To her complete devastation, he hadn't been able to give the obvious answer. He'd stayed silent, clearly weighing up both sides. The only side should have been hers.

'Wow,' she'd said, too hurt to even challenge him.

Josh hadn't even tried to make it right. 'Look, we're not getting anywhere here. I'm going for a shower. We'll talk about it in the morning.'

An hour later, he was asleep beside her, but she had been awake, staring at the ceiling, letting the truth sink in. He would never defend her. This wasn't 'good times and bad'. This was whatever suited him best. Tears had run from the outer corners of her eyes into her hair, as a realisation dawned – she couldn't marry someone who wasn't going to be there for her when she needed him. She had no idea where to start, but she knew she couldn't go to Hawaii with him, couldn't wear her white dress, couldn't promise to love him and vow to always stand by him, when he hadn't stood by her.

She'd quietly slipped out of bed, padded into the huge cupboard in the hall that she used as a wardrobe, packed her biggest suitcase and a black plastic bag with the first things that came to hand, then went into the kitchen and wrote him a note.

I would always have defended you. I want someone who will always defend me too. I can't marry you. Goodbye, Josh.

Silently sobbing, she'd walked back into the bedroom and left the note and her engagement ring on his bedside table. Then she'd walked right out of their lives together.

Now, as the memory of that night made her chest tighten, she sniffed. *Don't cry. Do. Not. Cry. Keep on packing.* Where were the sarongs, the SPF50 and her favourite flip-flops? Got them. Passport? Yep, in the drawer. Sunglasses? The next drawer. *One thing at a time. Just keep on packing. Just keep on packing.*

'Please stop packing.' The voice came from the doorway and

made her jump. She hadn't even heard him come in, too wrapped up in her thoughts.

'How did you know I was here?'

'The doorbell app,' he replied, holding up his phone.

Ah. She'd forgotten about that bloody thing. Traitor.

'Look, can we talk?' he went on, and for the first time, she noticed the dark circles under his eyes. Did it make her a horrible person that she was glad he was having sleepless nights too?

'On behalf of your clients?' she asked, archly, as she tossed the ESPA skincare set that Drea had bought her for Christmas into the bag. She might have lost everything, but at least she'd be well moisturised.

'Kara, it's my job. You know that. I represent both Corbin and the studio – they're my biggest clients. What was I supposed to do?'

She couldn't believe she was going to have to spell this out for him yet again. Hadn't they already covered this on the night it happened? 'You were supposed to defend me. That's it.'

'And lose my clients?'

'Or lose your fiancée.'

That must have struck home, because, for once, he didn't seem to have anything more to say. Speechless. Silent. And it was completely out of character.

Josh's talent for spinning any subject and charming everyone he met made him great at his job, but she'd realised not long after she met him that underneath all that affable professionalism, there was the laser-focused mind of someone who'd grown his company to be one of the largest PR firms in the city, landing a catalogue of impressive clients, including the Clydeside Studio and its flagship TV show. The role of his company was simple – to generate great publicity and squash anything that depicted the studio, the show or its stars in a negative light. He'd gone into full-scale damage limitation mode a couple of years before when one of their biggest names, Rex Marino, had made a complete arse of himself at a public event and been exposed as a serial cheat. And at the same time, he was strategising long into the night to counter the backlash when the show ousted the beloved Odette Devine after forty years in the lead role. In hindsight, it shouldn't have been a surprise that he was there today with Corbin, because a star being involved in an incident that could reflect badly on him was right in Josh's wheelhouse.

There was one difference with this situation, though. Usually, it wasn't down to Josh to make judgements on the situation, just to cover it up or fix it. On Hogmanay, he'd been forced to pick a side and he'd picked the wrong one. Now, she just wanted to get out of here and away from the guy who'd just made it clear that he valued his clients more than he valued her.

The sight of her throwing things in the holdall must have jolted a thought, because he suddenly blurted, 'So you're still going then? To Hawaii?'

She nodded. 'Of course. I'm going to see my sister get married.'

'You know she cancelled my flight?' he said. 'I got the notification yesterday and the refund today.'

'Makes sense, given that we're no longer getting married. Unless you were still planning to tag along?' There was a challenge in her words, and he didn't meet it.

Instead, the shake of his head gave the answer. 'No,' he said.

'Didn't think so,' she retorted. A mixture of anger and anxiety took over and she knew she had to get out of there.

Deciding to leave everything else behind, she grabbed the handles of the holdall, ready to flee.

'Kara, don't go. I'm asking you, please. Don't throw away eight years of our lives. Stay here and work through this.'

'For the sake of your favourite client or for me?'

'For us.'

She stared at him for several seconds, before blurting out the thought that was right at the front of her mind. 'There is no "us", Josh. You showed me that the other night. Tell me something – did you come straight here after me today, or did you take the meeting with Corbin and HR first and then come here?'

'Oh for God's sake...' he replied, agitated. 'Look, I had to stay and be professional. I couldn't just go running out after my girlfriend.'

All she wanted to do was curl into a ball and sob, but she managed to make her voice work. 'Your ex-fiancée. The one you let down. And you just did it again.'

'Okay, okay, I get it. At least give me a chance to sort this.' His voice was raised when he said that, and Kara could tell that he was transitioning along the emotional scale from pleading and semi-remorse to frustration and irritation.

'Tell me something else, then, Josh – if I agree to stay with you and get married as planned, will you drop the studio and Corbin Jacobs as your clients and stick up for me instead?'

She held her breath. In three days' time, they had been supposed to make their vows to each other.

> *'In sickness and in health.*
> *For richer and poorer.'*

She was about to find out if the next line was:

> *'Forsaking all others, including corporate clients and*
> *misogynistic scumbags.'*

11

_____

OLLIE

He'd been back home for ten minutes, and he still hadn't opened the video that purported to be a scandalous snippet of his wife doing some real-life close and personal stuff with Van Weeks, the actor who had played her love interest in the play that had just closed.

Calvin had offered to come in with him and handle the press, but much as he'd appreciated the offer, Ollie had declined. He had his own people for that, without putting demands on his old friend. His agent, his manager and his PR team – all of whom were based in LA and received a generous percentage of his earnings – were already blowing up his phone, and he was ignoring them all because he didn't want to deal with any of them until he understood exactly what was going on.

And the truth was, if he was going to witness something devastating, he would rather do it alone and when he was ready. That's why he'd come in, tossed his jacket on the coat stand, gone to the ridiculously well-stocked bar in the corner of his living room and grabbed a bottle of Budweiser from the self-service beer fridge. A Jack Daniel's or a shot of whisky would probably be more effective, but he wasn't a hard spirits kind of guy, so they'd only make this worse. As would a DUI, and he needed to drive to the airport later. One beer was going to have to be the limit.

After throwing back a slug of lager, he took the drink over to the kitchen island and leaned his elbows on the marble, holding his phone in front of him. With a churning stomach and an all-consuming feeling of dread, he pressed play.

The first thing that came into focus was a stranger, someone he'd never seen before in his life. It was a woman, maybe early twenties, sitting in what looked like an airplane seat in the business-class section of an airplane. He had an immediate flash of relief – Sienna only ever flew first class. That was followed by a second flash of dread as he remembered her complaining when she booked the flight that it was the only time that suited her schedule, and it didn't have a first-class cabin so she was going to have to slum it in business.

Shit. Back to the screen. The person filming was staring directly into camera, eyebrows raised as she mouthed three words. He didn't need a lip reader to confirm what she was saying. OH. MY. GOD. Then, ramping up the suspense, she moved the phone away from her face and began slowly turning it to her right, so that the passengers in the row one behind her, on the other side of the aisle, came into focus. A woman, her body partially turned away from the camera so that she was facing the guy in the window seat. Ollie's trepidation escalated another few notches as he focused on the woman – white T-shirt, black leather jeans, the same ones he'd bought for his wife when they had a session with a personal shopper at Bergdorf's a few weeks ago. But what he hadn't ordered was the hand that was trailing up and down her back. Or the other hand, that was clearly cradling her neck as the couple kissed, and kissed, and yep, they were still kissing.

Desperate to drag his eyes away from the woman, he switched his focus to the guy. He was wearing a beanie pulled down low, and gradient glasses that partially hid his eyes. His arms were muscular, his shoulders wide, and Ollie was pretty sure that grey T-shirt was Tom Ford. And he was almost definite that it had been another of his wife's purchases on that personal shopping trip. She'd claimed it was a gift for her brother. Ollie now doubted it had ever made its way back to her brother's penthouse in West Hollywood. He checked out the jaw, the colour of the tiny wisps of blond hair that were sticking out of the black wool hat. Ollie immediately recognised him.

Van Weeks wasn't a huge star. He'd done a few pilots, had a couple of minor TV roles, but he was far better known in the theatre world. Chances were, the average person on a flight wouldn't know who he was. No, the star attraction here was Sienna Montgomery, former child star and member of the Montgomery family dynasty, as recognisable as the Fondas, the Sutherlands or the Baldwins.

That was confirmed by the caption underneath the clip.

OMG. Am I crazy or is that Sienna Montgomery? Do you think Ollie Chiles knows that his wife is currently lip locked with some dude on a flight to LA? Come on, people, do the right thing and let him know. Tag me and tune back in for updates.
#milehigh #whathappensonaflight…

There was a time stamp on it of an hour ago, so at least he'd always know the exact moment that his life began to spectacularly unravel. It was Sienna. He didn't have a single doubt. It was the body that he slept next to whenever they were in the same city, the woman he'd loved for over six years, married, been faithful to since the day he met her.

But...

He paused while he clutched at a straw. Could it be a fake? All that AI stuff could do anything now. He'd seen a film clip of Tom Cruise buying tampons in Walmart last week. And the viral clip of an ex-President singing 'You Are My Sunshine' while sitting on the loo would live with him forever. Sure, it was highly unlikely that someone could mock all that up at just a few moments notice, but he supposed the person who filmed them could have used the in-flight Wi-Fi to send it to someone to be modified and...

Another ping. Then another. Then another. And his phone was vibrating so hard with a new wave of incoming notifications that it was making his hand tremble.

One of the messages that were running up his screen like some kind of mobile phone ticker tape stood out and caught his eye:

BREAKING NEWS – SIENNA MONTGOMERY LOSES IT IN MID-AIR RANT.

Oh Jesus. Maybe he should have gone for a shot of hard spirits after all.

He clicked on to TMZ's website and played the clip. Same airplane. Same couple wrapped up in each other. Then the woman slowly disentangles herself and stretches up as if waking from a long sleep. She turns her body so that she's facing the front and lifts the glass of clear liquid on the tray in front of her. Ollie knew exactly what it would be. Tequila Soda Lime. Sienna's drink of choice. Everything about this was looking way too real. The way she moved. Her body language. The dimples on her cheeks. And now, almost in slow motion, the way she reacted when her gaze flicked slightly to her left and she spotted that the other passenger had a phone camera angled in her direction. For a split second, she put her head down, her hand coming up to her face as if to shield herself from the glare of the lens, but then defence-mode must have kicked in because she suddenly moved towards the camera.

'Are you filming me?' she spat, but her words were now even more slurred than when he'd spoken to her earlier. She was drunk. Definitely wasted. It wasn't an uncommon thing of late. The slump in her career and the latest cancellation of her show had hit her hard. This Sienna Montgomery was almost unrecognisable as the carefree, driven, successful actress who'd been at the pinnacle of her career, lauded and drenched in accolades, when they'd met.

Ollie wanted to close his eyes or press stop because it explained so much. Sober Sienna would never risk misbehaving in public because she was very well aware that the majority of the people in their orbit had a phone with a camera now. Drunk Sienna was someone who tossed all her inhibitions and caution to the wind and did whatever she damn well pleased. Drunk Sienna was also more explosive than 100 per cent alcohol in a naked flame.

The person behind the camera didn't reply, so Sienna continued to stretch out of her chair and lean towards it. 'I said are you fucking filming me?'

The only thing her fury was achieving was putting her closer into focus, letting the watching world hear her voice, and confirm that there could be absolutely no doubt whatsoever that this was the real Sienna Montgomery, not some AI-generated spoof, or one of those uncanny lookalikes who made a fortune because the genetic lottery had given them a face that closely resembled a household name.

She turned back to the guy sitting next to her. 'Van, they've been filming us.' Slam dunk. Questions answered. Proof delivered.

Turning back, she was wide-eyed and her face twisted as she made a lunge for the phone, forcing the woman recording the whole debacle to pull back. The video was now jerking furiously as the operator tried desperately to avoid confiscation.

'I said give me the fucking phone,' Sienna hissed, and Ollie could hear the slur of her words again.

A rumble of noise and jarring movements emitted from the screen for the next few seconds, then a more official firm voice as a flight attendant intervened. 'Excuse me, please sit back down in your seat and put your seatbelt on.'

'No. That woman is filming me. She has no right to do that, and I want it deleted. It's my fucking privacy and she just invaded me. I swear to God if this gets out I'll sue this fucking airline until there's nothing left of it. Now get the fucking phone. I want to see exactly what's on it.'

'I'm afraid I can't take a passenger's phone.' The timbre of the voice changed as if the person speaking was now talking while facing the camera. 'Ma'am, are you willing to voluntarily hand the phone over or delete anything you've recorded of the other passenger?'

'No, I'm not handing it over. It's no one else's business what's on my phone. It's a free country – I can record anything I want.'

That activated Tequila Sienna. 'No you can't! How fucking dare you – I'm entitled to my private life.'

The flight attendant switched focus to Sienna. 'Ma'am, can you come with me please? I think for everyone's sake it's probably best if we move you to another seat for now, while I speak to the captain and ascertain the airline protocol here.'

Ollie was starting to feel sorry for the flight attendant. It was an impossible situation to deal with while all parties were at thirty thousand feet in a metal tube. And he also knew how it felt to take on Sienna in a rage.

The footage cut there, and he let his head fall onto his hands on the counter. Fuck. How could she do this to him? To them? Yet so many things were adding up in his head. Her drinking. The T-shirt Van Weeks was wearing. Their tactile affection at the beginning of the clip. This didn't look like a one-off drunken kiss. Was it a full-blown affair? How long had it been going on? Were they in love? Is that why she'd been so offhand with him lately? So angry all the time? And did it matter what it was?

He wanted to unsee everything he'd watched in the last half-hour and slam his phone off the marble. But before he got a chance to do that, his phone decided to torture him a little bit more.

Another text.

SIENNA

Just saw the video that's circulating. I know it's prob reached you too. It's not what it looks like, I promise.

Then another.

Babe, can you reply and tell me you don't believe it?

Then another.

Fuck. Don't do this Ollie.

And finally.

OLLIE, PLEASE TALK TO ME.

Capitals. Like that was going to make a difference.

He didn't cave in to her demands. Instead, he watched the video again. It was pretty hard to see in what world it wasn't exactly what it looked like – his wife getting it on with another guy. What other explanation could there be? By the way Van's hands were wandering, he was clearly still functioning, so she wasn't administering mouth-to-mouth resuscitation. And no, Ollie wasn't going to buy any kind of bullshit that they were rehearsing for a role. Which left the possible option that he'd been bitten on the lip by a snake and she was sucking out the venom. About as preposterous as it got on the JFK to LAX red eye.

No. There were no explanations other than the glaring reality that it was exactly what it looked like.

His phone began to ring. A WhatsApp call. And the screen was flashing with his wife's name. That made perfect sense. Wi-Fi calls were not generally allowed on most flights, but Sienna would often go into the airplane loos to make them. Just another example of how she thought that rules didn't apply to her. A bit like monogamy within marriage, apparently.

He checked his watch. Half past one. She would be landing around 3 p.m. his time, and maybe then they could have a proper conversation. He wasn't going to speak to her while she was huddled in an airline toilet or before he'd had a chance to think through what he'd just seen.

Ollie pressed decline.

He'd speak to her when he was ready and that wasn't now.

12

ALICE

'Och, that was such a lovely service, but the poor family was heartbroken,' Val said, as they pulled out of the crematorium, the last of a long line of vehicles that had filed out of the car park behind the family limos. 'And oh, that Celine Dion always hurts ma heart. I've told you before, make sure they play "Every Step You Take" at my funeral – I just want to remind all the lovely buggers that turn up that I'll be keeping a wee eye on them.'

'I thought you wanted Tom Jones "It's Not Unusual"?'

'Aye, right at the end. Just to get everyone moving after they've been sitting for so long. Don't want any DVTs on my conscience. Anyway, I'm so sorry you had to find out that Morag had passed away. I know you were hoping that you two could rekindle your friendship.'

'I was. In a strange way though, I'm still glad that I went. At least now I know. Although, selfishly, I was really sad when her family talked about how she came back to Glasgow every summer and New Year. I don't understand why she wouldn't get in touch.' Alice felt her throat tighten with sorrow. It just didn't make sense. They were such close friends then... nothing. She chided herself that there was no point crying about it now and tried to steer her mind back to the positive. 'Anyway, it was so lovely to meet Morag's son and I couldn't have refused his request to continue the conversation. Are you sure you don't mind coming back to the hotel, just for an hour or so?'

Val didn't skip a beat. 'You had me at sandwiches. Of course I don't mind. It seemed like the big fella was so keen to speak to you, bless him. He probably has loads of questions about his mum when she was a young lass.'

The snow and the fog that getting thicker by the minute, slowed the convoy of cars in front of them to a steady thirty miles an hour. Alice was grateful – Val had a heavy right foot and Alice was frequently whipped up to a state of sheer terror when they drove to ASDA for their shopping.

She shared a few anecdotes about Morag on the way, making Val laugh, then tear up when she heard the story of their goodbye at the airport.

'That's what she said?' Val asked, eyes widening. '"Watch out for Larry, he's not who you think he is"?'

'Or words to that effect,' Alice confirmed. 'Mint?' she asked, as she popped a Polo into her mouth, then leaned over and slipped one between Val's cerise pink lips too.

'Thanks. And you've no idea why she thought that?'

Alice shook her head. 'None. Larry could be arrogant and cocky – what does it say about me that those weren't red flags? Anyway, I suppose I just thought she'd taken a dislike to him because of that. Or maybe the opposite – as I said earlier, I wondered if she actually had an eye for him. Now the only explanation that makes sense is that she saw what I was so blind to – that he was a vile and cruel excuse for a human being who cared for no one but himself.'

They were the last car in the line to pull into the car park at the hotel. There were no spaces left so Val followed a couple of the other cars and bumped up onto a concrete verge, making the car shudder. 'Jesus, that nearly took my teeth out,' she groaned, before switching back to their conversation. 'I guess that answers your question though.'

'What does?' Alice wasn't following.

'Well, if she'd taken a dislike to Larry, that's probably why she didn't get in touch again. You know what family grapevines are like – she must have heard you were still together, and didn't want to cast any kind of shade on your relationship. Maybe she thought she was doing the right thing for you.'

Hand on the door, Alice paused. 'Val Murray, are you trying to make me feel better about getting ditched by my friend?'

Val flipped down the window visor and dabbed on a bit more lippy. 'I am. Is it working?'

'No. But thank you. You are lovely, you know,' Alice said gratefully. Today was their last day living together and it was only a few hours before she had to leave for the airport. She wouldn't normally be so sentimental, but she wanted to make sure Val knew just how much she meant to her.

'You're not too bad either,' Val replied, but her voice cracked on the last word and she waved her out of the car. 'Now get out before I have to redo my eyeliner.'

Opening the door, Alice gasped as a blast of cold air hit her. Hopefully the weather four hundred miles south would be a bit warmer than Scotland in January.

They followed the other mourners into the hotel, and made their way to an empty table, glad to be inside. A waitress in her sixties soon appeared beside them, balancing a tray carrying a teapot, two cups and saucers, a matching white porcelain milk and sugar set, and a plate with a beautifully arranged serving of sandwiches and sausage rolls. As soon as she spotted Val, her face broke into a wide grin, but she kept her voice low, as befitting the occasion. 'Val, love, how are you? That's a terrible question given the circumstances right enough.'

This was something else that Alice would miss. They couldn't go anywhere within a ten-mile radius of Weirbridge without Val meeting someone she knew. She'd lived her whole life in this area, and held so many community roles: running playgroups, village fetes, mums and tots gatherings, knitting bees, book clubs, dances for the elderly, Christmas parties at the town hall. Sometimes Alice thought the social life of the entire county would grind to a halt without her.

The two women had a chat for a few moments, leaving Alice to scan the room. She could see Zac speaking to someone at the bar, but other than that there was no one she recognised, except... Her gaze fell on the older man she'd seen at the service. About her age. Grey hair. With the slender, athletic form of someone who exercised and took care of himself. She stared at his face. Yes, that had to be Cillian, Morag's boyfriend that she had moved to Ireland with. Wasn't it?

She was still trying to decide, when his gaze met hers and she saw instant recognition. Yes! It was definitely him. He'd been such a lovely guy, and if he was here at Audrey's funeral, that must mean that he and Morag had stayed together. That made her happy. She began to smile and raised her hand to wave to him, when he turned away sharply, as if he'd never seen her at all.

'Something wrong?' That was from Val, who was free again now that the waitress had gone off to replenish her tray. 'And do you want to start with egg mayonnaise on brown bread, or cucumber and tomato sandwiches on white?'

Alice wasn't sure if she'd imagined what had just happened. 'Egg mayonnaise please. And no, nothing's wrong. I just thought I saw someone I used to know, but I must have been mistaken.'

There was no time to think too deeply about it, because just at that, Zac crossed the room to their table. 'Thank you so much for coming. Do you mind if I sit?'

Alice gestured to the chair across from her. 'Of course not. Please do.'

Now that she had time to study his face up close, she could see such familiarity in him. He had Morag's smile, and her colouring. He had her thick dark hair too. His eyes, though… they must have come from Cillian's side because they were a pale blue, not hazel like Morag's.

'I hope you don't mind me persuading you to come here. It's just that, when you said you were Mum's friend, there were things I wanted to pick your brains about. I realise now that I've done that typical thing of leaving it too late to learn about Mum's younger life. I never asked her the right questions and now Aunt Audrey is gone, and she was my last link to Mum's life before she met my dad.'

Alice understood completely. She'd left it too late when it came to Morag too, and she'd always regret that now.

'Your dad… that's Cillian, isn't it? He and your mum were dating when she left for Ireland. I went with them to the airport that night. I was heartbroken to see her go. We'd been best friends for so long.'

To her surprise, a momentary frown crossed Zac's face, or perhaps it was a flicker of puzzlement. Strange, but the poor guy's emotions must be all over the place today.

He recovered quickly and nodded as he answered her question. 'Yes, Cillian's my dad. He's taking Aunt Audrey's death pretty hard. They were really close – almost like brother and sister – and we only lost Mum a year ago, so it's been tough on him. He and Mum did everything together, so I think he's a bit lost now.'

Alice put her cup back down on the saucer. 'I'm so sorry to hear that. It's lovely to hear that they had a happy marriage, though. They hadn't been together long when your mum left, so I was always worried that maybe they'd jumped in too fast. It's good to know that Morag was right all along.'

Another frown, and Alice didn't understand this one either. What was she missing?

He was thoughtful for a moment, and it seemed like he was trying to find the words to ask her something and not quite getting them. Val must have noticed it too, because she was giving him space to think. Alice wasn't sure she'd ever been quiet this long.

Another pang of sympathy made her want to hug him. He must be so weary and emotionally exhausted with all this. She wondered if it would be okay to ask him to keep in touch with her, maybe meet up some time if they were in the same city. There was so much more that she'd like to learn about Morag's life in Ireland and, by the sounds of things, he wanted to know more about her earlier years.

'I don't mean to offend you...' he began, a little awkwardly.

Alice smiled, trying to encourage him. 'I promise you, I'm pretty much un-offendable, so please go ahead.'

'The thing is...' he began, his fingers looping into his tie and loosening it as he spoke. He then opened the top button of his shirt, now clearly uncomfortable. 'Did you and Mum ever have a falling out? Is that why you lost touch?'

It was a perfectly understandable question, but Alice was still a little taken aback, and it took a moment for her to get the right answer.

'The truth is, I really don't know. I was just discussing that with my friend here this morning. When your mum left, we made so many promises to keep in touch and meet up, and then I never saw her again. There were a couple of cards, but when I wrote back and asked about coming to visit her, the contact stopped altogether. I know she didn't like my boyfriend at the time – she always was a good judge of character – but I can honestly say that from my perspective, there was no falling out. I've always thought we both just got wrapped up in our own lives and the distance was too much for us to navigate back then.' A thought struck her. 'Can I ask what made you wonder if we'd fallen out? Did your mum ever tell you that?'

'No, actually – please don't be offended by this – but she never mentioned you at all. And that's why, looking back, it's so strange that she never contacted you when we were in Glasgow.' He opened his jacket and reached into the inside pocket.

Alice felt her heart sink. There must have been something that she'd missed, some slight or comment that Morag had taken to heart. It was the only explanation.

She sighed, fighting back the tears she'd been determined not to shed all morning. 'I'm so sorry if I did something to hurt or upset her. It breaks my heart to think that something unintentional could have kept us apart for all these years.'

Zac was taking something out of his pocket now, but Alice noticed that he had a quick glance around the room, as if checking no one could see whatever he was about to show her.

'I actually think it might have been the other way round. Were you Mum's only friend called Alice?'

She flicked back through the Rolodex of her memory. 'Yes, as far as I know.'

Something in his mannerisms told her he'd just made a decision, and he placed a pretty notelet down in front of her, the kind she and Morag used back in those days to write letters. He turned it around, and in an almost synchronised movement, both she and Val got their specs out, slipped them on and then leaned forward and began to read.

> *Dear Alice,*
>
> *I've been trying to write this note to you for the longest time, but I never seem to manage it. I don't know where to start, so I'll just begin by saying I'm so, so sorry. When I explain what happened, I'll understand if you never forgive me. I didn't mean —*

She read it again, stunned, before sitting back in her chair. 'It just finishes there? Without any explanation? What was she sorry for?'

'I was hoping that you could tell me,' he said earnestly. 'And there's another puzzle too.' He glanced around the room again, before reaching back into his inside pocket and pulling out a strip of photo booth images. 'I wondered if you could help me understand something else.'

13

ZAC

Zac couldn't believe he was sharing these photos and asking these questions of a woman who, just a few hours ago, was a complete stranger. However, the lawyer in him knew that none of this was adding up, and that he might not have another chance to get information from someone who knew his mum back then. Of course, he could ask his dad, but there was a serious niggle that if this was all something completely irrelevant and just a weird mistake, then all he would be doing was upsetting his dad for absolutely no reason.

Besides, he believed this woman when she said she'd been his mum's best friend, and that was backed up by the obvious evidence that Morag had been agonising over making an apology for some unknown wrongdoing.

'My cousin, Jill, found a box of Mum's old letters and mementoes – that's where I found the note I showed you – and these photos were inside too. It's pics of my mum and dad and I know it was on their first date.'

He placed them on the table, turned them around, and then watched as the two women leaned in a second time to study what he was showing them. They'd struck out on the letter. He wasn't sure if he wanted them to be more successful this time. Maybe he should just let mysteries from the past stay back where they belonged.

The lady, Alice, stared down at them and to his surprise a single tear dropped onto the table, barely missing the old black and white prints. Her friend, Val, pulled a hanky out from up her sleeve and handed it over, something he remembered his mum doing so many times when he was a kid.

Alice blew her nose, and a couple of people at nearby tables glanced over, then went back to their conversations. People were starting to drift out now, and the rest of his family were sitting at the furthest table in the other corner of the restaurant, with some women he recognised as Aunt Audrey's closest friends. They were all far too engrossed in their own conversations to notice where he was, and if they did, they would just assume he was being sociable and making sure that someone from the family spoke to everyone who was kind enough to give up their time to be here.

'I'm sorry,' Alice said, dabbing her tears away with the hanky. 'It's just so emotional because that's exactly how I remember Morag. You can see how happy she was there – just pure sunshine. I loved her very much and I'm so sad that we missed so many milestones that we could have shared. I'm guessing you're around the same age as my son...'

'I was twenty-nine in October,' he replied.

'Rory is the same age. I was actually already pregnant with him when your mum left, but I didn't know. When we were growing up, Morag and I would talk about how we would have children at the same time, bring them up together, go through life as friends until we were old and grey.' She patted her hair, to make her point, before saying softly. 'Well, I'm grey now. I just wish we'd managed to do that.'

Her reaction made Zac pause to wonder if he should say anything else. Right now, there was no harm done, no big mystery about his parents revealed. He could walk away now and let all this lie. But... What if he never saw this woman again? Then his chance to get to the bottom of this without risking upsetting his dad would be gone. He put one foot out over the edge of the cliff.

'How long, exactly, had they been together before they left?' he asked.

Alice thought about that for a moment.

'I'm not sure. Your mum's birthday was early January, and I remember that year we went to London with some friends. Your dad wasn't with us, so they must have got together sometime after that, and then they left in the spring. Or maybe it was summer. I'm sure your dad will know for sure. They hit it off from the moment they met and were absolutely besotted with each other. I suppose that showed in the fact that Morag left her job after no time at all and went off to Ireland with him.'

'You're not wrong. My whole life they've been devoted to each other. I was lucky.'

Alice reached over and put her hand on his. 'You definitely were. She was a good woman.'

A voice in his head was saying, *Stop there. Just stop. Leave this alone.* He was considering that when he heard himself say as casually as he could manage, 'Was she seeing anyone else before she met Dad?'

If Alice thought that was a strange question, she didn't show it as she pondered for a few seconds.

'No. Not for a long time. She had a huge crush on one of the partners in our office, and she said no one else matched up, and she was going to hold out for him. But then she met your dad and well... He obviously blew the other chap out of the water.'

'Son, I think the answer to the question you asked earlier is right here.' The interruption came from Val. He'd been so busy concentrating on his questions and Alice's answers that he hadn't noticed she had picked the photo strip up. Now she'd turned it over, and was reading the scribble on the back.

9 March 1995 – Our first date!

'Yes, I just...' How could he say this in a way that didn't imply that he was questioning something he'd thought to be true his whole life. He took a breath. 'I just wasn't sure if that was a mistake, and I thought you might know?'

He left that there. That's all he was going to say. Nothing more. Time to drop it. He couldn't bring himself to spell out his fears or to carry on thinking about this. He was just going to go back to Dublin tonight and let it all lie. Maybe one day he'd ask his dad about it if it felt like the right place or time, but he very much doubted it. For now, he was just going to choose peace of mind, and be grateful for the parents he had.

But while all that was going through his mind, he watched as Alice picked the photo up again. Turned it over. Read the back. Then did the same with the note. He watched her eyes move from side to side as she read it. Then read it again. Then again.

It was only then that she raised her gaze to look at him. Part of his job was to read people, to sense their emotions, to interpret their facial expressions and their body language. Right now, Alice didn't seem to be able to tear her eyes away from his face and she hadn't blinked for many intense seconds.

'I... I... really don't know,' she finally blurted, but everything was different now.

If this was an opposing party in one of his settlement negotiations, he'd advise his client to hold firm, because there were clear signs of panic. And stress. And fear.

He watched as she reached around and retrieved her bag from the back corner of the chair, then picked up her gloves from the table. 'Zac, it's been an absolute joy to meet you,' she said, her voice tight. 'But I'm afraid we have to go.'

Beside her, Val froze, a sausage roll halfway to her mouth, her eyebrows raised in question. 'We do?' Then another glance, this time catching Alice's expression, before, 'Yes, we do. I've got my knitting bee in fifteen minutes. It completely slipped my mind.'

It was very clearly a fabrication, but Zac registered exactly what was going on here – the unmistakable shift in Alice's demeanour and desperate need to leave had been caused by some kind of realisation or thought that she wasn't prepared to share with him.

She stood up from the table, her friend scrabbling to do the same. 'It's been really lovely to meet you, Zac,' she said, her tone thick with emotion. 'I think your mum would have been so proud of you and I wish I had known you both every day of your life. Take care.'

With that, she began walking in the direction of the door.

'Bye, son. You take care of yourself and your dad. I wish all the best to your family,' Val added, before setting off after Alice, her steps clicking on the wood floor all the way across the room.

Zac hastily tucked the photos and card back in his pocket, then dropped his head, all the air going out of his body. What the hell was going on? And did he really want to know? This was like the kind of bizarre stories he heard way too often as a family lawyer, and he always took a moment to feel grateful that he came from a completely uneventful, loving family; with an uneventful, loving mum and dad; and an uneventful, loving history.

Now he was beginning to suspect that he'd been wrong all along.

'You okay, son?' He hadn't even noticed his dad coming to join him, just felt the hand on his shoulder and heard the question in his voice.

'Yes, I was just chatting to an old friend of Mum's from when she was younger. Alice. Do you remember her?'

Now his dad was frowning too. 'Erm, yes, vaguely. I didn't know her that well, to be honest. Just for a few weeks. Her and mum weren't that close. Anyway, son, I'm going to go say goodbye to everyone and then head off now, because I still haven't packed. What about you?'

Either he was turning into an irrational conspiracy theorist, or his dad really had flat out lied to him and then just brushed off the subject of Alice altogether. Something inside him flipped and he knew what he had to do.

'Yeah, I'll join you in a minute. There's just someone I have to speak to first.'

As he rose from his chair, he patted his dad's back, then calmly walked to the door. Only when he was out of sight of the mourners did he break into a sprint, running down the corridor and out into the car park. *Please make her be there. Please make her be there. Please make her...*

She was there. She was at the opposite side of the concrete square and despite the biting cold and the flurry of snow that was floating down around her, she had both hands on the side of the bonnet of a bright yellow Jeep, leaning forward, as if trying to catch her breath.

He was across the car park in seconds. 'Alice?' he said breathlessly. 'I'm sorry. Please don't think I've lost my mind, because I promise I'm normally very calm and rational. But... is there something you want to tell me? I know things don't add up, and I think you know why.'

'I don't,' she immediately countered, but he could see her heart wasn't in it.

He went in for another shot. 'Look, I know you loved my mum, and I can tell by that note that she felt the same. She never got to make amends for whatever she did, but she cared enough that she wanted to tell you about it. Now, all I'm asking is that you help me find out if there's something she might have wanted to tell me one day too.'

'It's none of my business,' Alice insisted. Val was watching all this play out from the other side of the car, but she stayed silent. 'And I really don't think it's my place—'

'But you're the only one left who can. At least let me talk to you. One way or another, for my own sake, I need to get to the bottom of this. I don't think she'd have wanted you to let me do that on my own.'

It was difficult to say which of those points swayed her, but one of them hit home.

'The problem is, I'm leaving for London tonight.' A weaker objection.

'I'm flying back to Dublin tonight, so I'm in a time crunch too.'

A change in her expression told him she'd come to a decision.

'Okay, but I don't think this is an appropriate place. Can you meet me? Say, in an hour?'

'I can do that.'

But even as he was saying it, he wasn't sure if he was about to make the biggest mistake of his life.

2 P.M. – 4 P.M.

14

KARA

'Tell me something else, then, Josh – if I agree to stay... will you drop the studio and Corbin Jacobs as your clients and stick up for me instead?'

Kara waited for the answer, praying she was wrong about what it would be.

'Kara, that's totally unreasonable. You know that they're my biggest clients. It would have a huge impact on my business and—'

'Stop. That tells me everything.' Another question struck her. Today he should also have been getting ready to leave for their wedding, but instead, he was in full crisis-management mode. Would he have chosen work over her, even if it were a different situation? 'Josh, if Hogmanay hadn't happened, and there was some other huge scandal at the studio this weekend, would you still have left it behind and come to Hawaii today or would you have asked me to postpone our wedding?'

His hesitation and a flash of panic that made him blink before he spoke, answered her question without words.

'Oh Josh...' she groaned, as she shook her head, horrified. How had she missed this? How had she managed to carry on with life, blissfully unaware that he was so non-committal about their marriage? There was an instant realisation that made her want to weep. Had they both just been swept along with this whole thing? Drea had been the one to organise it all, because given her job, she had all the contacts and the vision of what it should look like. Kara and Josh had both been asked for their input at every stage along the way, but they'd both been happy to go with Drea's choices. Somewhere in Kara's mind, she'd told herself that they were just leaving it to the expert. But maybe she'd been sticking her head in the sand? Maybe their hearts weren't in it. Perhaps she'd just been so carried away with excitement for Drea and Seb that she hadn't stopped to think about whether it was what she'd really wanted too. And maybe Josh felt the same. After all, Seb and his brothers were in Hawaii right now with a couple of friends having a mini-stag celebration and Josh had been invited but had declined, because he didn't want to step away from work for any longer than absolutely necessary. None of Josh's family were coming. And it had taken five blooming years for him even to propose in the first place.

What had they been thinking? Oh God. It was a mistake. Maybe their whole relationship had been a mistake. And getting married this week would have been the biggest mistake of all.

'Babe, I'm just being honest. I want to marry you, but I'd have been okay with doing it in a registry office, just you and me. The Hawaii thing... that's because you wanted it and I was happy to go along with it, but—'

'But you could take it or leave it.'

'I didn't say that.'

'You didn't have to say it.' There was no air left in her lungs. It was all gone, sucked out of her by the absolute knowledge that they'd been sleepwalking their way to the altar, followed by a massive kick of self-reproach for being so damn stupid. She'd heard all that she needed to. 'You get to play hero for your client, and now you don't have to take time out of your busy schedule to go to Hawaii. Win-win for you.'

Her shoulder strained as she pulled the strap of the heavy, bulky holdall on to it, then grabbed her other bag, turned around and walked straight out of the door, downstairs, and got into her car, before taking off down the street as fast as the crunching snow beneath the tyres would allow. Only when she knew she was out of sight did she pull over, rest her head on the steering wheel and then let out a roar of blind fury and pain so loud it made a little man walking past with a Yorkshire terrier in tiny snow boots jump.

When she managed to get some air back into her body, she pulled her handbag up from the footwell and rummaged for her phone. 'Hey Siri, call Ollie.' He was the only person she wanted to speak to right now. He hadn't been having the easiest time with Sienna over the last year or so either, so she knew he'd understand. The two of them could just make the trip to Hawaii together, drink too many pina coladas, dance on the beach and make each other feel better – just like they'd been doing all of their lives.

There was a pause while Siri got her act together, then the next thing she heard was an all-too-familiar voice. 'Hi, sorry, I'm busy. Leave a message and I'll get back to you.'

Bugger. What was he doing right now that made him too busy to answer the phone? Sometimes she felt like she spoke to Ollie's answering machine more than she did to the real person. Although, she couldn't exactly claim to be an ace communicator over the last couple of days either. Not that that was unusual for them. They could often go back and forward for days trying to nail down a moment when they were both free, especially when they were in different time zones. LA was the worst. The eight-hour difference there usually meant he was free when she was sleeping, and she was free when he was working. But around once a week, when they did manage to co-ordinate a time slot, usually when their partners were out – when Sienna was at the theatre and Josh was either at work or the gym – that's when they'd sit on a FaceTime call for four hours and talk through every detail of their week, all the latest celebrity goss, what they were having for dinner, and a hundred other inconsequential things that amused them.

If Josh was home, though, it used to drive him mad, especially if it was, say, a Sunday night and he wanted her all to himself. A rebellious, pissed-off little voice in her head piped up to remind her that she wouldn't have to worry about that any more. And another rebellious, pissed-off little voice in her head pointed out that she never threw a tantrum when Josh spent the night at the gym, or locked in his home office working, or out at some swanky client event, so why did she have to be there when he snapped his fingers? Well, now she didn't. And much as that broke her heart, her rebellious, pissed-off inner self knew for sure that she was doing the right thing.

She didn't bother leaving a message, figuring Ollie would see her missed call anyway. Instead, she put her foot down and set off on the drive back to Drea's flat, giving herself a pep talk the whole way. She could do this. She'd never been the type of person who felt she needed a guy to exist, so it wasn't as if she was scared to be alone. Maybe it was time she had some independence and could do whatever she liked for a change. Perhaps this was a decision she should have made a long time ago, because Josh wanting everything on his terms was nothing new. Years ago, he'd even spat his dummy out about her going to New York for Ollie's wedding. Her best friend! And she was only away for a few days.

Before she realised it, a glance in the rear-view mirror told her she was almost smiling as her mind went back to that night. In fact, it must have been... She did the calculation... six years ago yesterday. Wow. This was the first year she hadn't spent the anniversary of that date thinking about that night and the lovely, lovely Zac. Although, granted, she was a bit busy being pathetic and feeling sorry for herself yesterday. That had to stop. Part of her wished that Josh had found out what had really happened that night because he'd have called their relationship off back then and she wouldn't have wasted another six years of her life. Zac struck her as the kind of guy who would definitely have backed her up no matter what. And so, of course, would Ollie. Yet the man who was supposed to be her person couldn't do that. Well, sod Josh Jackson.

Feeling a nugget of strength and resolve grow in her gut, she pulled into the parking space outside Drea's flat and then lugged her holdall up two flights of stairs. The lift was from the 1970s and she was deeply suspicious of it, so she preferred the stairs, even if they made her hamstrings scream. When she reached their door, she dropped everything and fumbled for her key before practically falling over the threshold as she dragged her bag in.

Sweating, she puffed her cheeks out with relief when she got inside and closed the door behind her. When she got her breath back, the first thing she did was open the holdall and take out the thing that mattered most: the pic of her, Ollie and Drea with their mums, and put it on the console table on the hall.

'I thought I heard you come in,' Drea said, padding through

in white furry slippers, wearing a white terry robe and a turban with two large rollers sticking out of the front. She spotted the new frame on the table. 'Aw, I love that picture. Right, I want to know every detail of every single thing that's happened since you left here, but you need to tell me in less than five minutes because I'm not organised yet.'

She turned back to Kara and suddenly stopped speaking. Kara watched as her sister's gaze went from her head to her toes, taking in her sagging shoulders and her red-rimmed eyes. 'Oh no, what happened?' Drea asked, with an edge of wariness.

Kara slumped back against the wall. 'How long have you really got? It's a pretty big story and five minutes won't cut it.'

Drea checked her watch. 'The cars are coming at four o'clock, so that's an hour and a half from now. That means I've got approximately...' She paused and made the motion of doing a calculation in her head. 'Ten minutes max, because I've still got about three hundred things to do. Tell me you're still coming.'

'I'm still coming.' There was no wavering on that. Her own wedding was off, and her life was a shitshow, but she wasn't going to let that spoil Drea's big day. Time to park her own feelings and just get on with celebrating her sister and Seb, and then in a week's time, when she got back, she could fall apart and try to process everything that had happened. Only then, maybe, could she begin to work out what she wanted and where she should go from here.

'Okay,' Drea said, ever pragmatic, 'Let's get everything ready and organised first, and then you can tell me the whole story in the car. But just tell me the headlines now – did you get your job back?'

'No.'

'And did you see Josh?'

'Yes. Wedding is still off.'

Drea wrapped her arms around her and hugged her tight. 'I'm so sorry, hon.'

'It's okay. I'm fine.' She wasn't. Although, she was relieved that she wasn't going to have to recount the whole sorry saga right now. Before Drea could ask anything else, she gently disentangled herself and changed the subject. 'Do you need me to help with anything? I feel like it should be chaos here today, although I know you've got everything planned to perfection.'

Drea raised one eyebrow. 'I've been planning this day, and tomorrow, and the next day, and the day after that, for months...'

That threw Kara back to her earlier thought. Drea had been planning it for months. Even before all the drama, Kara had barely given today a second thought, other than making a mental note not to forget the dress that was hanging in the Vera Wang bag in Drea's wardrobe. 'And I'd only be in the way?' Kara asked, smiling despite the misery that was seeping from her pores.

'Exactly. I've got this. I've got everything. You just need to be ready, packed and good to go at four o'clock. That's all I ask. And then I want to hear everything.'

Kara glanced behind her sister. 'Did Mum come back here after the hairdressers?'

'No. She's meeting us at the airport.'

It was difficult to hide her relief. Much as she loved her mother, Kara couldn't face the inquisition or the inevitable discussion and judgement her mother would have about every aspect of the situation.

'Okay, well, I'm allowing myself to have one last bout of indulgent self-pity, so I'm going to go cry in the bath for an hour, and then a new positive, optimistic me will be out and ready for four o'clock.' Or maybe she'd just go lie in soapy subs and reminisce about the lovely guy she'd met at the airport once upon a time. At least that option wouldn't make her eyes puffy.

Kara followed Drea down the hall, then turned left towards the bathroom, while her sister turned right, into the bedroom. Usually, she'd pour herself a glass of wine, maybe grab a slab of Dairy Milk to go with it, but right now, she just wanted to be neck deep in coconut-scented soapy bubbles.

'I meant to ask...' Drea popped her head back out of the bedroom doorway. 'You haven't seen my black Louboutin stilettos, have you? They're not in their usual slot in my dressing room.'

Shit. Caught. How could she have forgotten to put them back? Hoping for the best, she went for nonchalant innocence. 'Erm, I might have borrowed them to try on with my Hogmanay dress. I think they're under your bed.'

Drea gave her a glare that would suggest she'd rather Kara had stolen a vital organ. 'You'd better not have worn them.'

Nonchalant innocence again. 'Of course not. I'd have broken my ankle in those shoes.' Or some misogynistic tosser's foot. Same difference.

Drea seemed to have bought that because she switched to a new topic. 'Oh, and Ollie called earlier. He's looking for you.'

Kara nodded, pulling her jumper over her head. Every minute spent fully clothed in this hallway was a minute less in the bliss of a hot bath. 'I just tried to call him on the way here – straight to voicemail. I'll try him again when I get out the bath.'

It was with a massive exhalation of relief that she twisted her long red hair up into a high bun, secured it with a scrunchie, then lowered herself into the vintage white, gold clawed tub a few moments later. Yessssss. At last. Peace. Relaxation. Soothing of the soul.

'Hey Alexa,' she said, powering up the sound system that was fitted in Drea's sanctuary of a bathroom. She'd miss this. Even if she got a job that paid the same as her last one, she'd be lucky to afford a bog-standard, gadget-free one-bedroom or studio in the city centre. Not that she cared. As long as there was room for her bed, her desk and a couch, she'd make it work. 'Play "Kara's Badass Women Playlist".'

She'd programmed that in when she used to live here and then added to it over the years whenever she hung out with her sister. Beyonce. Gwen Stefani. Madonna. Kelly Clarkson. Alicia Keyes. Stevie Nicks. Tina Turner. Pink. Blondie. Shania. Miley. Dolly. Taylor. Aretha. Ariana. Adele. No matter how the playlist was shuffled, whatever came on would make her feel better.

The gods of the sisterhood were listening, she decided, when the opening bars of 'Respect' blared from the speaker above her head. Yes. She might be unemployed, homeless and newly single, but at least Aretha was telling her she was right to have standards.

One after one, the others reinforced the message. Kara's shoulders had finally relaxed, and she was in a momentary state of chilled-out bliss, when there was a thundering bang on the door, then it swung open so fast she yelped, slipped under the water and almost choked.

She came up spluttering, to see Drea in the doorway holding up her phone, eyes bulging out of her head, face stricken.

'What? What is it?' Oh dear lord, the flight must be cancelled. It was the only explanation Kara could think of that would evoke this kind of reaction.

'Ollie!' Drea yelped.

'What about Ollie? He's on the phone?'

Drea shook her head. 'No. He's on a whole big pile of crap from that bint he's married to.'

Kara grappled to understand what was going on, but Drea

cut right to it, turning her phone around so that Kara could see the screen. There was Sienna. On a flight... Sucking the face off Van Weeks.

Another video. Sienna losing her shit at someone who, granted, was completely invading her privacy by filming her. But then, if Sienna hadn't been up to no good in the first place, there would be nothing to see.

'Oh shit, shit, shit! Ollie!' She went to grab her phone, but her hands were soaking. 'Drea, can you call him, right now.'

Drea immediately reacted. She dialled, then held the phone against Kara's ear. Straight to voicemail again. Fuck! This time she left a message.

'Ollie! I've just seen the video. Oh God, I'm so sorry. Where are you? I'll come to you right now. I've got you, pal. Call me back.'

She jumped up, and for once, Drea didn't give her hell for splashing water everywhere. Just handed her a towel and held out a hand to help Kara climb out.

She tucked the towel around her, as she stood dripping on the bath mat, both of them staring at the phone screen. Nothing. No call back. No text. Nothing.

'Fuck it, I'm going to his flat.'

Drea had a slight objection. 'You might want to put some clothes on, unless you want your arse to be all over the internet within the hour. Although, it might get you a new boyfriend.'

'You're hilarious,' Kara said, in the most sarcastic tone she could muster.

She was drying her body like it was a Fiat 500 in the last bit of a car wash, flapping the towel around her bits, when Ollie shocked them both by replying.

I'm on way to airport. Meet me in usual lounge.

What. The. Hell. Was. Going. On?

The sense of urgency switched on for the first time all day. 'Get a move on, Drea,' she blurted in her sister's direction. 'We need to get to the airport. And I might need your Louboutin stilettos in case I meet Sienna fricking Montgomery.'

15

OLLIE

It was strange how the mind and body reacted when something cataclysmically shite happened to you.

From when he'd started acting at twelve, until he'd landed the role in *The Clansman* when he was twenty-five, Ollie had had thousands of rejections, some of them for parts that he'd really wanted. Somewhere along the way, that had given him the ability to compartmentalise disappointment and rejection, to put it in a box and refuse to let it get him down. Before he'd married Sienna, he'd had a few semi-long-term relationships that lasted a few months here and there – even thought he was in love a couple of times. And when the flings ended, usually because he was going off somewhere for work, he'd refused to let it get him down for long.

'Dust yourself off, son,' his mum always said, 'and let's keep going. You and I can deal with anything life throws at us, because we know the great stuff is on the way.' She'd drilled that optimism and resilience into him since he was a kid, and it was part of his DNA now. The only time that attitude hadn't got him through unscathed was when he was fourteen and his grandparents died within months of each other. He hadn't been close to his grandad – he was a man who preferred the pub to his family and didn't even try to hide it. But his gran... She'd come to every show, every school concert, every football match, and every Sunday she'd taken him to church in that building he'd visited this morning. Like her daughter, she was also called Moira, and her loss had left a huge hole in his life. He still missed her and he knew his mum did too. Gradually though, with the help of Kara, Drea and Jacinta, they'd both picked themselves back up and got on with living again.

What happened today wasn't a death, but it was a massive blow and he felt like he should be experiencing some kind of devastation. He kept waiting for it to come. It had been a couple of hours now, and he'd had a few coffees. He'd even found a packet of cigarettes Sienna must have left on a shelf just inside the balcony door, and smoked a couple of them too, which did nothing more than make him feel queasy because he'd quit five years ago and not touched one since. He was surprised by what she'd done. Shocked. Blindsided. But he wasn't pacing the floor or feeling his heart being ripped from his chest. Was the love already gone? Was this blow failing to crush him because he'd already begun building protection? Deep inside, had he already known the end was coming?

That was going to take a whole lot of soul searching to work out, but in the meantime, he focused on the practical stuff.

He'd spoken to his agent, his manager, his publicist, and told them all he wouldn't be commenting. What did it say about his life that he'd spoken to the people who handled his career before he'd had a conversation with the woman he'd vowed to spend the rest of his life with?

Not that she could get through to him anyway, because he'd also put his phone on silent, muted all notifications and he hadn't gone near a social media website since he'd watched the video.

Instead, he'd spent twenty minutes letting the jets of the shower pummel his back (for the second time today), got dressed again, packed his case for Hawaii, pulled a beanie hat low down on his head and now he was leaving the building.

He took the back exit to the gated service area where he'd parked the hire car he'd picked up at the airport when he'd arrived last night. Nothing conspicuous. A basic Audi. The last thing he needed was a flash car drawing attention to him every day. When he'd landed the role in *The Clansman*, he'd blown his first big cheque on the down payment on a Lamborghini, but he'd realised almost immediately that he was in a constant state of anxiety when he was driving it, because every pothole could cause a blowout, every idiot on the roads could cause a crash and it came with a big arrow above it saying 'look at me'. After a week, he'd driven it back to the dealership to return it, and then he'd gone to another garage down the road and driven away in the black Ford F150 pick-up truck that he still owned and adored today. It sat next to Sienna's Porsche Cayenne in their driveway, and she rolled her eyes every time she looked at it.

As he drove out of the back entrance and round onto the street where he could see his main door, he spotted and recognised a couple of press photographers hanging out at the front of the building. He was pretty sure they were just there out of hope and optimism, because no one other than his closest circle knew he was in town. Hopefully he would be gone before the media even knew he'd been here.

There was no ping of an alert from his silenced phone, but the car's display screen, connected to his phone via Carplay, flashed up a message that he had a voicemail from Kara. He pressed play to listen.

'Ollie! I've just seen the video. Oh God, I'm so sorry. Where are you? I'll come to you right now. I've got you, pal. Call me back.'

He hadn't even considered not going to Hawaii. Why would he? The only people he wanted to speak to were about to fly with him to London for an overnight stay, before taking a flight tomorrow to Honolulu, via a brief change in San Francisco, so right now there was nowhere else he'd rather be. Everything that had happened deserved more than a rushed phone call, so he texted her to let her know where he'd be.

'Hey Siri, text Kara.'

The very efficient Siri checked the number with him, then told him to proceed.

> I'm on way to airport. Meet me in usual lounge.

Message sent.

Shit, what had happened to them? Both of them going through major relationship dramas at the same time. As far as he could remember, this had never happened before. Kara had been with Josh for what felt like forever, and even before that, one of them had always been in a relationship when the other one was single. At least they would have the time in Hawaii to drink, talk and suss out exactly what they were going to do with the carnage they were both dealing with.

The snow wasn't lying on the main road, so putting his foot down, he teetered on the speed limit. Music. That's what he needed. His phone was already linked up to the car speaker system, so he lined up some Chris Stapleton and drove with the raspy sounds of 'Fire Away' filling his head. He pointed the car in the direction of the M8 motorway, which would take him all the way to the airport, about twenty miles outside the city, but only a few miles into the journey, almost unconsciously, he veered off, and ten minutes later he was back in the same street he'd visited earlier.

The teenagers were gone from the corner now, and there were just a couple of elderly blokes shuffling up the street, both insulated from the cold by their flat caps, padded jackets, and judging by the sway of their steps, a few lunchtime whiskies.

He stared at the building he'd toured earlier with Calvin. Was he being crazy even contemplating getting involved with a project like this? He had a dream job that, in filming season, came with an intense schedule, a personal life that just got way more complicated, and he already lived out of a suitcase. Did he really want to add to his workload? His head was giving him a different answer from his heart. Just at that, his phone rang and he knew that the name that flashed up on the car's display system would come down firmly on the side of the heart.

He flicked the button on the wheel to answer.

'Hey Mum, how are you doing?'

She didn't even pause to consider her answer. 'My blood pressure is rocketing and I'm about ready to track down that wife of yours and give her a piece of my mind. Oh son, I'm so sorry. One of the dancers in the aerial acrobatic group just showed me that video of Sienna that's doing the rounds and, oh my goodness, it's a shocker. What's going on? Are you okay? Aaaargh, I just want to hug you.'

'Thanks, Mum,' he said, thinking that her opening outburst summed up his mother in a nutshell. Loving, protective, would fight anyone who crossed people she loved, and not one to keep quiet or ignore a problem if she had something to say. He'd never been so glad that he was going to see her tomorrow in Hawaii. When she first went offshore, she'd call from a payphone in a port whenever she could, but now that the ships had decent Wi-

Fi they managed to speak every week. 'It was a bit of a blindside moment, but to be honest I should have seen it coming. Things haven't been great for a while now.'

'I knew that, son. You've never been much good at hiding your feelings and acting like nothing's wrong.'

That made him laugh. 'Mum, I literally get paid a lot of money to hide my feelings and act like nothing's wrong. I got a Golden Globe for it last year.'

'Aye, well, you can't hide them from me,' she said. 'And I'm going to give you a pass on your cheek, given that you're thirty and you're an only child. If you desert me, I'm on my own in my old age.'

Her habit of using humour at inappropriate times was yet another of the things he adored about Moira Chiles.

'That's very true. You're lucky I'm devoted to you at the moment, but that could change...'

This was no time for jokes, but he knew that as long as he was firing back barbs and teasing her, the chances of her worrying herself sick would be lowered.

'Enough of your cheek. Anyway, it's been a long time since I felt you two were truly happy together. Do you think there's any hope of getting back on track with Sienna?'

He'd been mulling over that same question all afternoon. 'I don't think so.'

'Okay. Well, I'll hold off tracking her down until you're absolutely sure. I'm not sure Jacinta will have the same restraint. I spoke to her earlier and she is ready to take a contract out on Kara's Josh. What a spineless one he turned out to be.'

Thanks to a dozen instances of missing each other's calls, Ollie had still to hear the details of what had caused Kara to call off the wedding, but before he could interrogate his mum, there was a deafening sound of a horn in the background.

'Listen, we're just coming into dock, so I need to get going. Offloading at Miami always takes ages. One of the croupiers in the casino is giving me a lift up to Orlando in return for a promise to sing Adele songs to him the whole way there. I'm catching a direct flight to Honolulu from there and Seb is picking me up from the airport and taking me to the hotel, so I'll be there before you. Tell Jacinta to remember to bring me three large bars of Dairy Milk, two packets of shortbread and a couple of boxes of Tunnock's Teacakes. And hurry up and get there so I can hug you.'

'I will, Mum. Love you.'

'Love you back, son. And I promise you... there's loads of good times ahead for you.' There it was. The Moira Chiles Pep Talk in Optimism, number 3425.

He hung up feeling a whole lot better than he had five minutes ago. He stared at the building again. His mum would love it. His gran would have approved too. But was he ready to tie himself back to Glasgow again? Was there really not a shred of hope for him and Sienna?

He kicked the car into gear and pondered his indecision all the way to the airport.

When he came off the slip road, he went left at the round-about, in the opposite direction from the terminal building, and stopped at a layby a few hundred yards from the car hire drop-off point. This was going to be the last time he'd be alone for a while, so much as he had no desire to do it, it made sense to just get an update on the online shitshow his life had become today.

Emails first. All of them predictable. Another round of communications from his manager, his agent and his publicist – hear no evil, see no evil and speak no evil – flooding his inbox with requests for the comments he'd already said he wouldn't give, suggesting interviews he'd said he wouldn't do and offering damage-control strategies he'd said he wasn't interested in. All that spin, smoke and mirrors that came with celebrity life was bullshit to him. He'd rather just get on with living his life and let people think whatever they wanted.

Next, his texts. A rake of contacts from journalists asking for his thoughts, lots of 'I'm here for you' sympathy texts from dozens of acquaintances, offers of a chat from several friends and castmates, and yet another reminder from Drea that he had to be at the airport by four o'clock. He scrolled through them all and decided there was nothing that required immediate action, especially as he had no desire whatsoever to discuss his wife's indiscretions or the state of his marriage.

Okay, job done.

He'd just released the handbrake when another notification alerted him to an incoming video call. Sienna. Of course, she'd have landed now. Probably already in the terminal building at LAX. He considered ignoring her, but he knew she would just keep calling. Sienna Montgomery wasn't someone who let things go if she didn't get her own way.

Reluctantly, he accepted the FaceTime call. Her face came immediately into focus. In the background, he could see what looked like a lounge area, with strip lights on the ceiling. He recognised it immediately. LAX had a whole ecosystem and team for dealing with celebrities. They were brought in through a different entrance, and chaperoned through a series of corridors and rooms that had no public access. When he flew with the cast of *The Clansman*, they were ushered through to the lounge that Sienna was standing in now, to relax there pre-boarding. If they were landing, they were met off the plane and taken through that same area to shield them from the public gaze. He rarely used that service when he flew alone, preferring to travel with glasses on, a hat pulled down, and as little fuss as possible, but a certain female who was on his screen right now took it for granted. She'd been going through LAX that way, with her famous parents and grandparents, all her life, so although she no longer had that star status, she had enough influence to send a text and get swift passage to the VIP lounge.

His wife was one of those stunning natural beauties, but right now, she wasn't giving her best look. Her eyes were even more bloodshot than they'd been earlier, there were mascara stains under her bottom lashes, her hair was dishevelled and her skin blotchy. He couldn't remember a time when she had looked like this, not even after a two-hour workout with her thousand dollar an hour personal trainer.

'Ollie, I'm so sorry,' she said again, and he wondered what approach she was going to go with now. Repentant? Explanatory? Self-justification? Would she be mortified? Or would she stick true to form in her life and go on the offensive when she felt attacked?

'Is this when you say again that it wasn't what it looked like?' he asked her, but there was no challenge in his voice, just sadness and disappointment, which seemed to light the blue touchpaper.

'Oh piss off, Ollie. Is that how we're playing this?' Yep, cue a very definite lean into a 'fight fire with fire' position. 'What do you expect? At least he's there for me. When was the last time you came rushing to my side? Or helped me through any kind of shit? You won't even come back to LA when I need you.'

'Last time I checked I wasn't snogging the face off someone I wasn't married to though.' Low blow, but it felt justified.

Her perfect bone structure twisted into a snarl. 'You sure about that?'

Okay. So that's how this was being played. He wasn't rising to it.

'I'm sure.'

'Maybe you just didn't get caught. You honestly want me to believe there's nothing between you and your eternal side piece?'

This was exhausting. He knew exactly who she was talking about, but he wasn't getting into this with her again.

'You've put Kara before me since the first day we met,' she went on.

He'd heard this so many times. It was the same argument she'd recycled every time she was angry, insecure, or she'd messed up and was trying to deflect blame. Like right now.

'And you're doing it again. I'm asking you to come home and you're going with her instead. No wonder I did something stupid. You can't fucking blame me.'

He was over the manipulation. 'So it's my fault you've got a thing going with Van? Tell me something, Sienna – was it just today? Or the last week? The last six months?'

He saw her jaw tighten and her eyes dart to the side, and he knew whatever was going to come out of her mouth next was a lie.

'Today.'

It wasn't. He should be angry. Furious. He should be raging about the injustice of this, the betrayal of everything they'd promised to each other. Yet, he still felt nothing but tired of the whole thing. Maybe she had a point. Perhaps his calmness was a sign that he was already checked out.

'And I know it was stupid, but I was just feeling so shit when you said you weren't coming home.' The emotional pendulum had swung back to self-pity, but only on the way to petulance and emotional blackmail.

'So that's it? When you don't get what you want, you just hit up another guy?'

For a second, he thought she was going to throw her phone at the wall. Instead, her eyes narrowed, and her cheeks reddened.

'You really don't care, do you?' she hissed.

He said nothing. He did care. He loved her. They'd had a brilliant few years at the start of their marriage and he hated that he'd hurt her, even unintentionally, by not doing as she asked. But this wasn't serving either of them anymore and it was becoming pretty clear that they both knew it.

His silence was making her escalate and veer right back into the attack zone.

'You used me and my name to get a bit of fame, then you think you can just toss me to one side and treat me like shit? Last chance, Ollie. Forget your precious Kara and come back to LA tonight or we're done.'

16

ALICE

Val's yellow Jeep was barely picking up speed on the road home, when she turned to Alice, eyes wide.

'In the name of the Holy Mo Farah, Alice, what the hell was that about? One minute my sausage roll was approaching the landing strip, and the next minute you were out of there like yer arse was on fire. I haven't run that fast since the eighties.'

Alice couldn't answer because she was staring straight ahead, trying to contain the tornado that was swirling in her head, scooping up every memory and everything she thought she knew, and then shooting it all out in different directions.

The photos of Morag and Cillian.

The scribbles on the back that showed their first date was in March.

The fact that Zac had mentioned his birthday was in October.

There were only two possible explanations: he was premature. Or Morag had slept with someone else before she met Cillian.

If the first was true, then why would he be questioning the date his parents met? Surely he would know if he'd arrived early?

And if the second option was true, then who had Morag slept with? And why hadn't she shared that with Alice? They'd told each other everything. Absolutely every blooming thing. At least, she'd always thought that they did. But then... another realisation dropped into her consciousness. Morag must have been pregnant when she left for Ireland. Why hadn't she said anything? Or, like Alice, had she not been aware of it, even though she would have been a few months on? Morag had been a tiny size eight back then – maybe she'd just been one of those women who didn't show until later in their pregnancy, and didn't even realise they were pregnant until the baby was practically there? Alice's mind was whirling as she struggled to decide if that could be plausible. It felt like too much of a stretch. Morag was always way too switched on about her body to have missed that. Surely, she had to have known, but again, why would she have kept that from her? Unless...

Every synapse of her brain tried to prevent Alice from answering that question, despite the building blocks of coincidences that were piling up to a whole big pile of conclusions.

Morag's sudden dislike of Larry.

Her decision to leave a job she adored and flee the country with a man she'd only just met.

Her warning to Alice at the airport. 'He's not who you think he is.'

Her disappearance from Alice's life.

Maybe if it were just those things, then she could sweep it to one side and tell herself that she was being crazy. But there were two other vital pieces of evidence that were difficult to ignore.

The note. What was Morag apologising for?

And then, the final brick in that wall. It had only fallen into place when she'd registered the connections of all the other factors. But it really was unmistakable... When she looked into Zac's pale blue eyes, they were so familiar to her.

And that was because they were the same shade and shape as the eyes she looked at every single time she gazed at her son.

The son who had exactly the same eyes as his dad.

'Oh sweet Jesus, oh sweet Jesus, Alice! You're hyperventilating!' Val had one hand on the wheel and the other was clutching for Alice's fingers. 'Put yer head between yer knees. No! Don't do that. This snow is coming down like icing sugar falling off a Victoria sponge and if I have to brake suddenly, you'll end up in the glove compartment. Just close your eyes and breathe. Breathe. Nice and slow. That's it. Hang on, I'm pulling over.'

'No,' Alice managed to gasp. 'Just keep going. Please. Get us home.' What was happening to her? Why couldn't she breathe? Breathe. Breathe. Breathe.

Alice continued instructing her lungs to gulp in air for the next few minutes, until they were pulling into their street. Only when she could see the house at the end of the path did Alice feel her heart rate begin to slow, but her legs were still trembling as she got out of the car. If Val hadn't been supporting her arm until they got through the front door and into the kitchen, then she wasn't sure she'd have made it.

'Sit there and I'll get the kettle on,' Val instructed, taking charge.

Alice put her head in her hands. On the day she'd left Larry, she'd resolved right then and there that she would never let him affect her life again, never allow him to hurt her, and now she had a very real feeling that she'd just taken a cannon ball to the heart.

'I'll be back in a minute,' she whispered, before, on still shaky legs, she managed to go down the hall and climb the stairs to her bedroom. In the cupboard, she found what she was looking for – the suitcase that she'd kept with her for over a decade, the one that had concealed her escape fund when she'd been planning to leave Larry, as well as all her important documents, belongings and, most importantly, all her photographs.

Opening the case, she flicked through half a dozen photo albums until she came to the one she was looking for – life before she married Larry. It had been decades since she'd opened it, because she couldn't stomach to see herself when she was young and optimistic, before a malignant narcissist had sucked the life out of her. She'd even considered burning it at one point, just as she'd torched every photo of her wedding day, and the years that came after it. But somehow, she'd felt the need to keep this chronicle of her life before she became Mrs McLenn. Her parents were in it, before Larry used the subtlest of coercive control to alienate them from her life. Her teenage and twenty-something friends were in it, before they were all cut out too. By the time she got married, all she had was Larry McLenn, and she'd been too blinded by love to see that's what he'd wanted all along.

Tucking the album under her arm, she held on tight to the banister as she descended the stairs, still not confident her legs would hold her.

Back in the kitchen, Val already had the tea out and the biscuit tin open. It was like prescribed medication in this house.

'You okay now?' Val asked her, concern written all over her face.

Alice nodded. 'I think so. Sorry if I terrified you, Val. It was just all a bit of a shock.'

Val did what she always did – tried to make everyone around her feel better. 'Och, no need to apologise. My pal, Josie, once passed out in the front seat, because she'd accidentally eaten magic mushrooms. That was far more terrifying.'

Despite the shock of everything that had just happened, Alice felt the edges of her mouth curl up and the next thing, she was laughing and sobbing at the same time.

'Don't worry, pet,' Val assured her, holding her hand, that concerned expression still there. 'It's just all the emotion. Just keep breathing and it'll pass.'

Alice closed her eyes, and did as she was told. All those years with Larry, her only joy had been Rory. Other than that, she'd been so utterly miserable to her core, that her sole defence was to shut down her emotions to the point of being robotic. Now that she'd allowed that coil of numbness to unwind, it sometimes bubbled over, and she found herself sobbing over clips of rescue dogs on Instagram, or yelling with joy when nice people won *Family Fortunes*.

It took a few minutes, and several sips of hot sweet tea, but eventually she began to feel like she could function again. She tested that by recounting all her thoughts in the car to Val, and her friend was the first one who vocalised the conclusion she'd been skirting around since she'd said goodbye to Zac.

'Wait – so you think Larry and your pal, Morag, might have had...' Val paused and Alice was really grateful that she didn't say 'sex', even though that's what they were both thinking. Val settled on, '...a fling?'

'No!' was Alice's first reaction, but then, far weaker, 'Well, yes. Am I crazy?'

Val sat back in her chair. 'I'm not sure, love, but no wonder you're in shock. That would be a shred of the heart after all these years.'

Alice had already opened the album and was flicking through the mixture of old Polaroids and photos that came from the kind of old-fashioned film that had to be developed by Boots or Happy Snaps.

She found the first couple of photos she was looking for and took them out of the album. London. Morag's birthday. Larry had taken a group of their friends down there in early January to celebrate and they'd had a ball, staying in a posh hotel and trying out new bars and clubs, in which, of course, he made sure they were treated like VIPs.

'That's Larry there, obviously...' she said, pointing him out to Val, not that she needed to. Most people in Scotland – probably the UK too – knew what Larry looked like, because he'd been a highly vocal MP, and then he'd been plastered all over the press and the news when he'd been embroiled in the bribery and drugs scandal that had scuppered his career.

'He's not aged well,' was Val's only comment and Alice knew she said that from experience. After his downfall, Larry had pulled in old favours to get a job as a taxi driver and Val had the misfortune of getting in the back of his cab last year. Although, by a long and shocking chain of events, that journey had resulted in the two women meeting, so Alice would always be grateful.

'Look at how happy Morag is there,' Alice said, drawing attention to the wide grin on Morag's face. Larry was between them, one arm draped around Alice and the other around Morag, and her friend must have been giggling at something he'd said because she was looking up at him with the biggest smile, eyes all crinkled with laughter.

The next photo was the same. Then another. All of them taken on that trip, all of them joyful.

Alice flicked another couple of pages, until she came to the second lot of photos she had in mind. 'These are the ones we took the night Morag left. At the airport. It was a few months later.'

The images showed the two of them at the departure gate, Morag's eyes red and glowering at the camera with sadness, while biting her lip as if her heart was breaking. There were three or four, all of them just as awful. Back when she'd first had these photos developed, Alice remembered putting Morag's scowl down to the fact that she was sad to be leaving, but now, she saw something else.

Morag's expression wasn't sadness. It was anger. Fury. Disgust. And she was staring right at the camera. Which meant she was staring right at the man behind the camera too. 'Larry took that photo.'

Val puffed out her cheeks. 'I mean, it wouldn't be enough for a jury to convict, but I see what you're saying.'

Alice felt some kind of comfort that she wasn't going mad. 'It's not just that, Val. It's all the other things too. It explains it all. And I know it's not proof of anything, but looking at Zac today was like looking at Rory.'

As if he'd heard his name being mentioned, Alice's phone began to ring, and her son's name was on the screen. She picked it up quickly and tried desperately to make her voice sound normal.

'Hello, son.'

'It's the big day!' he announced gleefully. 'Are you excited? Honestly, we can't wait for you to get here. Sophie has been hoovering for a week and a half.' Alice heard a yelp in the background and then laughter from them both. Rory had moved to Reading to be with Sophie a few months ago, and it warmed her heart to see and hear them both so loved up and happy.

'I can't wait either,' she said honestly. 'I wish I was there already.' If she'd gone yesterday, then she wouldn't be dealing with this today.

'Listen, I'm just calling to say I checked the Glasgow Airport website and loads of flights are delayed. It's still saying you've to check in at the same time, but just in case you're delayed, we just wanted to say don't worry. No matter what time you get here, we'll be at Heathrow to pick you up.'

'That's great, son, thank you. I'll see you tonight. Love you.' It still warmed her heart every single day that her son had turned out to be such a good man, with no trace whatsoever of Larry McLenn's twisted, malevolent genes.

'Love you too, Mum.'

And then in the background she heard, 'Love you, Alice!' from Sophie, before they hung up.

Her stomach went back on to a spin cycle. If her suspicions were correct, then this would have repercussions for Rory too. He'd grown up an only child, regularly bemoaning the fact that he had no siblings. That had been deliberate on Alice's part. She'd refused to bring another child into Larry's world. By the time Rory was a toddler, the boyfriend and fiancé who'd love-bombed her was long gone, and in his place was a sneering, cruel husband who'd created a world she and her son couldn't escape from. There was the irony. Larry hadn't wanted Rory. She'd found out after the wedding that he'd only married her to preserve his image and his political aspirations and later, that was the same reason he wouldn't let her leave. All she could do back then was stick it out and do everything she could to protect her boy.

'Och, Alice, I don't envy you this one,' Val said, reaching for a second caramel wafer, which Alice knew signified a Defcon 3 alert level. 'Are you going to share your thoughts with the lad if he comes here?'

Alice wasn't sure how to answer that. Zac had obviously sussed out that something didn't add up, and Alice was fairly certain he'd realised that Cillian couldn't be his dad. But what right did she have to become involved? It wasn't her place to tell him. However... could she really withhold information like that when she might have the answers he was looking for?

She sent up a silent message. *'Come on, Morag, tell me what you would want me to do.'*

The sound of the doorbell interrupted her wait for a reply.

Val stood up. 'Actually, you don't need to answer that question, because it looks like we're about to find out.'

17

ZAC

For a couple of moments, Zac wondered if his mum's old friend had escaped the awkward moment at the funeral by giving him the wrong address. Or maybe she was in there, behind the couch, pretending no one was home. No, he discounted that one. Alice hadn't seemed like the kind of woman who wouldn't keep her word.

His head was still reeling from everything that had happened today. After the funeral, he'd nipped back to Aunt Audrey's house and... he caught himself. It wasn't Aunt Audrey's house any more. That was going to take a bit of getting used to. Anyway, he'd gone back there so that he could say goodbye to his cousins and their kids, before they hit the road for Center Parcs. Right up until the last minute, Jill had been wavering about going, too upset after saying goodbye to her mum this morning.

'You know she'd be furious if we wasted her money,' Hamish had pointed out correctly. Aunt Audrey was unfailingly generous, but also notoriously careful with her cash. 'We'd get nothing back and she'd hate that,' he'd added, a variation of the argument he'd used every time Jill had wavered over the last few days. In the end, the enthusiasm of the kids and her wish to cheer them up after losing their gran had won her over once again and when Zac had said goodbye to them, they were changing out of their funeral clothes and getting ready to go.

Zac had had a quick change too. He'd ditched the suit and pulled on his black jeans and a dark grey jumper, then added the padded jacket that he'd brought with him because it was always bloody freezing in Glasgow at this time of year. Everything else, he'd packed into his case and then it left at the door.

Last job was to find his dad. Cillian was in the back garden, sitting on the stone bench, with the gazebo above it protecting him from the snow that was coming down thick now. For a second, Zac had thought he was sleeping because his head was back, as if he was staring at the sky, but his eyes were closed.

'Dad?'

There was a pause, and his heart had skipped a beat, before his father had brought his head forward and opened his eyes. His dad was only fifty-six years old, and he was a handsome guy, who kept himself in great shape, but right then he looked as old and as weary as Zac had ever seen him. 'Sorry, son. Just having a chat with your mum in my head there. Helps sometimes.'

'I do the same thing.' It was true. Sometimes he'd catch himself telling her something in his mind, and it would make him smile because he knew that she hated to miss a thing.

'Listen, I just need to pop out for a while – I said I'd nip over and see one of Mum's friends that I met at the funeral.'

Had it been his imagination or had his dad turned even paler?

'Oh. Right. Which friend was that now?' There had been an unusual edginess to his dad's voice.

'Alice. She seemed really nice. I'm hoping maybe she can tell me a bit more about Mum when she was younger.'

'I don't think we've got time, son. We need to get to the airport.'

His dad had said that with such conviction, Zac had frowned, confused. 'But our flight is at nine o'clock. We don't need to be there until seven.'

'I know, but with this weather...' His dad's words had tailed off, as he obviously gave up on that argument.

Zac had immediately realised what the issue was. His dad didn't want him to speak to Alice. And it wasn't a huge leap to think that must be because she might tell him something that his dad didn't want him to hear.

Zac hadn't even begun to process how he would deal with this situation, if, as he now suspected, Cillian Conlon didn't share his DNA. The biggest part of him was praying that this was all a mistake, even though the tiny voice in his brain was telling him it wasn't. Either way, he wanted to tell his dad that nothing would change, that it was only biology, that Cillian would always be his father. But that didn't negate his need to find out for sure and put all these questions and fears to rest.

'Aye, well, I don't want to be sitting in an empty house, surrounded by Audrey's memories, so I'd like to get off to the airport early. We're as well there, where we can get dinner and a pint.'

'Okay, but I tell you what then – why don't you go on whenever you're ready and I'll meet you there, just in case I get held up. Text me and let me know when you're leaving. I've left my suitcase at the door—'

'I'll take that with me,' his dad had offered. 'May as well get it all checked in and then we're sorted.'

More and more lately, as the months went by without Mum, it had felt like his dad appreciated being needed or doing things that were helpful. He'd show up at Zac's flat to fill the fridge with beer. Or he'd buy tickets for a football game that he knew Zac would want to go to. Zac appreciated it all and he'd started doing the same. Including Dad in his plans for the weekend. Suggesting things they could do together. Dropping by on the way home from work. He could see Dad missed Mum's company and her sense of purpose too. She always had a plan and a list of things to do and places to go. When they got back to Dublin, maybe he'd suggest a holiday, just the two of them. His dad loved to ski, so maybe a week in the Alps over Easter.

He'd bent down and given his old man a hug. 'It'll be okay, Dad.' Neither of them had chosen to clarify what he was referring to. 'Love ya.'

'Love ya too, son.'

A car horn had blasted from out in the street, interrupting the moment. 'That's my taxi. I'll see you later, either here or at the airport.' For all he knew, he'd be back there within half an hour, if the conversation with Alice was a non-starter.

Now, standing outside her door, he'd begun to think that would be the case, when he heard the sound of a lock being opened and suddenly Val was in the doorway.

'Come on in, you'll catch your death of cold out there,' she chirped, then froze. 'Sorry. Not the day for comments about death. I'm always putting my foot in it.'

Zac laughed. 'That's okay. I'm pretty good at that myself.'

He couldn't help but notice the white furry mules on her feet because they clicked all the way down the hall, past two large suitcases that were just outside the door ahead of them.

'Are you off on holiday?' he asked, just to break the ice really.

'Ah, I wish. No, they're Alice's. She's off to London tonight. Moving there permanently. You caught her just in time.'

Her words triggered a memory of Alice saying at the wake that she was going to London. In the moment, he hadn't given it a thought, but now he realised their paths might have been destined to cross again whether he'd come here this afternoon or not. 'Is she flying?' he asked, struck by the potential coincidence.

'Aye, son, because her canoe has a puncture,' Val deadpanned with a wink, making him laugh despite the craziness of the circumstances. This woman reminded him of his mum and Aunt Audrey so much. One of them would come out with a quip like that and it would set them both off. That thought was just what he needed to calm the uncharacteristic clench of nervousness at the back of his throat.

Alice got up from the kitchen table to greet him with a hug, and as he reciprocated, he saw the open album of photographs on the table, and beside it a small pile of snaps.

'Have a seat, and I'll get you a drink,' Val offered, as he and Alice parted. 'Coffee, tea or beer? My Michael keeps some cans of lager in the fridge, so they're cold already.'

'Coffee would be great, please,' he said, spotting that there was a pot already brewing on the machine beside the cooker. 'Just black. No sugar, thanks.'

'I'm on it,' Val said, crossing to the other side of the room.

Alice still hadn't said anything other than 'Hello' and he could sense that she was as nervous as him. He felt awful that he'd caused that. 'Can I just start by saying I'm really sorry to have ambushed you at the wake. This has all been a bit of a shock. I only discovered the note and the photographs this morning and it's all thrown me. Especially today.'

'I understand,' Alice assured him. 'And I hope you don't think I was being unhelpful. It was all a bit of a shock to me too.'

Val brought the coffee over, then pushed the biscuit tin in his direction. 'There you go, Zac. I bet you were too busy to stop for so much as a sausage roll this morning.'

An ache in his gut reminded him that she was right, and he

took a chocolate digestive gratefully. There were so many questions he needed to ask, but he knew better than to charge in. He'd interviewed hundreds of clients and witnesses in his time, and he'd learned that no one responded well to cold questions, so instead of starting where they'd left off this morning, he gestured to the photo on the top of the pile on the table.

'My mum,' he said, spotting her face.

'Yes,' Alice said gently, picking them up. 'I picked out all the ones I could find of her because I thought maybe you'd want to take them? Or even make copies now by photographing them with your phone, if that would be okay? I'd hate to lose them.'

'That's a good idea,' he agreed, pulling out his iPhone.

Over the next fifteen minutes or so, they went through each photo one by one. Alice would tell him where it was taken and why, or perhaps share an anecdote, while he captured the image on his camera roll. Today was worth it just for these. They were in age order, and in the youngest she must have been about twelve, right up until her early twenties. In Aunt Audrey's house there had been old photo albums that had belonged to his gran, so he'd seen photos of his mum in her youth, but most of them were posed shots on special occasions with her family. These ones were different. She was with her friends. Laughing. Celebrating. Singing into hairbrushes. Being mischievous. Dancing. Blowing kisses. Giggling. And she looked so full of life it brought a lump to his throat.

'This one is your mum's birthday celebrations in London, a few months before she left.'

He turned the photo over and the inscription there hit him like a bullet between the eyes.

The birthday gang! Jan 1995.

The month he had to have been conceived.

He turned it back over and studied the faces there. His mum. Alice. Two other women. And one guy.

'Who is he?' he asked, trying to sound as nonchalant as possible.

'Larry. He was my boyfriend at the time. We got married shortly after that.'

Another bullet. And he could see by the red rash creeping up Alice's neck that she was taking shrapnel too.

The lawyer in him had already formulated a sequence of questions, but he held off, went gently, unable to bear causing her any distress. In the pause, he studied the photo, his stare almost entirely on the one male in the picture. There was something... something familiar. Bullet number three hit him with the answer.

'Hang on – is that Larry McLenn? The politician?'

Holy shit. He'd seen this guy all over the news for years. He'd even visited Ireland as part of a UK delegation for something or other, and then there had been a big scandal – caught on a covert recording accepting bribes and snorting cocaine, if Zac remembered correctly. The guy was a complete sleaze. No morals. No standards. No...

Oh no, no, no.

Realisation dawned and he ran that back.

No morals. No standards. The kind of guy who would sleep with his girlfriend's best friend, approximately nine months before Zac was born? Is that what his mother was apologising for in the letter?

He raised his eyes to meet Alice's, and found his answer right there, in the absolute horror and devastation that was in her eyes.

'Did my mum have a relationship with him?' he asked her,

seriously wishing that he knew none of this.

Alice took several seconds before she managed a quiet, 'I don't know. I had no suspicion of it at all until I met you today…'

He put the pieces together. 'And I showed you the letter. And questioned the date my parents met.'

Val leaned forward, said softly, 'You definitely weren't premature?'

Zac shook his head. 'No. Ten pounds. Full term.'

'Bugger,' was her whispered reply.

He didn't want to ask the next question. He really didn't. Yet he knew he had to. 'Now that you have all this information, do you think there's a *possibility* that they could have had an…' He couldn't make the words come out. Not in relation to his mother. She was the most honest, genuine person he'd ever known. He reworded the question. 'Do you think there's a possibility that there could have been something between them?'

Again, Alice thought about her answer before speaking. 'I would never have thought so. That wasn't Morag. She was good, and kind, and, sure, she loved to have fun, but I find it impossible to believe that she would do that to me. Or to anyone.'

There was some consolation that Alice had the same opinion of his mum's integrity that he held. But he sensed that she was holding something back.

'But…?' he probed.

Alice let out a long sigh and her shoulders sagged. 'Larry could be persuasive. Charming. He was a master manipulator, and he could make people do things that they didn't even want to do. Not through threats or violence, but just by finding their weak spot, or getting them at a vulnerable moment. He was a shark, and not many people were a match for him.'

Zac felt pure visceral anger begin to tighten his chest. This guy sounded like such a prick, and in Zac's line of work he'd met so many just like him. The husbands who controlled their wives, who were charming in public and narcissistic, megalomaniacal assholes behind closed doors. They didn't intimidate him in the least, but he could see how twenty-five-year-old Morag would be no match for someone like that.

'So I guess the bottom line is that the only person who knows is him. And possibly my dad, but I can't bring myself to ask him. Not now. Maybe not ever.'

Val put her mug on the table. 'Oh, your poor dad. I can only imagine how difficult that would be for him. Especially after losing your mum and your aunt. For what it's worth, my advice would be to let it lie, if you can. You are who you are because of the parents that raised you. Isn't it enough to know that?'

He thought for a moment, but he already knew the answer. 'No. I really wish it was, but that's a loose end that I can't leave. I'm a facts guy – occupational hazard – and not knowing the truth would keep me awake at night.'

'Well, maybe think about it for a wee while at least. It's a lot to take in,' Alice suggested, and he could feel that came from a place of care and concern. But this information had been lost to him for almost thirty years, and he couldn't leave it any longer.

'Where will I find him – Larry McLenn? Do you know where he lives?'

The shadow of horror that crossed Alice's face made him flinch. 'I do. But Zac, it's really not a good idea. Stay away from him.'

There was no doubt this was rash. Impulsive. But he only had a short time to get answers on this trip, so he checked his watch and then pled his case.

'I have a few hours before I need to get to the airport for my flight back to Dublin. I hear you're headed that way too.' Alice nodded, as he went on. 'The thing is... I don't know when I'll have a chance to come back to Glasgow, so I can either kill time until my flight or I can go and at least try to make sense of this and get an answer. If I don't find him, fair enough, but at least I won't have missed an opportunity.' He watched as the colour drained from her face and he felt terrible for upsetting her, so he immediately clarified his thoughts. 'Please don't think I'm pushing you to be part of this, though, Alice. If you're not comfortable sharing his address with me, I can use my own resources to locate him and I'll grab a taxi there. Thank you so much for your help and for sharing those photos with me. They're really special. I can see why my mum loved you.'

He stood up and, with a grateful smile, gave them both a hug. First Val, then Alice. He then pulled his jacket off the back of the chair, but as he did so, he spotted Val's raised eyebrows and pursed lips, then then two women had yet another one of those unspoken conversations.

Suddenly, Alice exhaled, shaking her head, as if making a decision to do something even though it was against her better judgement.

'Zac, forget what I just said. Wait right there while I get my coat.'

Val nodded her approval. 'I'm with you too. Let me grab my lippy and the keys for the Jeep.'

18

KARA & OLLIE

Glasgow Airport – 2014

'Kill me. Kill me now. Put me out of my misery,' Kara groaned. 'I'll miss my twenty-first birthday, but at least I'd be spared this eternal embarrassment.'

Ollie was finding the whole thing hilarious. 'I would, but then I'll have no one to call if it all goes to shit. Besides, my ego is loving this.'

They both turned their focus back to Jacinta McIntyre, who was speaking to both the people in front of them, *and* the people behind them in the check-in queue at Glasgow Airport. 'Yes, he's my nephew. Ollie Chiles. Remember the name because he's going to be a huge star. He's off to Los Angeles to audition for a part in a movie. I can't say what it is – confidential. Isn't that right, Ollie?'

Standing a few feet away, he watched all eyes fall on him and he felt himself blush.

'That's right,' he said, practising his best actor-like grin.

Beside him, Kara was still in a state of high-grade embarrassment. 'She's a beamer, she really is. Why does she have to make herself the centre of attention every time? It's mortifying. I'm really sorry.'

'Don't apologise. This might be the closest I ever get to stardom. If I don't land this part I'll be back in a week looking for a job.'

A shudder went down his spine as he said that, and he immediately regretted even vocalising the thought. The truth was, he had to get this job, because he had nothing else. No other options. No plan B. He'd just completed four years of drama school – he'd got accepted at sixteen because he had aced his Highers and given the best audition of his life – and the roles out there for a twenty-year-old, six foot two Scotsman with a Glaswegian accent, were pretty few and far between. Besides, he'd been living in Aunt Jacinta's box room since his mum left to take up her job on the cruise ships, and it was the size of a large cupboard. It was going to be worth going all the way to America just to get a couple of nights in a proper bed, at someone else's expense.

The casting scouts sent over from the USA had auditioned just about every Scottish aspiring actor his age. The role was a small part on the latest movie in *The Clansman* series, based on the books that big shot Hollywood writer and producer Mirren McLean had written and adapted for screen. They'd all become huge global hits, a bit like *Mission Impossible* or Bond, but set in sixteenth-century Scotland and with a lot more blood and gore. It was a pretty small role, but the rumour was that the studios had decided to break the books down into a spin-off TV series, and if that went ahead, they'd go into production in the next couple of years. To get a part on a recurring TV show was what Ollie had been dreaming about his whole life, and he'd be one step closer if he at least got his foot in the door with the studio and the production team and especially with Mirren. If she liked him, she might keep him in mind when she was casting the new show. Anyway, that was a pipe dream for the future. He had to get this part in the movie first. He already knew that he was one of three actors who were being flown over to the Clansman production offices for a final interview. A 30 per cent chance of getting his first decent step on the ladder.

He was excited about every single aspect of this, except leaving Kara. It would be like losing a limb. Or, say, his DVD player. Or his original signed Guns N' Roses poster.

They finally reached the front of the queue, and of course, Jacinta led the way. 'Ollie, hand over your passport and ticket and put your suitcase on this belt here,' she said, before turning to the airline agent. 'This is my nephew, Ollie Chiles. He's on his way to America...' and there she was, off again.

Kara dropped her head onto his shoulder and groaned. 'I can't take any more. Save me. Take me with you.'

That made him laugh, mostly because he absolutely knew she was joking. Kara was in her second year at The Royal Conservatoire, studying costume design, but she'd already landed a part-time role as an assistant in the wardrobe department at the Clydeside Studio. It was an entry-level role and didn't come close to utilising her talents, but he knew his mate – she'd work her arse off and she'd win everyone over and by the time she graduated and needed a full-time role, they'd definitely offer her a job. He was sure of it.

The woman behind the check-in desk handed back his passport with his boarding pass and an encouraging smile. 'There you go. And good luck in Hollywood. I hope we'll see you in the cinema soon.'

She was just being nice, but Jacinta loved every second of it.

'Oh, you definitely will. You remember this face!' she said, pointing to his cheeks.

Okay, so he was beginning to think Kara was right, and Jacinta was mortifying, but she meant well.

They took the escalator up to the departures floor. Drea had already been despatched to the café up there to save a table.

'Right then, I need to go to the ladies' and then I'll meet you both in the café. I told Drea to get cans of Coke and some crisps for you two and make sure she remembered that I want three Sweetex in my tea.'

With that, Jacinta swanned off in the direction of the toilets, her floaty kaftan wafting behind her.

Kara took his hand and dragged him over to the floor to ceiling windows that over-looked the runway and the tarmac that currently housed at least a dozen planes. 'Which one do you think is yours?' she wondered, aloud, while Ollie got slightly distracted by three stunning flight attendants who were walking by, one of whom gave him the most beautiful smile.

He felt a punch to the side of the arm. 'Yo! Can you at least wait until you're on the plane before you start flirting? This is supposed to be our big sad farewell and you're already distracted. Honest to God, you're like a puppy with too many shiny new toys.'

Of course, it was Kara, so she was just taking the piss and laughing as she said it. And she wasn't finished.

'You do know it's 2014 and you're no longer allowed to objectify women like that?' she said, with an arched eyebrow.

'Objectify? I was just being friendly. Last time I checked, that was still allowed.'

'Only today, and only because you're leaving and only because I'm going to miss you sooooo much. But I know you're going to do great. Do you want your pep talk now or will I just write it all in a note, so you don't forget it?'

'A note. Definitely. That way, I can read it every time I get a door slammed in my face.'

'That's not going to happen,' she said, with such conviction it was impossible not to believe her.

Ollie was going to miss her too. She'd been his number one supporter for as long as he could remember and if someone's belief in you could make you successful, then he was destined for big things because she'd been telling him he was great their whole lives. And he'd been doing it straight back.

His mates had always given him stick for having a best pal who was a girl, but he couldn't care less. Besides, although they weren't actually related, they were family, so she counted as more of a sister than just a friend.

'But come on...' his mate Ross said at least once a month. 'You must have got off with her at least once. Or even just thought about it.'

Ollie shook his head and told him to stop being a tosser every time. He just didn't think of her that way. And she didn't think of him like that either.

'I think that one's yours,' she said, pointing to a British Airways plane to their right. He was flying BA to London, then on to Los Angeles. 'Oh, I meant to say, I met your pal, Ross, today. He said to tell you goodbye, and that he was taking your place as striker on the football team, and that he still doesn't believe you and I never hooked up. He tells me that every time he sees me.'

'He thinks we're weirdos,' Ollie told her. 'He's probably right.'

It would be the easiest thing in the world for them to have got together in that way. They'd even talked about it a few times over the last few years, usually when they were drunk after too many snakebites at the student bar.

'Never going to happen,' Kara said, every single time. Sometimes she'd elaborate. Last time they'd discussed it had been a few months before, when he'd been hanging out with her at a pub in the West End near her uni, and she'd gone into fairly incontrovertible detail.

'And I'll tell you why,' she'd said, before chugging back another drink.

'Tell me,' he'd replied, amused.

Her snakebite – a potent mixture of lager, cider and blackcurrant – was getting dangerously close to tipping over the edge of the glass, because she was talking with her hands, as always.

'Well, because… a) I don't fancy you. Sorry. Will I scar you for life if I say that because it questions your firm belief that there isn't a woman on earth who can resist that face and that charm?'

He'd feigned devastation. 'I might never leave the house again.'

That had made her chuckle, before she got back to the point.

'Okay, well… b) I know all your bad habits.' She'd ticked that off on her fingers. 'And c) – brace yourself because this is major.' She did a drum roll with her hands on the pub table. 'We could never split up. Never ever. Because if we did, we'd lose our best mate and that's just not worth it.'

Even thinking about that prospect made him feel a bit sick inside.

'And did you hear the bit where I don't fancy you?' she'd checked, teasing him while finding herself highly hilarious. Snakebites did that to her.

A quick glance at the huge clock on the wall to the side of them jolted him back to the present, and the busy departures area at Glasgow Airport.

'Shit! I'm boarding in fifteen minutes and I'm not even through security yet.'

Kara's chin dropped. 'Noooooo! We didn't even make it to the café.'

She threw her arms around him. 'I love you, Ollie Chiles. You're going to be brilliant. A huge, big, massive success. And then you'll come back to Glasgow and scoop me up so that I can design all the costumes for your movies. Not that I'm making it about me.'

He squeezed her tightly and that was normally the point where he'd come out with some daft comment to make her laugh. Not today.

'I love you too, Kara McIntyre. Don't get swept off your feet by some smart bloke and forget about me.'

'Oh, I'll have done that by tonight,' she teased him, just as her mum and Drea came rushing over. They both smothered him with hugs and kissed. Even Drea. 'The café queue was a mile long and just when I got near to the front, I realised it's time for you to go.' she wailed.

'No worries, I'll get something on the plane. Okay, time to shift.' He put his arms around Kara again.

'Thanks for being you, and thanks for... you know, always being team Ollie.'

'Team Ollie? Will your head be okay going through that door?'

He was still laughing when he released her and picked up his carry-on backpack. With a final wave, he turned to go, and that was when she body slammed him with another hug.

'You take care, Ollie Chiles,' she said, her voice husky. 'And come back safe and in one piece, because you never know... Maybe one of these days I'll fancy you.'

'And maybe one of these days I'll fancy you too,' he shot back, grinning, before turning, and walking away.

But he was pretty sure that neither of them could ever imagine a day when that would be true.

4 P.M. – 6 P.M.

19

KARA

It was already dark, cold, foggy and there was three inches of snow on the ground when Kara opened the boot of the taxi van to load it up with luggage.

'How can you have so many suitcases?' Kara asked Drea, using every ounce of strength her biceps possessed to haul yet another suitcase into the back of the vehicle that would whisk them to the airport. 'Just how? Are we going for a week or are you fleeing the country?'

She'd counted four cases so far, and the driver had helped with the first two before claiming a bad back and retreating into the vehicle. At which point Drea had given her a desperate shrug and said, 'I can't risk breaking a nail. I'm getting married.'

Kara put her hands on her hips, bent over, trying to get her breath back. 'Can I just check how often you're going to use the "I'm getting married" card. Only, if it's going to go on, I'm going to start using the "I've called off my wedding and I'm heartbroken" card to get me out of manual labour.'

Drea put her perfectly manicured hand through hers. 'Are you heartbroken? Still? Because I feel that other than taking to your bed for two days, you don't seem to be sitting with your feelings.'

Kara wrapped her in a hug, appreciating the concern. 'I don't want to sit with my feelings because it only makes me want to go smash Josh's windows and I'm trying really hard not to get arrested before your wedding.'

'Good plan. Okay, let's go before you change your mind.'

Desperate to get out of the snow that was beginning to fall thick and fast again, they clambered into the back seat of the van. While Kara shook out her feet to get the thick white slush off her boots, Drea clicked her seatbelt on while having a minor moan to herself. 'I told Mum we'll meet her at the airport because I'm trying to minimise my exposure to her. She has an opinion on every detail of the next week and I'm scared too much gritting my teeth will pop off a veneer.'

Kara didn't respond. Their mum being a lot was nothing new. As the car pulled out of the street, she took in the dark sky above them and was grateful that in less than twenty-four hours she'd be in the sunshine. And yes, she should be wearing a white dress and saying, 'I do', but right now she'd settle for a pina colada and double scoop of coconut ice cream on the beach.

'Anyway,' Drea went on. 'I want to hear everything about your encounters at work and with Josh this morning. What happened?' Drea asked. 'And leave out nothing.'

Kara rewound her day, back to the start when she'd walked into the Clydeside Studios with Tress, and then pressed play, mapping out everything that happened afterwards. Drea didn't interrupt until they got to the bit where Kara left the meeting and Josh was in the reception area with Corbin Jacobs.

'He was not!' she gasped. 'You know, screw it – we could still detour and pan his windows. So what did you do?'

'Erm,' Kara said, a little shamefaced, 'I very boldly and bravely ran out of there like my arse was on fire.'

Drea pursed her lips. 'Not exactly a superhero move, but okay.'

'I know. Not my finest moment. But anyway, so then...' On she went, laying out chapter two of the sorry tale, the one that was set in her old flat and that ended with her putting him on the spot. 'I hit yet another all-time low by giving him a hypothetical scenario – if I agreed to still marry him, would he drop Corbin and the studio as clients and defend me instead? He didn't say yes.'

'Oh love, I'm so sorry. What an arse he truly is.' Drea took her hand, her sympathy making tears pool on Kara's bottom lids. She blinked them back and cleared her throat before answering Drea's inevitable question. 'What would you have done if he'd agreed? Apart from panic, because I already cancelled his flight.'

'Yeah, he did mention that.' Kara said, before falling silent for a second, as she contemplated Drea's question. 'I don't know. The weird thing is...' She was admitting this to Drea before she'd even admitted it to herself. 'There was part of me that was relieved that he didn't. How could I marry him when I couldn't count on him to have my back? Or to put me first? I know Clydeside is one of his biggest clients, but he could have handled this another way. Instead, he just went straight into damage control, and this time, I was the damage.'

'I get it and I agree. You deserve better. I told Ollie he should have married you when you asked him.'

'I was eight and I just wanted his bike,' Kara spluttered.

Drea cackled so loudly the driver did a welfare check in the rear-view mirror. 'That's exactly what he said when I spoke to him earlier. Anyway, you can stay with me and Seb as long as you want.'

'Thanks, Drea.'

It was one of those beautiful sister moments, until Drea added, 'But not too long because you spend an inordinate amount of time in bed and in the bath. There's always your old room at Mum's.'

Kara shook her head, a rueful smile. 'I'd rather go back to Josh. Or sleep in my car. A Mini can be surprisingly roomy when it's the best option.'

'See, you should have married Ollie. You'd have got the bike, half of that swanky townhouse in Park Circus and an LA crash pad. You really are such a disappointment.' She pivoted to the next fleeting thought that went through her mind. 'You know what I don't understand though?'

'Empathy?' Kara went with her best guess, but Drea refused to rise to it.

'I don't understand what's happening with Casey Lowden. I feel like she's letting you take the fall and all you were doing was defending her.'

Kara nodded thoughtfully. 'I know what you're saying, but the bottom line is that she didn't ask me to step in. It was my choice, so everything that's happened to me since is down to me. I don't blame her in the least. Maybe she'd rather have handled it a different way.'

'Yeah, well, I hope you hear from her.'

'Doesn't matter,' Kara countered honestly. 'I don't regret it and I'd do it again, so it's all on me.'

Before Drea could respond, the car veered off the motorway and onto the slip road to the airport, sending her into a full-on flap. 'Eek, we're only five minutes from the airport. Okay, let me just check everything again. Passport, itinerary...'

While Drea lost herself in her oversize bag, Kara took the moment to check her phone. Two more missed calls from Ollie.

Argh! The sooner they were in the same place the better because all this phone tag was driving her crazy. She cleared the notifications, before flicking onto social media. The story and video of Sienna was trending on X, and all over her Facebook and Instagram. She no longer had TikTok, after realising she could spend endless hours scrolling IKEA hacks, even though she didn't need any furniture and she couldn't use an electric saw if her life depended on it.

She was about to shut it down and put her phone away when she spotted a pap photo of Corbin Jacobs, walking out of his house wearing a medical boot on one foot. According to his spokesman (his name wasn't mentioned but step forward Josh Jackson), it was 'a minor injury sustained while taking part in martial arts training for a potential movie role. More details to be released at a later date.'

Suffering from a sudden bout of dickhead-induced nausea, Kara tossed her phone into her handbag, just as they pulled into the drop-off zone at the airport.

The driver grabbed a trolley from the stand, but that was as far as his help with the luggage went, so it was down to Kara to wrestle the cases into the luggage equivalent of a Jenga tower, and then push it, while trying to hold on to the top case so it didn't fall off.

The terminal building was packed, and Kara presumed that was because it was a busy time, with people returning home after spending the New Year celebrations in Scotland. Once upon a time she'd known a lovely Irish guy who did the very same thing.

'I'm a gold member of their loyalty programme, so we get to go in this queue,' Drea directed her to a priority queue, and Kara changed course like an F1 driver taking a hairpin bend. 'Mum texted and said she's running late and we should go on through. She'll meet us in the lounge.'

Kara didn't want to admit that she was a little relieved. She couldn't face recounting the whole story of her day to her mum right now. In fact, there was only one person she was desperate to see. Their wait was only twenty minutes or so to get to the front of the line and the whole time, Kara anxiously scanned the terminal for Ollie, but there was no sign of him. She'd been fretting about him ever since the Sienna story broke. All she wanted was to sit down with him and a large glass of wine and make sure he was okay.

When they finally got to the desk, they handed over their passports to a slightly harassed-looking lady behind the counter, who scanned them and then requested that the suitcases be put on the scales. Again, Drea eyed Kara with a pleading expression.

'All right, all right,' she said, manhandling the cases from the trolley one by one until her biceps were on fire. She'd need to collect them tonight at Heathrow, and then do all this again tomorrow morning when they flew out to San Francisco, en route to Honolulu.

'I'm afraid your flight to London is currently delayed for two hours, so you're now scheduled to depart at 8 p.m.'

Drea visibly paled. 'But I just checked it before we left home and it said no delays.'

'I'm sorry. It's the snow and the fog. We have had a weather warning running all day...' The tension showed in her tight smile. She'd probably had the same reaction from every single passenger she'd checked in.

Kara struck 'ground crew' off the list of potential jobs now that she was unemployed. She'd rather deal with Corbin Jacobs than with hundreds of irate customers in one night.

Drea was still under the impression that arguing would make this woman phone the pilot and say, 'Get your tea down, and get your jacket on – ignore the fact that it's like pea soup out there and fire up the 747 because this lady needs to get to London tonight.'

'I saw that, but when there were no delay notifications I assumed it was fine. Sorry, I know it's not your fault. I'm just worried about the next leg of my journey. We're staying overnight at Heathrow and then tomorrow morning we're flying onwards to San Francisco and then Hawaii, because I'm getting married there the day after tomorrow.'

Drea had also inherited the oversharing gene.

'Congratulations. At the moment, it's only a two-hour delay, so I'm sure you'll be fine.' Kara watched the woman scan the packed hall and suppress a sigh. It was going to be a long night.

'At the moment...? You mean it could be longer?' It was impossible to miss both the rising panic and the rising volume in Drea's voice. People in the queues on either side were turning to stare.

With an apologetic smile, Kara took the passports and boarding passes from the woman's outstretched hands. 'Thank you so much. Hope things calm down here soon and your night gets less hectic. Happy New Year.'

Was it still okay to be saying Happy New Year, on the third?

'Okay, breathe, just breathe,' she urged Drea as she gently nudged her sister in the direction of the lifts that would take them up to security. 'It's only a couple of hours.'

'But what if they extend it for another hour? Then another. What if we're here all night and then miss the flights tomorrow?'

'If we're here all night, I'll treat you to a swanky suite in the hotel across the road. They've got Toblerones in their minibar and cashew nuts that cost a week's wages, but you're worth it.'

They went through the barriers and joined a security line that was approximately seven miles long.

Two little lines appeared between Drea's eyebrows as she frowned. 'How do you know?'

'How do I know what?' Kara asked, gulping back the realisation of what she'd just said, and trying desperately to come up with a way to dial it back.

'About the hotel across the road. When did you stay there?'

Of course Drea would remember that kind of stuff. She was a travel professional who booked all Kara's trips and who stored that kind of info in her travel professional encyclopaedic brain.

'Erm, it doesn't matter.'

Drea knew her too well. She immediately zeroed in on Kara's reddening face, flustered with a side dish of guilt.

'Ohhhhh. Kara McIntyre, I think it does. And I think I'd like to hear about it.'

'You wouldn't.'

'Oh, I would.'

The good news was that Drea's anxiety over the delay seemed to have subsided. The bad news was that the reason for that was because she was now laser focused on Kara.

There was no point resisting. The only smart choice was surrender.

'Okay, fine!' She glanced around and decided there were too many people in earshot for that conversation. 'I'll tell you all about it when we're somewhere more private... but let's just say that Josh wasn't the only one in our relationship who made a mistake.'

20

OLLIE

It was rich that Sienna had been the one giving the ultimatums. You couldn't knock that level of confidence. Or arrogance.

'Last chance, Ollie. Forget your precious Kara and come back to LA tonight or we're done.'

'Really?' He'd reacted with a sad smile and shake of the head, before delivering the answer in a quiet, resigned tone. 'You know I don't respond to ultimatums, Sienna.' Even after the whole debacle with Van Weeks, the viral humiliation and betrayal, he still didn't know for absolute certain what his answer would be until it came out of his mouth. 'I'm not coming back.'

There had been no point raging. Or getting angry. Or making this any worse than it already was by treating the other one with contempt.

'Then it's over. Go fuck yourself, Ollie.'

Apparently, she hadn't got the 'no contempt' memo.

After she'd hung up on him, he'd sat in the car for a few minutes, debating his options. He could let her cool down and then call her back and discuss this like two calm adults. Although, given her reactions so far today, he wasn't confident about the 'calm' bit. Nevertheless, he could give that a try. Or he could walk away and accept what he'd known deep in his soul for months now. It was over. It had been amazing, and he'd never regret it, but it was done. And even if either of them wanted to, there was no point in going to couples therapy, or trial separations, or any other half-assed attempt to get them back on track. Whether today was the first time or not, Sienna was already onto the next thing. She'd checked out. Time for him to do the same.

He'd sat with that for a few minutes, waiting for some kind of internal reaction, an objection to rise from inside his soul, but it hadn't come. All he'd realised was that he wanted to be anywhere but sitting in a car, at Glasgow Airport in the fog and the snow, so he'd restarted the vehicle and now, a few minutes later, he was steering it into the rental return site. He parked it up, pulled his beanie back on, added the specs and then went inside to drop off the keys.

'Thanks, pal. Any problems or damage?' the gent behind the desk asked, without looking away from his screen.

Ollie put the keys on the counter. 'Nothing. It was all good. I didn't get a chance to fill it up though, so just add the charge to my credit card.'

The bloke was typing something on his keyboard, paying Ollie no attention at all, and that was just the way he liked it. 'Will do. We'll check it over and your deposit will be returned to your credit card in the next three to five business days, Mr... Mr...' He was peering closer at the screen now, reading what was there, and if this was a cartoon, a lightbulb would have started flashing above his head.

'Oliver Chiles?' For the first time he raised his gaze to Ollie's face. 'Bloody hell, it's yourself! My missus loves that show you're in. I mean, not that I watch it because it's all that historical pish – I prefer a bit of footie or a good murder – but she'll never believe this when I tell her. Can we get a selfie? Hang on, where's my phone?'

He patted the top of piles of paper on his desk until he located it, then he came round to Ollie's side of the desk, put his arm around Ollie's shoulders, went for his very best grin and snapped.

'Got it. My Margaret will be gobsmacked, so she will. Hey, Harry...' he yelled, in the direction of the door behind the desk. 'Can you come man the shop for five minutes? I'm just going to give my pal, Ollie, here a lift over to the terminal building.'

'Oh no, that's okay...' Ollie began to object.

'Nonsense. We canny have you getting the shuttlebus. My Margaret would never forgive me.'

An older gent emerged from whatever was behind the door and gave Ollie a disinterested nod.

'Harry, it's Ollie Chiles!' his new best friend said.

Nope, Harry still had no clue. 'You play football, son?' Harry asked Ollie, in that very Glasgow way of assuming everything revolved around football.

'Only in the garden,' Ollie told him, before his newly appointed chauffeur interjected with, 'He's an actor! He's in that show... Ach, never mind.' He picked a set of keys off a hook on the wall behind him. 'Right then, let's go, Ollie.'

Five minutes, a couple of skids in the snow, two more selfies, an autograph, a vigorous handshake and slap on the back later, Ollie got dropped at the terminal building. Inside, it was the busiest he'd ever seen it, so he put his head down, made eye contact with no one and made his way to the check-in queue to drop off his suitcase.

He'd done so many miles over the last few years that he'd made it to the top of the airline loyalty scheme tiers, giving him access to the much shorter priority line. He kept the same

posture as he shuffled forward a few feet at a time, using the
pretext of being on his phone. To his relief, no one appeared to
recognise him and if they did, they didn't say anything. Since the
whole fame thing had happened, people were mostly great, especially in his home city, but he couldn't face the 'It's you!' conversations today, especially with his wife currently trending on both
X and TikTok. #sloppySienna.

'I'm afraid your flight is delayed for two hours at the
moment,' said the lovely lady behind the desk.

'More time for beer and tequila,' he quipped, then he heard
his publicist in his head reminding him comments like that were
off limits. If there was a pap or a press mole anywhere nearby,
he'd soon know about it because, based on that comment alone,
there would be headlines for the next two weeks, talking about
how he was devastated about his wife's antics and using alcohol
to numb the pain. Or how he couldn't get through the day
without a drink and was on his way to rehab. He'd once visited a
drug treatment clinic as research for a role and, by the following
day, several press outlets had reported he'd checked into rehab
for his addictions to both drugs and sex. Ironic, given that he was
the married bloke, who didn't sleep around, and the only drugs
he did were Rennies for the occasional heartburn.

As soon as his case whisked off on the conveyor belt, he made
his way upstairs, still head down. He always paid extra for
Priority Security, avoiding the general security line that he'd
noticed snaked back almost to the entrance barriers. He briefly
wondered if Drea and Kara were stuck in that, but he didn't want
to put his head above the parapet to search for them. Hopefully
they were already through and waiting in the lounge.

A few of the security officers were familiar to him, because
he'd been travelling in and out of Glasgow for years, so he made
a point of saying hello. Not that it got him off trashing the bottle

of water he'd mistakenly left in his backpack, and nor did it get him any favours, like being able to leave his boots on when going through the scanner. Apparently fame only got him perks in LA and the car rental return office here.

Reunited with his boots and backpack, he made his way straight to the BA lounge and had a look around for Kara and Drea, but they weren't there yet. He grabbed a can of Budweiser from the beer fridge and settled in the furthest corner from the door, his back to the world, so that no one would give him a second glance. One of his favourite memories was of coming to the airport when he was twenty and going to LA for the first time. Kara had come to see him off, and they were just skint hopefuls who couldn't ever have grasped what was to come. He'd got the dream... he just hadn't realised it would come with shadows in the corners.

He pulled out his phone and hit the #sloppysienna hashtag, only to discover that #OllieCallMe and #CryOnMyShoulder-Ollie were trending too. He could already gauge Sienna's reaction to that development, and it wouldn't be pretty. What a shitshow this day had turned out to be. This morning he'd climbed out of the shower, pretty chilled and happy, and now...

His phone burst to life in his hands and he answered it straight away to hear Calvin's melodic tones. 'Well, hello! Apparently #OllieCallMe is trending, so I thought I'd save you the bother and get in there first, just in case you suddenly realise I'm the man of your dreams.'

'Appreciate that,' Ollie replied, laughing. 'And if there was going to be a man of my dreams, it would be you, my friend.'

It was all in jest – Calvin and his husband, Pierre, had been married for years and they were devoted to each other.

Calvin's laugh was infectious. 'My ego thanks you. But enough about me... I'm just calling to check in. How are you doing, what's the latest on everything that kicked off this morning, and is there anything I can do to help?'

Making sure no one was in earshot, Ollie filled him in on his conversation with Sienna, rounding off with, 'Feels weird saying it out loud, but I guess that's it. And what's even weirder is that it honestly feels like it's the right thing to do. I don't think we've made each other happy in a long time.'

'Maybe that's what you need to think about going forward then – do the things that make you happy, Ollie, because otherwise what's the point? Listen, no pressure, and I know that today isn't the day, but at some point, come back to me on the theatre school. I'm going to make a decision on whether to go ahead with it in the next few days. No pressure though. If being part of it isn't for you, I'll completely understand.'

With everything that had happened in the last few hours, that had slipped down the list of things that were taking up headspace. Sienna no longer being part of his consultation process was a plus – but if he was going to have to reshape his life post-marriage, did he really want a commitment this big and to have more people depending on him? He needed to think it all through.

He nodded, even though Calvin couldn't see him. 'Yeah, I will do, pal. Let's catch up again later in the week. And, Calvin, sorry to drag you into my mess this morning.'

'Any time. Mess is my specialty.' Ollie knew he wasn't joking. Over the years, Calvin had managed some of the most notoriously difficult talent in the business. His client, Odette Devine, was a legend and a brilliant actress, but it was well known in the industry that she could give J.Lo a run in the diva stakes, yet Calvin had been her manager forever. 'And like I said, if you suddenly realise you're besotted with me, call me. You're my celebrity hall pass, so you won't be wrecking a home.'

That made Ollie laugh. 'Good to know.'

He said goodbye and put his phone back in his jacket pocket. He rarely left it on a table in public just in case anyone managed to swipe it.

Picking up his beer, he took a sip, thinking about what Calvin had said about focusing on things that made him happy. Now that his life had blown up in his face, he was going to have to rethink what that was.

He got up to go for another beer, but as soon as he turned, he spotted a couple of new arrivals entering the lounge.

One of the things that made him happy had just walked in the door.

He rose his hand and waved to Kara and Drea.

21

ALICE

Alice was feeling wave after wave of nausea, and not just because of Val's driving. This was such a bad idea. A terrible one. The last time she'd seen Larry, he'd been in a hospital bed, recovering from a crash that had almost killed him and Sophie, the young woman her son now lived with. Larry had been driving his taxi, drunk and high on drugs, and Sophie had the misfortune to get into his vehicle that day. Thankfully, Sophie had survived, and when Rory had gone to her to apologise for his estranged father's despicable actions, it had sparked a friendship that had led to where they were now. That, and Rory's birth, had been the only two positive outcomes of Larry McLenn's existence on this earth.

Back then, Larry's injuries had been far more serious, and Alice was fine with the knowledge that one day she'd go to her grave, and be judged because every single minute of that day of his accident, and the days that followed, she'd wished he would die.

The bastard had lived. The only consolation was that while he was in hospital, she'd got the breathing space to escape him, with Val and Rory's help. When she'd also discovered that he was having an affair with his workmate, Sandra, it had only been a relief, because the other woman had pressured him to let Alice go. Alice had tried to warn her what she was getting into, but Sandra had brushed her off. At the time, Alice had nothing but scorn for her, but she'd soon realised that the woman was no different from the young Alice, who'd been too besotted with Larry to see the monster that he truly was.

Every word of their exchange during that last meeting with Larry still played out in her mind on the nights when she couldn't sleep. Over the years leading up to that moment, she'd been accumulating damning evidence against him, photos, notes, recordings, and she'd used the threat of exposing it as her final goodbye, in the Intensive Care unit at Glasgow Central Hospital.

'If Rory or I see you or hear from you again, I'll make it all public. Every. Last. Word. Of. It. And it will bury you under so much shit you'll never breathe again. So I'm going to get up from here and I'm going to walk away. And Larry? You can rot in hell.'

She'd already been on her feet when he'd snarled, *'I was tossing you out anyway. Sandra is moving in with me.'*

Alice had stopped. Turned. *'You know, I think that's the first time you've made me happy in thirty years.'*

That should have been it. Case closed. Over. They weren't divorced yet, because he'd refused to engage a lawyer or sign the papers, and she couldn't afford the cost of the legal action it would take to force him to do that, but it had been enough to know she never had to see him or speak to him ever again.

Until now.

There had been no other choice though. If this lad was Larry's child, then he would be her son's brother – so for that reason, and for the memory of her friend, Morag, Alice couldn't have let him do this alone.

It was dark outside, as they left the village of Weirbridge. The fog was getting thicker and the snow was still falling. The snowploughs hadn't been out yet so the couple of inches of white that now covered every surface was turning the village into a scene from a Christmas card – one that Alice really didn't want to go for a drive in. She was glad it was only ten miles or so to the rough estate in a neighbouring village, where she'd lived with Larry after they'd lost the huge, opulent mansion in the West End of Glasgow that had been their home while he was the MP for that area. Alice hadn't cared about leaving the luxurious surroundings because it had been a gilded cage, with malice and dishonesty in the very fabric of every wall. In some ways, she'd actually preferred the dilapidated hovel that they'd moved to, because living there had been absolute torture for Larry, a daily reminder of his downfall and disgrace. After almost thirty years of abuse, threats and coercion, Alice had welcomed the pain going in his direction.

And now it was flowing her way again.

The thought of seeing him had sent every one of her nerves to the surface of her skin, making it crawl. She couldn't even pinpoint the emotions that were twisting her gut. It wasn't fear. She'd stopped being terrified of Larry McLenn when he could no longer hurt her or threaten their son. This was something different. Horror. Like falling asleep and watching an old nightmare return, one that had taken her to hell and almost decimated her to the core the first time around. There was nowhere in the world she dreaded going more than Larry McLenn's house. All she could do, for all their sakes, was hope that he wasn't there. He'd spent four months in prison after the crash, but Alice had spotted a story in the paper a few weeks ago that said he'd now been released. If he wasn't at the house she'd lived in with him, then she had no idea where else he would be.

Zac was in the back seat of the Jeep, and Alice was the front passenger, so she turned around to speak to him. 'Are you really sure about this, Zac? I promise you, he's not a good person and nothing good has ever come to anyone from meeting Larry McLenn.'

She could see the tension on his face and her heart ached for him. The poor guy. He had only said his final goodbyes to his aunt this morning, and now he was dealing with what had to be one of the biggest shocks of his life.

'The truth is, I don't know,' he admitted. 'Part of me thinks I've lost the plot, but the other part of me needs to know the whole story. I can't stand the thought that he might have hurt my mum, or at least caused her to lose her best friend, change her whole life, keep a secret for a lifetime. But then, what if...' He stopped, choking on the last few words of that sentence, but she knew what he was going to say. *What if he's my dad?*

Over time, she'd come to realise that it was incredibly diffi-cult for anyone who'd had a happy, loving upbringing to under-stand that people with the opposite experience sometimes had to walk away from their parents because they were just not good people. It was a lesson her son had learned, when he had cut his dad out of his life, but even then, it had taken a lot to get to that point. She suspected Zac would follow his natural instinct and try to find some good in Larry McLenn, some redeemable feature. Alice wanted to save him the pain and convince him there was none, but he would have to see that for himself. She could only warn him and be there for him no matter how it panned out and that was why she'd agreed to this insanity, even if she still didn't feel it was her place.

A picture of Cillian, at the service this morning, came into her mind. She was sure he'd recognised her, yet he'd turned away. But before he did, there was something in his glance – fear, maybe? Why hadn't he spoken to her? If Zac was someone else's son, then he must know, surely? So many unanswered questions.

'I think my biggest question is why Mum didn't tell me,' he went on. 'She was always so honest and when I was growing up she told me time and time again that if I made a mistake I had to own up to it because that was the only way to make it right. And she held me to that. I mean, it's not quite on the same level as this, but I can't tell you how many times she marched me round to a neighbour's house to apologise for booting the ball into their garden and damaging something, or round to a friend's house if she thought I was out of line. Keeping something secret, not righting a wrong, it's just not who she was and that gives me hope that there's some innocent explanation for all of this. Am I crazy to think that?'

Alice's neck was beginning to hurt with turning around in her seat, but she said, 'No, not at all and I truly hope so too. I just don't want you to be disappointed.'

'I appreciate that.' There was a pause, before Zac leaned forward until his seatbelt was straining. 'Can I ask you something really personal? I totally understand if you'd rather not answer.'

Alice was desperate to say no, but of course... 'Sure.'

'I was just thinking how, if we're right about this worst-case scenario and Larry McLenn is, you know...'

Alice realised he couldn't say it out loud, but they both knew what he was referring to.

'Well,' he went on, 'that would make me your son's half-brother. How would he feel about that?'

Alice thought it over for a few seconds.

'I think it might take him a beat to get used to the idea of Larry having yet another effect on his life...' It sounded like Zac was holding his breath, so she followed up quickly with, 'but I think he'd love it. He always wanted a brother and Rory is a really decent, good man. Obviously I'm biased, but he truly is. I think you'd like him. And I think he'd welcome you to the family. I would too.'

Zac cleared his throat. 'Thank you. I hope, however this turns out, that I get to meet him some day. I always wanted a brother too. I just never thought it would be this way.'

A pause, before Alice brought up something else that was on her mind. 'While we're asking questions, have you thought about how it would affect your dad if you do uncover a connection to Larry? I have to guess that it would be devastating for him.'

She watched Zac sigh, as he slowly nodded his head. 'I have. But if the date on the photo is correct, then he already knows the truth, so if I find out for sure that he's not my biological father, then I guess I'll decide then what to do about it. Maybe nothing at all. I don't want anything in my life to change, and it won't change how I feel about my dad – I just need to know for me.'

The car fell silent again, other than the low background music coming from the speakers – Tom Jones' Greatest Hits, a classic according to Val – for a few moments, until Val gave her arm a nudge. 'You okay there, Alice?' she asked, and Alice thought again how much she'd miss her friend.

Right on cue, the opening bars of 'The Green Green Grass of Home' filled the air. She still hadn't fully absorbed that home was going to be a completely different place after today.

'I am. Thanks again for driving us, Val.'

'My pleasure. Although, Zac...' She glanced at her back seat passenger in the rear-view mirror. 'Alice is right in everything she's saying about Larry. He's a bad one. There's still time for me to stop and turn around…'

She didn't get the rest of the sentence out because suddenly there was a massive bang, and then the Jeep lurched to one side, then began to spin… and spin… and the last thing Alice heard before it stopped was her own scream.

22

ZAC

They came to a halt with a thud, and Zac was the first one to find his voice. 'Alice? Val? Are you okay? ARE YOU OKAY?'

He wasn't sure if the crushing feeling in his chest was down to panic, or the seatbelt, or a bit of both. What had he done? These two women wouldn't even be here if it weren't for him, so if anything happened to them... Fuck, why couldn't he get this seatbelt off so he could get out or get up front to check on them?

'Alice?' he blurted again, still scrabbling with the seatbelt clip.

'It's okay. I'm fine, I'm fine,' she repeated, then he heard her say, 'Val?'

'Just give me a wee minute until my heart stops racing,' Val answered, and the blood coursing round Zac's veins flooded with relief and gratitude. They were both okay. He'd never have been able to live with himself if they weren't.

Val shook out her arms and shoulders. 'Everything's still attached and working. I think we're fine.'

'What happened?' That came from Alice, who was now opening her door. 'Did we hit something?'

Zac finally managed to get the seatbelt unclipped, and followed her out, leaving the door open.

'You don't have to tell me what it was, I already know,' Val said, in a tight, furious voice that shocked him because he'd only heard her being funny, calm, supportive.

Thankfully, there were street lights on this part of the road so they could see in the darkness, but Val came right in with the correct answer at the same time as he and Alice spotted the problem. Even with the white coating on the ground, it was impossible to miss.

'It's a pothole the size of a fecking duck pond. I've reported it to the council twice in the last month and they haven't done a bloody thing about it. My pal, Jessie McLean from the hairdressers, lives in that house just there and she lost her whole front end on Christmas Eve. And usually I'd have a joke about that last sentence, but I'm too bloody mad to think of one. I knew the damn thing was there, but I was too engrossed in our conversation and lost concentration for a second.'

He could see she was right. The bang had obviously been a result of the wheel hitting the pothole, and it had blown the tyre, causing them to spin on the snow-covered road. They'd been so lucky there wasn't another car anywhere near them or they could be dealing with so much more than just a flat tyre right now.

'Val, can you drive the car slowly into the side here, just to get it to a safer space?'

Still in the driver's seat, Val switched the engine back on and slowly edged the Jeep around so that it was facing the right way, then switched it off again and climbed out.

He had a closer look at the wheel, but other than the shredded tyre it didn't seem to be damaged. 'Have you got a spare tyre?'

'Aye, son – in the boot.'

'Okay, let me have a go at changing it.'

'I did a car mechanic course back in 2012 – I'm perfectly capable of doing that too,' Val countered, and Zac didn't doubt it for a second.

'I'm sure you could, but, Val, it's freezing and it's snowing and I've got this huge jacket…'

'True. And I did just get my hair done yesterday,' she added. 'It'll get wrecked with this snow and I'm trying to make it last past our bingo night tomorrow.'

Zac never thought he'd see that day that he was grateful for high-maintenance hair.

Alice and Val were now sheltering under a very sparse tree a few feet away. 'We could just go knock on Jessie's door,' Val suggested, nodding at the house, which had lights on in a couple of windows. 'It looks like she's in, so we could have a cuppa so we're not in your way.'

'That's a really good idea,' Zac agreed, already round at the boot, checking that he had everything he'd need. Spare. Jack. Locknuts. Yep, all there.

'Are you sure, Zac?' Alice asked and he immediately responded with a nod.

'Absolutely. You can't sit in the car while I'm doing this and that tree isn't much of a shelter. It'll only take me fifteen minutes or so, but at least you'll be out of the snow.'

He could see Alice's reluctance in her face, but she agreed after Val gave her a tug on the sleeve. 'Come on, love, we'll only be in the way. And I can get Jessie's statement about this bloody pothole while we're in there. I'll be at that council office first thing tomorrow morning.' Zac felt a pang of sympathy for the council official who was about to meet the wrath of Val, but he had no doubt the pothole would be repaired before the week was out.

'We'll watch out of the window, and when you're done, we'll be right back out,' Alice assured him, before they both went off down the thirty yards or so to the house.

Zac got busy, jacking the car up, then removing the wheel. Practical stuff always gave him time to think. Whenever he had something on his mind, he'd go to the gym and work out, or go out into the back garden and chop wood for the log burner in his lounge.

Or change a tyre on a bright yellow Jeep on a dark, slushy road in the West of Scotland. What was he doing here? And why? He'd lived perfectly happily for almost three decades without the knowledge of any of the puzzles that had been raised about his origins today, so why did he have to stir this up when he could just walk away, go to the airport, meet up with the man he called Dad and get on with his life? That would be the most sensible solution.

But then... He'd never been good at ignoring questions. What happened if he needed medical treatment that only a blood relative could provide? A long shot, for sure. And given what he knew of Larry McLenn, he was fairly positive that a liver transplant was off the cards. But what about when he had kids? He wanted to know the genetic history he was passing on too. And... His legal brain ran dry on justification, and his heart took over. The truth was he wanted to know exactly what, if anything, had happened between this guy and his mum. He needed to understand if and how she'd been manipulated into acting so out of character. He wanted to know his origin story, because not knowing the truth would haunt him.

The snow had eased off by the time he had the new wheel on and released the jack, lowering the car back onto the ground. He'd just put the damaged wheel in the boot and cleaned his hands with some wet wipes that were in there, when he saw Val and Alice hugging another woman at the door of the house, then walking speedily back towards him.

Val held out two lidded cups. 'Coffee or tea? We weren't sure which one you'd prefer so Jessie made both. I'll pop the cups back into her at the hairdressers tomorrow.'

'Coffee please,' he said, taking the one from her right hand. He wasn't even so bothered about the beverage, it was more just that the heat from the cup would defrost his frozen fingers.

They all climbed back into the car, and only the rich smell of the coffee gave a clue that there had been an interruption to proceedings. At least, until Alice spoke...

'Zac, are you still sure that you want to do this? You know, I'm not one for paranormal or spiritual theories...'

'She's not, but I am,' Val interjected, but her tone was gentle, as if broaching a difficult subject. 'And I'm thinking maybe your mum was using a wee bit of divine intervention there to tell us something?'

The thought had crossed Zac's mind too. Would his mum want him to do this? Would she be horrified? Disappointed?

'Maybe. Or maybe it was just the council's roads policy.' He managed a conciliatory smile. 'Ladies, I honestly appreciate everything you've done for me, and I don't want to put you out any more than I already have.' He felt terrible for everything that had happened in the last hour and for any stress he'd caused Alice before then. If his mum really could do the divine intervention thing, then she'd find a way to give him a piece of her mind for troubling folk. 'I promise it would be no bother at all for me to get a taxi the rest of the way.'

It was Alice who shook her head, and she seemed to have a new air of resolve. 'Nope, if you go, we all go. Right, come on, Val, let's get moving. We've only got an hour before we need to head to the airport, so let's get this over with.'

They got back on the road, and Zac sipped his coffee as he looked out of the window. When the warm liquid hit his stomach, he realised that other than a biscuit at Val's house, he hadn't eaten anything since breakfast, but his appetite was gone, replaced by the knot of apprehension that he hadn't been able to shake all day.

He watched as they turned off the country road and into what looked like the outskirts of a village, and then into a housing scheme that was very different from the streets of the surrounding areas. Many of the homes were well kept and pristine, but there were several that were clearly neglected, along with a couple of burnt-out cars on the communal grass area and every bus stop they passed had been smashed to bits.

Alice had told him that this was where she'd lived for the last year or so that she'd been married and he couldn't help but compare it to where she lived now with Val. Both were council estates, but Val's was clean and well maintained, very similar to where his mum and Aunt Audrey had grown up, whereas this one definitely looked like it had more challenges.

'Left here, Val,' Alice said, quietly but calmly, before pointing at a row of five or six terraced homes. 'And then it's the last house on the left there. You can turn into the side alley next to it or park out the front.'

'I'll stick to the front,' Val said, pulling in behind a white transit work van and stopping. 'Right, I'm going to stay here in case we need a quick getaway. I feel like an extra on an old episode of *Taggart*.'

He could see that Alice was peering out of the window at the house and he understood how difficult this must be for her.

'Alice, please stay here with Val too. I'm fine to go in by myself. Like I said, I can get a taxi to the airport from here, so there's no need to wait.' He was just trying desperately to let them go, because he felt so awful about the trouble he'd caused. 'And, Val, I'll be in touch because I'm going to pay for that tyre.'

'Och, don't be daft. My pal, Bob, down at the garage in Weir-bridge, will sort that for me in no time. And, anyway, I'll make sure the council pays for it. That pothole was a disgrace.'

'And it's a "no" from me too,' Alice added, taking off her seat-belt. He saw the steely determination on her face and then she inhaled like someone who was just about to jump off the ledge on a bungee rope. 'Let's go, Zac. And I apologise for whatever happens in here because there's no civility in this man at all.'

The next thing he knew, she was out of the door, and he was racing to keep up with her. He reached the small front gate first, although it was hanging off one hinge, so he guessed it wasn't there to prevent intruders.

The whole house looked neglected. Dilapidated even. One of the windows was smashed, with what looked like cardboard taped across the cracks. The door had splinters down the side, as if it had been kicked in at some point. The front garden was completely overgrown and full of junk – a sharp contrast to the immaculate lawn and flower beds next door.

To his surprise, it was Alice who took the lead, swerving and reaching the front door before him. He was seeing she had a core of inner strength just like his mum. It made so much sense that once upon a time they'd been best friends.

Alice raised her hand at the door, then paused, turned to him. 'Ready?'

Was he? Absolutely not. The calm, capable guy who spent his working days helping other people sort out their lives, their problems, their finances and their futures, was now absolutely, to put it mildly, bricking it.

'Ready,' he nodded. His first lie of the day.

Alice banged on the door with a violence that was unexpected, then stood back and waited. And waited. And waited. Nothing. Not a sound. No answer.

He thought she'd turn and walk away at that point, but, instead, she stepped forward again and banged even harder. 'He'll be passed out,' she said, with cool, calm, but utterly unmistakable scorn.

Another wait.

'I don't think anyone is home,' he murmured, deflated, his mind already racing ahead. He was going to have to come back here. He had loads of holiday days carried over from last year, so maybe he could take a long weekend next week. He was just thinking through the logistics of that when he heard a noise from inside. He and Alice met each other's gaze, eyes wide. Someone was there. A suspicion that was confirmed when they heard shuffling footsteps coming down the hall.

'Brace yourself,' Alice whispered, and he saw that her hands were balled into fists of tension.

He had no idea what to expect, but he could never have predicted the sight that was in front of him when the door was slowly opened.

A woman. It was hard to tell what age. She had long dark hair pulled back in a ponytail. She was wearing a dressing gown that reached the floor.

But her face. Holy shit, her face.

It looked like she was the one who had been in a car that had hit a pothole and then spun out on a deserted road. Only in her case, it seemed like the car only stopped when it hit a wall.

6 P.M. – 8 P.M.

23

KARA

Kara's phone began ringing as soon as she walked into the executive lounge at the airport, and the *Ghostbusters* ringtone made everyone stare at her, turning her face bright red. Drea, meanwhile, found that hilarious, so Kara immediately knew who'd set that up.

'*Ghostbusters*?' she said to her sister, one eyebrow raised in mortification.

Drea didn't even have the decency to blush. 'Sorry, did it earlier, when you were loading up the luggage on the trolley. Thought it might make you smile and put you in the holiday mood.'

Kara eyed her with incredulity. 'My whole life has fallen apart, I've lost my fiancé, my home and my job, and you thought a *Ghostbusters* ringtone was going to have me drinking pina coladas and doing the Macarena?'

Drea shrugged. 'Well, I suppose when you put it like that. Anyone ever told you you're a tough crowd?'

Her sister didn't wait for an answer, because she'd spotted

one of her favourite people across the other side of the lounge. And Ollie Chiles was waving and grinning right back at them.

Two couples sitting to the left of the door had just registered the identity of the bloke who had had his back turned to them for the last half-hour, and they were now surreptitiously lifting their phones and positioning themselves so they could take selfies with Ollie in the background. Kara threw them an icy stare and reminded herself not to be too over the top, otherwise photos of Ollie with his 'new girlfriend' would be viral within the hour. That had happened once before, a few years ago, when Ollie and Kara were in LA celebrating his wedding anniversary. Sienna was with them, but she'd gone off to the loo, and while she was away, Kara and Ollie had been messing around, laughing so hard they were buckled over. Of course, the photos were all over the internet in no time at all, and from a certain angle it appeared that they maybe, possibly, almost, could have, in a dim light, been kissing. Only they weren't. They were both huddled over Kara's phone because she was showing him one of those videos where people do voiceovers while their dogs are moving their mouths. Not exactly a salacious, illicit affair, but the worst of the internet believed it for a while, and Sienna had, aptly, put them in the dog house for days afterwards.

One of the lounge bartenders passed by and took a drinks order – another beer for Ollie and two glasses of Prosecco for Drea and Kara.

'How are you doing, pal?' Kara asked, feeling her soul soar just because she was in the same room as him. It was tough to have a lifelong best mate who lived in another country, and who also hobnobbed with Julia Roberts and Reese Witherspoon. Could give a girl a complex if she didn't know with absolute certainty that he'd drop both Julia and Reese and fly to be by her side at a moment's notice if she needed him. 'I want to give you a huge hug and a smacker right on the face, but the two couples behind me have their cameras out and they're doing the surreptitious photos thing. I don't want to make your life even more complicated today.'

Ollie was either two beers past caring or had decided that he had nothing to lose, because he grinned, said, 'Screw them' and tugged at her arm. She knew that he just meant to pull her towards him to give her a hello hug, but he caught her at the wrong angle, when she was off balance, and she fell onto his knee, forcing him to react at lightning speed to grab her and prevent her from face planting on the carpet. So much for trying to keep their greeting low-key.

'Well, that went well,' she quipped, figuring it was already on its way to TMZ and giving him the tightest of hugs. 'I've missed you, pal. Thanks for still coming with us. My horrible boot of a sister is ignoring my pain and making me go celebrate her half of our double wedding.'

'Your horrible boot of a sister has arranged for you to have a swanky bungalow with an ocean view and a personal butler.'

'I've always loved you, Drea,' Kara giggled, finally climbing off Ollie's knee.

She sat in the bucket chair next to him and she desperately wanted to take his hand, but they were probably in enough trouble. Instead, she just said, 'Okay, so obviously I saw the video.' Her nose wrinkled as she cringed. 'I'm so sorry, Ollie. How are you feeling? Because you know I'll come with you and slash her tyres. Or bribe her beauty therapist to overdo her Botox. There's no gutter I won't crawl into in the name of revenge.' She was trying to make him feel better and make him smile, but they both knew there was a grain of truth in there. They'd been backing each other up since Gary Diller from the end of the street stole Ollie's scooter when they were about six, and Kara had marched right up to his door and demanded it back or she was calling 999.

'Weirdly, I am okay. I keep waiting for it to hit me, but in the meantime I'm strangely fine. You know it's not been great for a while…' Many of their weekly FaceTime calls over the last year or so had slid into discussions about the issues in both their relationships, so none of this was a surprise. 'But I have to say, the Van Weeks thing came out of left field. I knew they'd become good friends and it was pretty obvious that he was always in awe of her, because, well… she's Sienna Montgomery. But I just didn't see him coming. Which probably says a lot about me. I guess I should have been paying more attention.'

'Or maybe she should have been paying more attention to the fact that she was married,' Kara retorted. 'Don't you dare take this and put it all on you. It's not you who made the mistake here.'

Drea's eyes suddenly swivelled towards her and there was a mischievous grin there, making Kara quickly regret the mention of 'mistakes', because she knew she'd just jogged Drea's memory about the mistake she'd mentioned earlier when it slipped out that she'd been to the hotel across the road. Dammit. There was no way she was discussing that with her now, so she was going to have to try to keep the conversation on other subjects until Drea's Prosecco kicked in. Kara knew how that would play out. For the last year, as soon as Drea got three glasses of vino in, she'd start talking about her wedding and she wouldn't shut up for hours. It was a plan that wouldn't be tough to implement because it had been a shitstorm of a week and they all had so much to catch up on.

The nice bartender appeared with their drinks and put them down on the table. Kara thanked her and then waited until she was out of earshot before steering the conversation back to Ollie's situation. 'So what's the move then, Mr Chiles?'

'Dunno. I haven't got much further than run away to Hawaii with my pals and stick my head in the sand until all my problems disappear.'

'That's so spooky,' Kara exclaimed, laughing. 'I thought long and hard about my situation, analysed it from all angles and then came to the very philosophical conclusion that I was going to run away to Hawaii with my sister and my pal and also stick my head in the sand until all my problems disappear. There's a reason we're friends,' Kara laughed, which felt great, given that it was probably the first time all week.

'I've just realised something,' Drea blurted, picking up her Prosecco and pausing for effect. 'This is the first time you've both been single at the same time. Can you not just do us all a favour and get together? It would save me a fortune at Christmas and birthdays, and it means I'd never have to pretend to love the terrible people you both choose as partners. Honestly, it's exhausting. Acting as if I liked Sienna required so much forced smiling that I had jaw pain on your last visit. And as for Josh...'

'Don't do it, Drea, because I was with him for eight years, so if you suddenly tell me you didn't like him, I'll never trust you again,' Kara warned.

She then watched as Drea held it in, held it in, held it in, then as if someone had kicked a brick out of a dam, let it all flood out. 'Urgh, I always thought he was an arse.'

'Seconded,' Ollie admitted.

Kara threw her hands up, aware that neither she nor Ollie had actually answered Drea's question about getting together, but too incensed by the twist in the conversation to address it. Besides, all three of them knew that Drea's happy picture of Kara and Ollie riding off into the sunset together was just the stuff of her sister's imagination and too many romcoms. Back to the point.

'Well, you don't have to worry about Josh any more, because he's gone. And for the record, I was in love with him for a long time.' That was true. Although she just realised that she'd had that thought in the past tense. 'And yes, he might be an arse, but I'm the only one who's allowed to say that out loud.'

'You still haven't told me what he did,' Ollie prompted her.

Kara groaned. 'I much preferred the version where my head was in the sand. I don't suppose we can just talk about Drea's wedding instead?'

'For once, I'm declining that offer,' Drea countered, obviously not quite at the Prosecco level required to unleash her inner bridezilla.

Kara knew that there was no getting around this, so, after a deep breath, she turned the clock back to Hogmanay, which felt like three days and a lifetime ago. 'It started with me dancing with Casey Lowden...' she began, only to be immediately interrupted.

'She's joined your show? How did I not know that? I worked with her on that play Sienna and I did last year while my show was on summer hiatus. She came in for the last week, after Sienna got food poisoning, and she knocked it out of the park. She was great.'

'Yeah, she's lovely. Although we're going to be here all night if you don't let me get to what actually happened.'

Ollie put his hands up. 'Sorry. Okay, so you were dancing with Casey...'

She took the prompt and rolled out the rest of the story. Corbin. Grabbing at Casey. Holding on to her. Kara going for a diversionary foot break with... with...

'My black block heels,' she finished, praying Drea wouldn't

put two and two together and solve the mystery of why her Louboutins had been moved.

'That arrogant fucker,' Ollie hissed, and Kara watched as his jaw clenched in fury and then he pulled out his phone.

'What are you doing?'

'Calling him. There's no way he's getting away with this.'

Kara's first thought was that this was exactly how Josh should have reacted. This was all she'd needed from him. Some support. Maybe a little action. But as for Ollie phoning him right now? Too late and wrong guy. She reached over and took his phone from his hands. 'Whoa there, Rocky. I appreciate the support, but I don't need you to fight my battles. I did okay by myself.' She didn't add that by 'okay', she actually meant 'my whole life has gone tits up', but that became perfectly clear as she recounted the rest of the story, right up until the showdown with Josh at their flat earlier.

'Kara, you don't deserve any of this,' he said softly when she was done. 'What can I do? I can speak to the chiefs at The Clyde-side, tell them they're out of order and—'

'Ollie, no. Thank you so much and I love you for saying it, but I've got this. I really have. I've decided to view it as the universe pushing me in a new direction. I loved my job, but it wasn't 100 per cent fulfilling. I loved my flat, but it never really felt like mine, because Josh owned it, and he was already living there when we met. And I loved Josh, but I don't ever want to come second. And now I'm beginning to realise that maybe I didn't love him enough.'

Drea leaned forward in her chair. 'Is that why you ended up in the hotel across the road? Don't think for a single second that I've forgotten about that.'

'Forgotten about what? What hotel across the road?' Ollie asked.

Drea slumped back in her chair, astonished. 'Oh wow. I've finally found something that you two didn't tell each other. Well, hallelujah!'

Kara felt her face burn, deeply aware that Ollie was looking at her quizzically.

'I think you're going to have to tell me about this now then...' he said, and she could see he was intrigued and maybe having a little bit of fun with her discomfort. 'Was there another guy involved?'

'Okay, yes.'

Ollie's gorgeous face was still concentrating intently.

She definitely wasn't getting out of this. 'Fine! Do you remember—'

'Well, here you all are!' The voice was so loud and exuberant that there wasn't a person in the lounge who'd been able to ignore it. All eyes were now on the little group in the corner, who'd been minding their own business until that instant.

Kara wanted to put her head in her hands, but instead, she looked up and greeted the new arrival. 'Hello, Mum.'

Jacinta McIntyre stood there in all her chiffon, colourful glory, platinum locks flowing down her back, red ruby lips outlined to within an inch of their lives.

And beside her stood a bloke that Kara had never seen before in her life. 'Everyone, I'd like you to meet my brand-new friend. This is Cillian.'

24

OLLIE

Ollie adored his Aunt Jacinta. She'd stepped in and taken care of him when his mum left, and she'd treated him like her own ever since. However, no one could ever accuse her of being shy and retiring. Humble and modest were a stretch too.

'Cillian helped me get my case onto the luggage cart – it's my Louis Vuitton one that you bought me for Christmas,' she gestured to Ollie. 'And then he helped me when I got all in a fluster and thought I'd lost my passport. Anyway, we've been having a lovely drink in the bar next door, but I told him he had to let me thank him by signing him in to the VIP lounge here. It's the least I can do.'

Ollie noticed that neither Kara nor Drea countered the 'VIP' thing – this was just a standard airport airline lounge – and he didn't speak up either, because they all knew that it was invari-ably easier to let Jacinta live in her own world, with her own interpretations. It was all part of her vivacious, over-the-top, utterly infectious charm. Although whenever he pointed that out to her daughters, Drea would comment that herpes was also infectious, and she didn't want to be in close proximity to that either.

'Cillian, this is my nephew, Ollie Chiles. He's just flown in from Hollywood to travel with us to the wedding I was telling you about. He's the TV star in the family. You might have seen him on *The Clansman*.'

Behind him, Ollie struggled to suppress a laugh and he heard Drea mumbling to Kara. 'Golden boy gets first billing as usual. She'll get to us eventually.'

It had always been a topic of much derision and teasing from Drea and Kara, that Jacinta was prouder of Ollie because he was famous. And much as he'd like to blush and say it wasn't true, the reality was that they were absolutely on point. There wasn't a person Jacinta encountered in her day who didn't hear the boast about her famous TV star 'nephew'. In fact, he could only remember her nose being out of joint once, and that was because she met Ryan Reynolds' mother in the ladies' at a Hollywood event, and realised that there was the potential for her to be out-boasted. It took her a couple of days to recover from that, and her equilibrium was only restored when he took her to the TV Choice Awards and she was sitting next to the mothers of two reality stars. Apparently, in the Boasting Hierarchy, trained actors beat reality TV.

'And these are my daughters. Drea...' she pointed to her elder offspring, 'is the one who is getting married, and Kara is the one who was supposed to be getting married, but it's all gone horribly wrong.'

'Thanks, Mum,' Kara responded with a cheesy smile and a thumbs up.

As for Cillian, the poor guy looked like he'd just stumbled into the epicentre of a hurricane and was somehow still standing, so Ollie felt sorry for him as he reached out and shook his hand.

'Pleased to meet you, Cillian. You're very welcome to join us.'

Jacinta's new very best friend shook his head. 'Thank you,' he said, in an unmistakable Irish accent. Ollie had done some work with a voice coach for a movie set in Dublin, and that was his first guess for the origin of Cillian's brogue. 'But I'm actually meeting my son, who'll be joining me shortly, so if you don't mind, I'll sit over at the bar and wait for him there.'

Jacinta obviously took that as an implied invitation. 'Ah well then, I'll have one with you and we can leave these young ones to chat,' she said, before turning back to them. 'I'll be back in a tick. Just don't want to leave the poor man drinking alone.'

'Good to meet you, Cillian,' Ollie said again, while Drea and Kara smiled and added variations on the theme.

Only when they were out of earshot, did Kara deflate and put her head on the table. 'I might have made this request on many occasions before, but kill me now,' she groaned, making Ollie laugh.

He hadn't forgotten the niggling emotions from a few moments ago though, and he just hoped that they hadn't shown on his face. It was the strangest thing. When Drea had said that Kara had a secret, he'd felt... Jealous. And when he'd established it was about a guy who wasn't Josh, the jealousy had ramped up a notch. What the hell was that about? Since when had he ever been jealous? Maybe if one of his mates landed a role he'd been after, then there would be a small and easily disguised tug of envy, but what he'd experienced just now was something different altogether. He made a mental note to give it some more thought later.

In the meantime, Drea took charge and steered them back to where they'd been before they were interrupted. 'Right,' she said, nodding to the departing figures of Jacinta and her new friend.

'You've got until that poor guy's ears start to bleed to tell us the story, so go.'

Kara blew out her cheeks, obviously deciding resistance was futile. Drea had been bossing them for a lifetime and she was a pro.

'Okay, so rewind six years ago. Remember when I was coming over to LA for your wedding, and my flight got delayed and I had to come the next day instead...'

Ollie racked his brain, flicking back through his Kara Memory Book until he got to that one. 'Yeah, you said that you went back home and then you got a flight the following morning.' Another memory assailed him. 'Actually, Sienna mentioned that on the phone earlier. I don't think she ever got over the fact that I postponed our wedding so that you could be there. Anyway, I'm now sensing your story wasn't entirely true?'

Kara shook her head dolefully. 'Not exactly. Full disclosure, and I didn't want to tell you this at the time, but Josh was mighty pissed off with me for coming to New York for three days for your wedding. So when the flight was cancelled, I was going to go home, but by that time I'd got talking to a really nice guy in the airport bar who was also supposed to be on the same flight... and I'm not really sure how it happened...'

He wasn't sure that he'd ever seen Kara this embarrassed or flustered. Her face could melt the ice on the runway right now.

'Anyway, we went to the hotel, and I swear we didn't request this, but we ended up in adjoining rooms.'

'Not the old "adjoining rooms" excuse,' Drea cut in, chuckling and very obviously enjoying Kara's shame.

Kara carried on, face still beaming. 'We opened the middle door between the rooms, and then we watched ten episodes of *Friends* and worked our way through half the minibar. The Toblerone nearly took my teeth out.'

'And...?' Drea prompted. 'Get to the good bit.'

Kara seemed confused. 'That was the good bit. Well, apart from us both falling asleep on the same bed, *fully clothed*!' she stressed. 'And then waking up the next morning in a bit of a cuddle position.'

'So you didn't have sex? Or even lock lips?' That came from Drea again. Ollie couldn't seem to find the words.

'No!' Kara exclaimed. 'I told him I had a boyfriend and made it clear at the outset that nothing would happen. He respected that. He was a really good guy, actually. Far nicer than fricking Josh, if I think about it now. I probably backed the wrong horse there.'

Drea still wasn't letting her off the hook.

'What was the big mistake then?'

Ollie was so glad she was here to ask the questions because his throat was suddenly dry.

Kara sighed. 'The fact that I didn't tell Josh about it. I said that I'd gone and stayed at Mum's house. I knew he'd never ask her, because he avoided her as much as possible. And then I flew out the next day, and I never told a single soul what happened. I think I was just embarrassed. I don't do stuff like that. I'm the boring one, remember?'

Drea shrugged. 'I think you just lived up to that description. I was hoping for a mass orgy. Or maybe at least a bit of wild kinky sex.'

Ollie swallowed, a weird sensation in the pit of his stomach again. More jealousy? What was going on? And why were Drea's words from earlier echoing in his head?

'This is the first time you've both been single at the same time. Can you not just do us all a favour and get together?'

He took a sip of his beer, while CIA Agent Drea carried on the interrogation.

'So that's it? That's the whole story. Over and done. And that's the only time you met?'

'Yeah,' Kara insisted. 'Definitely.'

He watched as Kara's neck flushed just a little, the way it used to do in school whenever she had to lie to a teacher.

'Really?' he asked.

'Absolutely...' she nodded.

As far as he knew, she'd never lied to him before. It just wasn't in her nature. So why did he have a feeling that his best friend in the world still wasn't telling the whole truth?

25

ALICE

'Sandra? Oh my God, Sandra, what happened to you?'

Alice couldn't quite comprehend what she was seeing. The bolshy, arrogant Sandra she'd met at the hospital on the day that Alice had discovered her husband had a mistress bore absolutely no resemblance to the poor soul who was standing in front of her right now, her eye swollen shut, and one cheek raised and bruised to deep purple.

'Alice?' Her voice was a croak of hostility. That part Alice remembered well. Back in the hospital, she'd tried to warn Sandra what she was getting into with Larry, and she'd advised her to run a mile from him, but the other woman had gone on the attack, telling Alice she was just bitter and twisted and jealous that Larry had replaced her with a younger model. Alice had walked away, satisfied that she had tried. What else could Alice say to the mistress who was absolutely convinced that the man she was having an affair with adored her and was the love of her life?

Now, no matter how Sandra had treated her, Alice felt nothing but horror and sadness that this had been the outcome.

'I walked into a—'

'Please don't say "a door",' Alice prompted gently, making it known that she wouldn't believe that.

Sandra shrugged. 'I couldn't care less what you think. What do you want?'

Zac cleared his throat. 'It's actually me who wanted to come here tonight. I'm looking for Larry? My name is Zac Corlan. My mum was a friend of Larry's and I just wondered if I could ask him a couple of questions about her. She's dead now, but there are some things I'd like to know that only Larry can answer.'

Alice was impressed by his improvisation, and she immediately realised that there was more chance of a positive outcome if she detached herself a little from the aim of the visit.

'I'm just here because Zac asked me to help him track Larry down. His mum was my friend too, so I was just trying to help out.'

Sandra took a step backwards. 'Larry's not here. He went down to the off licence to get some beers. Come back tomorrow.'

'Erm, I can't come back tomorrow,' Zac said, with a sense of urgency. 'I need to go back to Ireland tonight and I was really hoping that I could speak to him, just for five minutes before I went. Could we come in and wait for him?'

Under normal circumstances, it wouldn't have been Alice's choice of moves. She'd much rather have fled the scene, or waited in Val's car, but she remembered that Zak was a family lawyer who would probably have experience in dealing with abuse and domestic violence. Also, if he had Morag's heart, then there was no way that he would walk away from someone who could be in danger. And the truth was, for Alice, right now personal feelings didn't even come into it – she didn't want to leave either, until she knew Sandra was safe.

Sandra didn't seem to take issue one way or another. 'Suit

yourself,' she shrugged, then turned and walked back down the hall, leaving the door open for them to do as they pleased.

Alice and Zac made eye contact, agreeing without words, then followed. With every step Alice took, her body trembled more, as her soul recognised the smell, the tattered wallpaper, the broken floorboards revealed by the threadbare carpets. This was her house of horrors. The last time she'd walked out of here was on the night she'd finally left Larry and she'd sworn to herself and to her son that she would never step foot in this house again. Yet here she was. And all she wanted to do was run.

Instead, she fought down the nausea that was swirling in her stomach and tried to stop the tremors that were coursing through her. When they reached the living room, Sandra sat on the sofa and lit a cigarette, while Alice quickly glanced around the room. Nothing had changed. Same couch and armchairs. Same battered old tiny dining table, with two rickety seats. Discoloured and broken kitchen units that she was fairly sure had been fitted when the house was built in the sixties. This wasn't a life for anyone, let alone someone Alice knew had a good job and her own flat only six months ago. Let alone someone whose face looked like it had met something hard and fast coming the other way.

'May we sit?' she asked Sandra, even though absolutely no part of her wanted to touch the sofa or the burst armchair that had once been Larry's mum's pride and joy, but that was now so old and dirty it belonged in a skip.

'Please yourself,' Sandra retorted, still going with indifference and disdain. To some extent, Alice recognised all of those things. Three decades ago, in the early days with Larry, she'd shrugged off anyone who criticised him, and had been single-minded in her defence of him. When the emotional abuse and the cruelty began, she was so embarrassed and scared that she shut down anyone who tried to get close to her or to question what was going on. Larry had never laid a finger on her, but she had absolutely no doubt that he was capable of this.

'Sandra, can I ask you again what happened to your face? Did Larry do this to you?'

Sandra took a puff of her cigarette and at first Alice thought she was going to ignore the question, but instead she challenged her with, 'Why? Did he do this to you too?'

Alice ran that back. *Do this to you too?* She'd confirmed it. And Alice heard a slight waver in her voice, as if the bravado was slipping. Alice chose to brush over the question, because she didn't want to make Sandra feel any worse. Instead, she tried to forge some kind of connection.

'Sandra, I know this is none of my business, and I'm the last person you would want to talk to...' Actually, Alice wasn't sure that was true. There might be a tiny part of Sandra, the scared, vulnerable part that was undoubtedly there, who would want to speak to someone who'd been in the same position. Someone who'd escaped.

All those months ago, when Larry was in the ICU, and Alice was in the hospital family room, ostensibly there out of concern for her husband, but actually hiding from the world while praying that his injuries would kill him, a nurse called Bernadette had popped by on the pretext of checking on her. In the course of their conversation, Bernadette had shared how she'd left her husband, a prominent heart surgeon, after three decades of emotional abuse. Bernadette hadn't pried. She hadn't asked questions. She'd later told Alice that she just recognised the signs and wanted to support her, to give her hope. Alice had been volunteering at Bernadette's weekly support group for abuse survivors since she'd founded it shortly after that. Now was her chance to help someone who was still in that situation.

She carried on with the point she'd been putting to Sandra. '...But if Larry did this, you need to leave him. You can't stay with someone who hurts you.'

'Didn't you stay for, what, not much short of thirty years?' Sandra shot back.

Alice nodded. 'I did. And there were lots of reasons for that. Fear, mostly. And threats that I was too scared to call Larry's bluff on. But every single day of my life now, I wish I'd left sooner.'

Throughout this whole exchange, she appreciated that Zac stayed silent, and figured he probably knew that his voice wouldn't help in this situation. This was woman to woman. Survivor to someone who hadn't yet found the strength or the opportunity or the resources to leave. The last thing that they needed was for Sandra to feel backed into a corner and go further on the defensive.

It seemed Sandra was already there. 'And if I left, where would I go? He's gone through all of my savings. My landlord found an excuse to kick me out because my boyfriend was in prison, and I was constantly being doorstepped by journalists who wanted the inside scoop on the story of why you left and he was with me. And I lost my job, because the taxi company needed to cut ties with both Larry and me to wash the stink of Larry's accident off their company.'

The "accident". Not exactly an accurate description of the day Larry had got high on booze and drugs then smashed his taxi into the central reservation of the motorway with Sophie in the back seat. Sandra would have no way of knowing that had been one of the contributing factors in propelling Alice here tonight. When they'd hit that pothole earlier, all she could think about was how Sophie must have been terrified that day, yet she'd survived. It had given Alice the little bit of extra courage she'd needed to walk up that path to Larry's front door.

Sandra was still raging on. 'And all my friends and family have ditched me, either because they don't approve, or because they think Larry is scum, or because he's tried to borrow money from them. I have no one left. Nowhere to go. Nothing.'

Alice felt a crack run right through her heart. That was exactly how she'd felt for far too long in her life.

Zac sensed this was the time to step in. 'Sandra, I know we've never met, but I'm a family lawyer, and I deal with situations like this. You can come with us right now, and he never needs to know we were here. I'll find you a refuge where you'll be safe, and I'll do everything I can to get you back on your feet. I know it's a long shot to ask you to trust me, but I promise I'll help.'

The fracture in Alice's heart just got wider, but this time it was because she was so proud that Morag had raised such a decent man.

'Listen to him, Sandra, please. We have a car outside, and I have other friends that will help too. Women who've been through this. My friend, Bernadette, runs a support group and she has resources...'

'No.' Sandra's objection was clear and final. 'I'm going to get myself out of this. I've got a job interview this week and I'm going to get it. Then me and Larry will be fine because things will be good again. I don't need anyone sticking their nose in and—'

There was a shout from outside, and Alice recognised it immediately. Larry. No doubt yelling at the teenagers who always congregated in the alley at the side of the house. It was a nightly ritual, yet they returned time and time again to taunt the old bastard.

Damn it. If they had more time with Sandra, maybe they could persuade her... But even as she had that thought, she knew it probably wasn't true. Sandra needed to make the decision on her own terms and when she was ready.

Her gaze darted to the notepad that she'd pinned to the kitchen wall when they'd first moved in here, and the pen that still dangled on a string from it. She jumped up, grabbed a sheet, and jotted down her mobile number, then shoved it in Sandra's hand.

'This is my number. Please, please, just say the word, and my friends and I will arrange somewhere safe for you to be. I promise. Don't stay here, Sandra. Your life is worth so much more than him.'

They all heard the front door opening, and Alice saw Sandra slip the note into her dressing gown pocket. Alice wasn't sure if she'd ever call, but it was a start.

She'd just sat back down in her seat, when the door opened. Every cell in her body recoiled. Her stomach clenched. Her throat became so tight she could barely breathe. Larry McLenn. And as his gaze fell on her, that familiar sneer curled his top lip.

'Well, well, well… What the fuck are you doing here?'

26

ZAC

Zac had never hit anyone in his life. Never had a violent urge. Never thought that physical force was the answer to anything. Yet right now, he had an almost explosive desire to pummel this man's face until there was nothing left of that sick, twisted snarl.

He remembered Larry McLenn's TV appearances and press conferences as a politician. Trying to correlate this vile specimen of a human, with his bloated, almost purple face and the long, greasy hair, with the MP who had stood in the Houses of Parliament and wandered the corridors of power was impossible.

Trying to imagine him with his mum or with Alice... His brain just wouldn't go there. Somehow, they had to get his current girlfriend away from him too, but he could sense that was going to be a challenge.

It was a question that came up time and time again with clients – both female and male – who were in abusive situations. They often said their family and friends would ask them why they didn't just leave their tormentor. He knew the answer to that was far more complex than just walking out the door. All they could do here was provide an exit route and pray that Sandra would take it.

Meanwhile, the overwhelming part of his brain now realised that Alice had been absolutely right. It was a huge mistake coming here to chase down answers, because now he couldn't bear the repulsive possibility that he shared any kind of genetics with this man.

Zac recognised the wide pupils and erratic gestures of someone who was high. Larry hadn't given up the cocaine habit that had been one of the contributions to his downfall then.

'*Well, well, well... What the fuck are you doing here?*' he'd crowed to Alice.

Zac hadn't even given her a chance to answer.

'Actually, it's me who's here to speak to you. Alice was just kind enough to come with me.'

'Aye, regular fucking superhero she is. Who the fuck are you?' he asked, plonking himself down on the one unoccupied chair, and taking a bottle of vodka out of the bag he'd come in with. He didn't even try to disguise what he was doing – just opened the top and took a long, slow swig of it. By the looks of things, he'd been doing that on the way back from the off licence too, because the bottle was already half empty.

Zac had contemplated going with some kind of fabricated story designed to elicit the truth, but in the end he decided to go with a vague version of the truth.

'I'm here on behalf of the family of Morag Corlan. You knew her as Morag McTay.'

Larry immediately switched focus to Alice. 'Who the fuck is this guy, in here talking like he's the fucking CID?'

'Just answer the questions, Larry.'

'Or what?' he challenged her.

'Or I'm going to call the police and tell them you violated

your parole by snorting cocaine in front of me and have them down here within minutes. Zac is a lawyer and he'll corroborate that story. I'm sure your probation officer will be delighted to hear about that.'

Zac didn't know whether to be astonished or impressed. He went with both.

Alice was still speaking.

'He's talking about my friend, Morag, from back when we first met. You remember her.'

It was a statement, not a question.

'Of course I remember her. Do you think I'm stupid?'

No one answered that question, so Zac went on, trying desperately to frame this in such a way that he'd get answers. Larry wasn't going to tell him what he needed to know out of the goodness of his heart. And he wouldn't be afraid of physical threats. The only thing that just might work would be a more tactical, psychological approach that hinted there might be something in it for Larry if it were true.

'She was my mother. And as Alice said, I'm a lawyer. Some new evidence has come to light that would suggest that you had an affair with Morag before she left for Ireland back in 1995.'

Larry snorted at that, apparently finding the whole thing amusing. 'Did I fuck,' was his only retort.

'I'm afraid we have evidence that says otherwise. Photographs. Witness statements.'

'Wait, wait, wait – why would you care?' Larry challenged him. 'What's this got to do with you?'

Zac found it interesting that there was nothing in Larry's demeanour that was connecting a potential affair with the appearance of Morag's son thirty years later. Even someone who wasn't too smart would probably have connected those dots if there was a possibility that was the case.

'Because, like I said, I'm her son. And I was born roughly nine months after the alleged affair.'

Larry choked on his vodka. 'Wait a minute – you think I could be your dad? Mate, I don't know what you've been smoking. First of all, I never shagged that bird. She was all over me, but nah, she wasn't my type. Too needy and nothing going for her.'

The urge to pummel him was back, but the desperate need for information overrode it. For now.

'So there's absolutely no chance that you could be my father? The thing is, when I find my dad – and only after a DNA test proves that he actually is my father – I want to be in his life. And, you know, make sure he's taken care of.'

He'd switched to the carrot and stick method of eliciting information now. It was a lie. Even if this was his father, he wanted nothing to do with him, but the promise of some financial gain for Larry might just make this horrible bastard open up.

'A DNA test?' he asked, but Zac could sense it was half-hearted.

'Of course. I mentioned I'm a lawyer, Mr McLenn. I only deal in proven facts. That's why there would be an irrefutable DNA test, and anyone knowingly falsely claiming to be my father would be liable for potential legal action for fraud.'

Not strictly accurate, but it got Larry's attention, as he knew it would. There were two options here – that Larry went for it because there was indeed a possibility that it could be true and there could be a little pot of gold at the end of the genetic rainbow.

Or...

'Aye, well, you can take your care and shove it, because it cannae be me. Which is a shame, because the son I've got is fucking useless and I could do with some bastard taking care of me.'

Yep, there was option number two – Larry knew there was no way he could be Zac's dad, and he didn't want any more legal issues in his life so he didn't even try to bluff it.

He saw Alice balling up her fists again after the comment about her son, and he admired her restraint because he wasn't sure he'd manage the same.

'You know what? Get the fuck out of my house. I don't know who you think you are, but you can just go. Piss off.'

Neither Zac nor Alice needed to be asked twice. He had his answer and could walk away, but as he stood up, towering over Larry, he made a point of distracting him, by spitting, 'Don't worry, we're going.'

Alice took advantage of Larry's focus being on Zac. Out of the corner of his eye, Zac saw her take the opportunity to make a 'Call me' gesture to Sandra. The other woman looked away.

'Sandra,' Zac said, hoping that he was doing the right thing. 'I hope you're feeling better soon and that your face heals well.' He racked his brain for the right thing to say – something that wouldn't inflame the situation or make Larry think she'd grassed him. 'I hope the police find the person who assaulted you. Terrible, the crime on the streets these days. I've got a friend who's a police officer in the area – I'll make sure she knows about your injuries, just in case it ever happens again.'

Sandra raised her eyes and they both saw Larry flinch and knew the point had been made. It wasn't perfect but hopefully it would help for now.

He thought the conversations were over, but he hadn't realised that Alice wasn't done yet. As she passed where Larry was sitting, she leaned towards him, clearly trying to show that she wasn't intimidated. Larry flinched for a second time. 'And,

Larry, the promise about my call to the police still stands. Sign my divorce papers by the end of the week, or expect a knock at the door. Zac, here, will be a very willing, and very credible witness.'

With that, she straightened up and walked on by. Zac paused to let her go past him too, to protect her from any random lunges from Larry. Nothing came, and they both walked at speed down the hall. They couldn't get out of that door fast enough.

He managed to wait until they got to the end of the path before blurting out, 'Do you believe him?'

Larry had said it wasn't him, and Zac had already formed a judgement on whether or not he was being honest. However, Alice knew him better than anyone else, so she was the one person who could give an informed opinion on whether his gut was telling him the right thing.

Alice nodded. 'I do. Two reasons. Not to make this about me, but if he'd had an affair with Morag, he'd have been desperate to tell me, to cause me pain and rub my nose in it.'

It was a good point and even in the short time Zac had known Larry, he'd got a measure of him and suspected that would be true.

'And the other?'

Alice was walking quickly, and he was having to rush to keep up with her.

'If he truly thought there was even the slightest possibility that you were his son, he'd have accepted the DNA test in the hope that he could take you up on the offer to take care of him. He used to demand money from my son all the time – just one of the many reasons that Rory cut him out of his life.'

Bingo. Alice was right. There was no doubt about that.

For the first time since the prospect of Larry McLenn being

his father was raised, Zac felt the twist of anxiety in his gut unwind just a tiny bit.

They were almost across the communal grass area in front of the house, close enough to see that Val was watching them, ready and waiting in the Jeep.

'The thing is though... The photos of Mum and Dad still don't make sense. The dates still don't work. If I didn't get half my DNA from that vile human being in there, then who was it?'

Alice looked like she could weep with either the relief or the stress of it all. 'I honestly do not have a single clue, Zac.'

She climbed into the front seat of the Jeep, while he folded his way-too-long limbs into the back.

'Well?' Val asked urgently, and he saw that she had the expression of someone who was watching something terrible unfold but couldn't look away.

'It's not him,' Zac said, relief oozing out of every word.

Val threw up her hands. 'I knew it! You couldn't possibly be related to that old bastard.' She put the car into drive, and then he could see an expression of puzzlement cause her to frown. 'But, hang on, if it isn't him, then who...?'

Zac sagged back in the seat, his body suddenly giving in to the exhaustion and turmoil of the last couple of days. 'I don't know. I think I need to get to the airport and speak to my dad.'

Val Diesel took off like she was auditioning for *Fast and Furious*. 'No bother, son. Just pray we don't hit another pothole and I'll have you there in no time.'

27

ZAC

One Year Before...
Glasgow Airport – 2 January 2024

Getting through security had taken twice as long as normal – partly due to the usual crowds of people leaving Glasgow after the New Year Celebrations. All his life, Zac had been coming here at New Year, and he'd always loved the buzz of the airport almost as much as the buzz of the city. The return journey, however, was his least favourite part. Everyone exhausted. Hungover. Skint. Sad to be leaving the party. Unexcited about the prospect of twelve full months until they got to do it again.

This year he felt that more than ever. At the last minute, his mum had decided that she was going to stay behind in Glasgow with Audrey, and his dad had, of course, stayed too. Zac wasn't completely surprised. His mum wouldn't admit it, but he could see that the liver cancer she'd been fighting for the last couple of years had been causing her increasing pain over the last month or so, so it was only natural she'd want to stay with her sister a bit longer.

He'd have stayed too, but his mum had been adamant that he go. 'For goodness' sake, son, you need to take that concern right off your face. You'd think I was dying, the way you're looking at me. I'm fine. I just need to get my meds increased a little. Now go get your flight, because you've got that case to prepare and I'm not having you being shite at your job on my conscience. Too many people depend on you.'

With that, she had gone up on her tiptoes, as she always did, and wrapped her arms around him, then kissed him on the cheeks. 'Now, I know you're a grown man, but do what your mother tells you, okay?'

He'd reluctantly agreed, mostly because Morag Corlan was the not the kind of woman who was easily contradicted.

He'd finished packing the few clothes he'd brought with him into his carry-on bag, and then sought out everyone else in the family, hugging them goodbye. By the time he'd got back to his mum, she was lying on the sofa. He'd told her not to get up, but she'd insisted. She'd put her arms around him for the second time that day, not an unusual thing at all. His mum was someone who loved fiercely and held on longest to every hug, kissed everyone twice and told him she loved him every time they spoke.

He'd kissed her goodbye, then picked up his bag. 'Right, Mam, see you back in Dublin. I'll put some bread and milk in the house for you if you give me a shout and tell me what day you decide to come back.'

She'd nodded, smiling. 'I will do, son. Now you take care and don't be talking to strangers.' That always made him laugh. He was a fully-fledged adult, over six feet tall, a trained legal professional who'd lived on his own since he went to university at eighteen years old, and yet she was still worried that someone would steal him, or he'd fall into mortal danger by striking up a conversation in a check-in queue at the airport.

He'd now been in the airport for over two hours and had safely managed to avoid being kidnapped or murdered. He'd grabbed a coffee in Starbucks and was making his way down the long pier of gates that stopped with the British Airways hub at the end. His flight to Dublin was leaving from a gate about halfway down – a relief because the corridor was packed and he was dodging passengers who'd arrived at the BA hub and were coming in the opposite direction. Glasgow airport was one of those airports where departing and arriving passengers passed each other in the same walkways, so it was a collision course of bodies. If he managed to get to his gate without spilling his cappuccino, it would be a miracle. He was focusing intently on it, when…

'Zac?'

He didn't even have to look up to know who it was. Kara. The woman he'd met at the same airport on the same January day, years before. On that occasion she'd been travelling to LA for her best mate's wedding, and he'd been going home. By some brilliant twist of fate, their flights had been cancelled, and they'd spent the night at an airport hotel, during which he'd laughed more than he had before or since. If she hadn't already been in a serious relationship, he'd have been all in.

'Kara! Were you just hanging out here, hoping I'd be here?' he feigned suspicion, making her laugh.

'Ah, shit – busted. I was hoping it wouldn't be that obvious.'

Zac was aware that he was standing still, and they were staring at each other, grinning, while waves of people tutted and puffed their way around them.

'Have you got time for a coffee?' he asked, his own still in his hand. 'I think there's a coffee bar along at the BA gates?'

'There is – I just passed it – and sure,' she shrugged, making a lot of irate people happy when she stepped off to the side and followed him all the way back along to the very last gate.

'You're looking great,' he told her honestly, as he put her coffee and two huge chocolate chip cookies down on the table she'd snagged while he waited in the queue for her drink.

'Thank you. Fake tan and a decent haircut. Works wonders. Are you on your way home to Dublin?'

He took the lid off his coffee to let it cool. 'I am. And you?'

She took a deep breath, and he suddenly remembered that she had a tendency to overshare. He'd loved that about her when he'd met her the first time, and now? He grinned as he settled down for the ride. 'My friend who was getting married that last time we met? Ollie? Well, wait until I tell you – a few months later he landed the best job ever. A starring role on that *Clansman* TV show.'

'I love that show!'

'Me too. He plays Cam McGregor...'

Zac realised immediately who he was. Ollie Chiles. He'd shot to stardom as soon as the show aired a few years ago, and Zac was sure he had seen him on the cover of *Rolling Stone* last month – the top twenty hot young stars in Hollywood, or something like that. Zac had always thought he was excellent in the show – and his mum and Aunt Audrey adored him.

'Check you out, with your famous friends,' he teased her. 'That's amazing. He must be pretty chuffed that it's going so well.'

Kara nodded. 'He definitely is – he's loving life. He's shooting in Croatia right now, but his wife is in New York in a play there, so he was on his lonesome for New Year. Which is all my round-about way of saying that I'm on my way back from Croatia because I spent New Year there with my pal.'

'And your boyfriend didn't mind?'

'I forgot that bit. He's been in Paris for the last five days with a big corporate client who was launching a new product on the Eiffel Tower at midnight on New Year's Eve. They're still there, although I suspect it's now more of a jolly than work. Oh, and it's more than boyfriend now.' She held up her hand and he saw the large solitaire sparkling in the light. 'Fiancé now.'

'Congratulations.'

'Thank you. We're getting married next year in Hawaii. A double wedding with my sister.'

'Congratulations again.' His face was smiling, and his words sounded convincing, but both were masking a mighty pang of disappointment that was thumping the inside of his chest.

'Thank you.'

He could end the conversation right there and go catch his plane. He could, but he didn't want to. He'd thought back to the last time they'd met on a thousand occasions, and nothing else since had quite matched up. This felt... right. Natural. He'd met her twice and yet, clichéd as it was, he felt like he'd known her forever. So no, he didn't go. Instead, he took a sip of his coffee and decided that the rest of the world could wait.

'And how's your work going?' he asked her, and then settled back to listen as she chatted about her job, then asked about his, and an hour later their coffees were cold, the final call was made for his flight, and he realised that he didn't want to go.

He made a split-second decision. 'Can I ask you something?'

She didn't hesitate. 'Shoot.'

'If I were to go and change my flight and catch the first one tomorrow morning, would you have dinner with me? Only I feel that we have several more conversations to get through. We haven't even scratched on world peace or the history of the boy band.'

Her laugh was one of his favourite things about her. She

didn't even break eye contact and her smile widened as she answered his question with one of her own. 'Can I ask you something?'

'Shoot.'

'Can we have dinner in exactly the same place, in exactly the same way that we did last time? Because I think that was one of my favourite nights ever.'

'I think we can manage that,' he agreed. 'And for the record, it was one of mine too.'

Thankfully, he hadn't checked any luggage in, so he just let a harassed gate attendant know that he was no longer taking the flight.

Less than an hour later, they were lying, fully clothed, on a bed in the hotel across from the airport, drinking beers, eating room service and chocolate from the minibar. They watched ten more episodes of *Friends* and Zac thought how he hadn't laughed more in one night since the last time they'd done this.

It was almost midnight when she rolled on her side to face him. 'I'm glad we got to do this again.'

'Me too.'

'You know, I never told a soul about the last time we met.'

That surprised him. She'd said she shared everything with her sister and her actor mate. 'I didn't either.'

'I think it felt... special. And innocent. I didn't want to let anyone make it something it wasn't.'

'I get that. Don't get me wrong, if you didn't have a boyfriend...'

'I know,' she said, and they didn't have to say all the words in the sentence because they both knew what they were thinking.

He wasn't sure who fell asleep first, but he remembered waking in the middle of the night, and they were spooning, and then waking in the morning and she was gone.

He glanced around for a note. Nothing. Just a Toblerone, sitting on the bedside table next to him. They hadn't kissed. They had barely touched. He was sure he'd never see her again. Yet it had totally been worth it.

The shower beckoned, so he got up, spent twenty minutes under the jets, then, when he was dried and dressed, checked the flight app to see that his rescheduled midday flight was on time.

Pulling his bag up on to his shoulder, he was about to leave the room when his phone rang. Dad.

He answered the phone with a breezy, 'Hey, how's things?'

The reply was a choking sob. 'Son, it's your mum. She took a turn during the night and she's in hospital. I don't know how to tell you this...'

'Don't say it, Dad. What hospital?'

'Glasgow Central. But I needed to tell you because there might not be enough time for you to get back here.'

Zac swallowed, trying to force his vocal cords to work. 'Dad, I missed my flight.' There was no need to explain the details. 'I'm at a hotel at Glasgow airport. I'll be there soon. Please, please tell her I'm coming.'

Half an hour later, he was at his mum's bedside. She was slipping in and out of consciousness, and he felt immediately it was close to the end, but he got to say everything he wanted to tell her. At one point she squeezed his hand and whispered his name, and that's when he knew with every beat of his heart and hers, that she'd heard it all. Shortly afterwards, she slipped into a coma, and three days later she passed away.

For the rest of his life, he'd be grateful to Kara McIntyre for giving him that time and that last conversation with his mum.

And he knew that he'd never again walk through an airport without checking the crowds to see if she was there.

8 P.M. – 10 P.M.

28

KARA

Kara was squirming under the glare of the interrogation light. Or it might just have been some fancy ceiling fixture in the posh airport lounge.

'So that's it? That's the whole story. Over and done. And that's the only time you met?' Ollie had asked her. Or was it Drea? She was too busy panicking inside to take in the details.

'Yeah,' she'd insisted. *'Definitely.'*

'Really?' he'd asked.

'Absolutely...' she'd nodded.

But she'd never lied to him in her life, and she couldn't do it now. She cracked like an old windscreen in a car crusher.

'Okay, that was a lie. I met him one more time, but it wasn't planned, I swear. I bumped into him again here at the airport last year. On the same date as we'd met before. The second of January. I was on my way back from spending New Year in Croatia with you and he was going home to Dublin.'

Kara watched as Drea's chin dropped and now her sister was staring at her as if she didn't recognise her at all. Which was probably true. Kara was the least likely out of the three of them to ever do something illicit or scandalous.

'And that was what? Just an accident?' Ollie asked.

'Yes,' Kara blurted, before backing down again. 'Well, a happy accident. That was maybe a little hopeful. Since that first meeting, I've found a reason to fly in and out of the airport on the second of January a couple of times. On the years that I wasn't travelling, I'd make an excuse to Josh that I had to pop into work and instead, I'd come here for a coffee, hoping I'd bump into him, just to see how he was doing. Last year was the first time it actually worked and our paths crossed again.'

She could feel her toes curling inside her boots. This was so embarrassing. She hated being on the spot and she hated being the focus of attention. Right now, she was both, and the two people she loved more than anyone else on earth were clearly finding this all to be shocking.

Ollie reached for his beer. 'You know there's a thing called social media now, right? You can track down just about anyone. Maybe even drop them a text to see how they are. It would have saved you a fortune on flights.'

If they were still fifteen, Kara would have punched him on the arm for his sarcasm and for the amused grin on his face that showed he was making fun of her.

'I was aware of that little development, yes. But that would have felt... disloyal. Like cheating on Josh. Whereas, if we just happened to bump into each other...' She let them fill in the blanks, before going on, 'Look, I didn't say it was the most logical plan in the world, but in my head it made sense.'

'And so, last year, you just had a nice chat and then went your separate ways again?' That was from Drea, who was clearly in need of fortification for this confessional and had just signalled the swirly finger thing to the waitress.

'No, he missed his flight again, maybe a little deliberately, so we booked a room at the hotel across the road again and spent the night fully clothed, watching TV and snacking from the minibar – exactly the same as the first time.'

She didn't want to add that it was, and would always be, one of her favourite memories.

'I'm still struggling to understand why you didn't tell us. Or why you didn't call things off with Josh and see if there really was something between you and… What was his name?' Ollie never did have a great memory for names.

'Zac,' Kara said, already preparing her justifications and hearing how lame they sounded in her head. 'And I didn't tell you because I knew you'd both have the faces that you've got on right now. I know it sounds crazy…'

'It does.' It freaked her out when they spoke in unison.

'Yeah, okay, Mr and Mrs Judgemental there. But I liked having a secret that didn't have to go anywhere. The two of you are fixers. Action people. I'm the one who just goes with the flow all the time and that wouldn't have been good enough for you. You'd have grilled me to death, and you'd have wanted me to act on it, to rethink my relationship with Josh, to make the thing with Zac more than it was. Kind of the way you're doing now. But that was the whole thing about Zac – there was no pressure. We were just two strangers who met up by chance. Sliding doors. Coincidences that threw us together. It was romcom stuff. Without the riding off into the sunset thing at the end.'

Ollie seemed to be missing the point and introducing safety concerns into her romcom bubble. 'A romcom that could actually have turned into a slasher movie if he'd been some kind of maniac stranger who lured you into a hotel room and then murdered you while you slept.'

Kara rolled her eyes. 'You really need to work on your sunny optimism.'

Before he could say anything, Drea piped up. 'So what happens now? Are you going to look him up and see if there's something real between you? Something that could maybe become a thing?' she asked, then got distracted before Kara could answer. 'Ollie, are you okay? You're looking really flushed.'

Now Kara could see it too, but Ollie shrugged it off. 'Just warm in here.'

'You sure?' Drea checked. 'Because not that I'm the only important one here, but if you drop down sick or give us all some mad flu and it affects my wedding, I will bear a grudge for the rest of my life, and it won't be pretty.'

Kara exhaled, feeling the change of subject had finally taken the pressure off her.

Or maybe not. Drea was staring at her again. 'You didn't answer. Are you going to track him down or am I just going to have to book flights in and out of Glasgow on the second of January for you until the end of time?'

Kara shook her head. 'Nope. That's why I didn't find an excuse to come here last night. I've given up on relationships. I've spent eight years in the same one and walked away with nothing, from a guy who let me down. What a total waste of time. So from now on, I'm officially off all that romantic stuff because I'm clearly crap at it.'

'Or maybe you just picked the wrong guy,' Ollie shrugged.

He was still a bit flushed. Kara couldn't remember if she'd packed any paracetamol, so she made a mental note to pick some up at Heathrow, if they ever got there.

Just at that, a murmur of discontent went around the room, and they saw that it was coming from all the people who were now staring up at the information board on the far wall.

'Oh no. Oh bugger, no.' Drea was up and speed walking towards the board to find out what was causing it, leaving just Kara and Ollie.

'Can't believe you're full of secrets, Miss McIntyre.'

'Not full. Just one,' Kara corrected him, but there was an edge of apology in her voice. Ollie was just being concerned about her safety and all the points that both he and Drea made were completely valid. 'I'm sorry. Don't hate me. It was just a special little interlude from real life, and I didn't want anyone to burst my bubble... even for the right reasons.'

Drea returned and slumped down in her seat. 'My nerves are shredded. Half of tonight's flights have just been cancelled, but ours is still going, so we should still make it to the hotel at Heathrow for tonight, and be on schedule for the Hawaii flights tomorrow.'

Kara knew that Drea's travel expert brain was all over this. She'd obsessed for days over the best way to get to Honolulu before settling on the Glasgow-Heathrow-San Francisco-Hawaii route, with the layover at Heathrow tonight. Kara was 100 per cent positive that the gods of the airways wouldn't dare mess that up for fear of Drea's ire.

'They've delayed it another hour though, so we're just as well hunkering down here. Any other deep dark secrets you want to tell us to pass the time? A side hustle working in a morgue? A bondage fetish?'

'Only on the weekends,' Kara said, making her sister grin.

'Good to know,' Drea retorted, before getting up and grabbing her bag. 'I'm just going to go find Mum and tell her about the delay.' She turned to Ollie. 'If this one confesses to being a serial killer or having a stamp collection while I'm away, get it on tape.'

As she strutted off, Kara's phone buzzed on the table, so she picked it up and turned it over to see an alert notification:

CLYDESIDE STUDIOS SHAKE-UP

What? Surely they weren't making an announcement about her leaving? She was no one in the Clydeside sphere. There was no way they'd even notice she was gone, never mind send out a press release about it.

'Hey Kara, the stuff Drea was saying... you know, about us being single at the same time... Do you ever think about...?'

She could hear Ollie speaking, but she wasn't really paying attention because she was furiously clicking through to the article mentioned in the headline.

When she reached it, she gasped. 'Ollie, look at this!' She turned her phone so that he could see the article's tagline on the screen.

Corbin Jacobs out. In a surprising move, the fan favourite's contract has not been renewed, with the studio citing, a 'new direction for the show'.

She scanned the rest of the story and got the gist of it pretty quickly. Whatever language they used to soften the optics, Corbin Jacobs had been fired and Casey Lowden had agreed to a new contract that would see her stepping up into a directorial role on one show per week, while still maintaining the spotlight on her current character.

Wow. Just wow.

Ollie sat back in his chair. 'What does that mean for you?'

Her phone began ringing and Josh's photo flashed up on the screen. It was her favourite pic of him. On the beach last year in

Greece, after they'd had the most amazing lunch in a little taverna and then walked for miles along the golden sands, hand in hand, totally in love. If someone had told her then that she would call off their wedding, she'd never have believed them.

'I've no idea. But I think he's probably calling to tell me.'

29

OLLIE

'Are you going to answer it?' Ollie asked, his heart beating just a bit faster than usual. What the hell was going on with him today? Okay, so his marriage had fallen apart, he'd been globally humiliated, and he'd realised he was going to have to rethink his whole life, but still... This was more than that. He hadn't been able to get what Drea said out of his mind. Him and Kara. Getting together. Could that work?

'No,' she said, jolting him, and he had to rewind to clarify what she was objecting to. 'I'm not picking up. He's got nothing to say that I want to hear.'

Ah, okay. She wasn't going to answer Josh's call. He was still in the game.

'Kara, do you ever wonder...'

Her damn phone started ringing again.

'Will you tell him to fuck off!' he said, just a little too loudly, and an elderly bloke at the nearest table gave him a raised eyebrow of disapproval.

Kara was looking pretty confused too. 'It's not him. Look.'

She turned her phone around again so he could see what it said on the screen.

Casey Lowden. FaceTime.

Kara was looking at him questioningly, as if undecided on whether to answer this one too, but before he could respond, she took the call.

'Hey Casey,' she was saying into the phone now, her eyes darting to make sure no one was close enough to overhear. She was safe. Even the old bloke with the disapproving eyebrow wouldn't be able to pick up her words unless they were shouted.

Ollie stayed quiet, picking up his phone to check on his emails. Kara nudged his leg, gesturing to him to listen in, so despite her often-repeated doubts that he could manage it, he proceeded to multitask.

From his side view, he could see Casey Lowden's face on the screen. Predictably, the press always went for the obvious, dubbing her the 'new Jennifer Aniston', but actually in this case they weren't far wrong. There were definitely similarities, in her looks, her quirky mannerisms and her absolute genius for comedy. According to Kara, she'd not long joined the cast of *The Clydeside*, but Ollie had a feeling she wouldn't be there long, because she had three movies already in the can and scheduled for release over the next year. Word on the inside was that they were fantastic and that she might just be the next big thing. He was reserving judgement, but it was great to see another Scot getting a bigger platform in the industry.

'Thanks for taking my call, Kara. I want to apologise for not getting in touch before now. I was in deep with the lawyers and the chiefs at Clydeside, and my team insisted I maintained total confidentiality until we'd reached a conclusion. Have you seen the news?'

'I did. Jacobs is gone. I'm guessing now that's down to you and your team? You did every woman in that studio a service.'

'Not just me. Josh Jackson from the PR company was a big help too. Although, I still think he might have played both sides at the start, but he soon realised who was winning the battle.' Ollie knew that Kara kept her personal life out of work and the public eye, so it wasn't surprising that a fairly new addition to the cast wasn't aware of the connection with Josh. 'And Abigail in HR was fricking mighty,' Casey said, with a wide grin. 'She's got the best poker face ever, but as soon as she knew the whole story, she held his feet to the fire. Or at least, the one good foot he had left. Sorry. Sometimes things just come out of my gob.'

'I know that feeling,' Kara agreed, and he could see the weight lifting off her shoulders with every second of the call.

'So anyway, two things – first, I just wanted to let you know that the studio are going to call and beg you to come back. It's not a good look for them that they didn't support you right from the outset.'

Kara nodded and he could see she was taking it all in and processing what that meant for her.

'And the second thing is what I've been dying to say to you for days now – thank you. Thank you so, so much. The way you stepped in and defended me... It was hardcore fricking epic, and I wanted you to know how much I appreciate that. I'm so sorry too, for all the stress it must have caused over the last few days. We just needed to get everything in place so that we could get the right outcome. Please, please come back to work, and thanks again, from the bottom of my heart. You're 100 per cent my kind of lady, Kara McIntyre.'

'I really appreciate that,' Kara responded, with a typically bashful smile. 'But no thanks are necessary. I'll wait to hear from the studio before I decide what I'm going to do.'

'They'll be in touch tomorrow. But, you know, with those reactions and that attitude, you should really consider a role in an action movie...'

That made Kara laugh, and when she did, the phone momentarily tilted in Ollie's direction.

Casey responded immediately. 'Wait, are my eyes playing up or did I just see Ollie Chiles?'

'Your eyes are fine,' Kara assured her, laughing. 'Ollie's my best mate – we're just heading off to Hawaii for my sister's wedding.'

Ollie leaned into the scope of the camera and Kara tilted it to make it a bit easier for him. 'Hey Casey, good to see you.'

'Good to see you too, Ollie. It's been a while. Listen, I'm sorry about all the shit you're dealing with. That was rough today.'

With everything going on, all the crap with Sienna seemed like forever ago – it was still crazy to him that he'd woken up this morning with not even the slightest idea of what was coming.

'Thanks, Casey,' he said, meaning it.

'And next time you're in town, shout me for a beer.'

'I will do.' Those kinds of exchanges happened all the time in their industry, and the beer/drink/dinner never materialised, but he was pretty sure this was real. They'd had a few nights out with some of the other cast members when they were working together the previous year and they'd definitely struck up the beginnings of a friendship.

'Oh, and by the way – anyone who's been anywhere near you two in the last year knows Sienna's statement was bullshit. Saving her own arse. She must pay her publicist the big bucks. See you later. Bye, Kara, and thanks again.'

With that, she blew them a kiss and then the screen went black.

It was Kara who reacted first. 'Statement? What statement?'

Ollie felt a deep, depressing inevitability sink from his shoulders to his gut. Of course Sienna would release a statement. His team had been urging him to do the same all day and he'd refused, because the negative optics weren't on him. Sienna would claw at every possibility to restore her image.

He clicked onto Instagram, knowing that if she'd posted something it would be everywhere. As soon as he pulled up her profile, there it was. A tear-stained and emotional Sienna, who, despite her distress, was sporting flawless make-up and perfect hair, stared straight into camera.

'Hi everyone. Thank you so much to all of you who have reached out after the horrendous invasion of my privacy this morning. You guys know I'm an open book, and I always want to be fully transparent with my fans, but the reality is that Ollie and I have been keeping something to ourselves for the last few months.'

Kara reached over and paused the video. 'You have?'

He shook his head. 'News to me.' He pressed play.

'We actually separated last summer...'

Beside him, Kara gasped and murmured, 'Cow.'

'And we've both moved on. As you all saw, I'm now in a really great relationship with Van Weeks, who has a brilliant new show coming out shortly on Netflix...'

It was almost laughable. She was hustling even in this moment.

'And I won't speak for Ollie, but I can say that he has someone new too.'

Again, Kara questioned him. 'You do?'

Same answer. 'Also, news to me.'

'We wish each other well, and we're both grateful for the wonderful times we had together. We'll go on as best friends...'

'I'll scratch her eyes out,' Kara joked. 'I'm your best friend.'

'...who want only the best for each other. I hope that this update puts this morning's video in perspective and all I'd like to say is be kind. You don't know what other people are going through. Thank you and I love you all.'

Ollie had to give it to her – she'd just cleaned up her image and scored a PR win at the same time.

'In case it wasn't already clear, I now can't stand her. Any time you want to talk or bitch, I'm here and ready.' Kara nudged him playfully and he felt such a wave of gratitude and love that he finally snapped and got to the point of the conversation he'd been trying to have for the last two hours.

'Actually, I kinda want to talk now,' he said, turning to face her, leaning forward in his seat so that they were only a few inches apart.

'I don't know how to say this, so I'm just going to blurt it out. Have you ever thought about you and me?'

'All the time. It's why I spend half my life on FaceTime with you.'

She wasn't getting this, so he went back in. 'No, I mean, actually you and me. Together. As in, a relationship.'

Her eyes widened as the message got through. 'Wait... with the naked stuff?'

Even in the tensest moments she could still make him laugh. 'You don't have to act so grossed out. There are a few million people in my fan club that might find the naked stuff appealing.'

Her mouth was now open and moving, but there was nothing coming out. He hadn't thought this through for long enough to envisage what her reaction would be, but this definitely wasn't it, so he immediately pressed on, desperately trying to reinforce his point.

'I was just thinking about what Drea said, about us both being single at the same time. We'll be in Hawaii for a few days together. Maybe we can... I don't know. Start slow. Maybe see whether it's something that could be a possibility for us. You're always going on about the romcoms. Isn't it always the good-looking best friend they end up with?'

She was still staring at him, eyes wide, stunned into silence.

That's when Drea returned, plonked herself down on her chair, then immediately sensed the weird vibe as her gaze went from one of them to the other, and back.

'Okay, what's happening? What did I miss? She told you another secret, didn't she? It's the bondage, isn't it? I fricking knew it the minute my black stilettos went missing.'

30

ALICE

It had taken until they were halfway to the airport before Alice's heart rate had returned to anywhere near normal. As soon as they'd left the home she'd once shared with Larry, Val had put her foot down and they'd raced back to her house to pick up Alice's cases. On the way, Zac had filled Val in on all the details of his exchange with Larry McLenn.

'What a relief,' Val had said, and Alice heard her voice catching with emotion. 'I was heartsore and worried for you. I'll admit, I wasn't on board with going to see him in the first place, but you were right, Zac, because if you hadn't, you'd always wonder. But I can't tell you the joy of knowing that you're not related to that man. If I get to heaven and get a free pass to wipe someone off this earth, Larry McLenn will be the one.'

Despite the stress of the day, that had made Alice smile. 'Do you have any evidence of these free passes, Val, or is it just a wish list item?' she'd teased. Even in the semi-darkness of the car, Alice had spotted the side-eye that was coming her way.

'If they're not there when I arrive, they will be available as soon as I get the place sorted out,' she'd joked, but Alice had decided there might just be an element of truth in there.

When they'd reached the house, they'd raced inside, and picked up her travel bag.

'Okay, have you got everything?' Val had demanded. 'All your IDs – passport, driving licence, Tesco Clubcard. And your purse. And where's your jewellery? Have you put one of those Air Tig thingies in your jewellery bag?'

A year ago, Val had lost her most precious possessions while travelling and it had scarred her for life. She'd then been introduced to the power of tracking devices and never left home without them. 'Air *Tag*,' Alice had corrected the title. 'And yes, one in my purse, one in my bag, one in my jewellery...'

Val had ticked them off on her fingers. 'And pop one in your bra, just in case you get lost. Me and the Jeep will come save you.'

Alice didn't doubt it for a second.

Zac – lovely guy that he was – had grabbed the suitcases and lugged them down the path and into the back of the Jeep. She'd checked her watch – they were cutting it fine, but they should make it with about twenty minutes to spare.

Now that they were well on the road and making good time, Alice could begin to breathe normally again. The relief was still coursing through her. Larry wasn't Zac's father. Morag hadn't done the unthinkable. Now Alice could go back to thinking of her friendship with both joy that it had happened and regret that they'd let it go. And unless she ever learned differently, she was also going back to her previous belief that they'd lost touch because youth, time and distance had got in the way.

'Val, there's one more thing about what happened at Larry's house that we have to tell you. When we got there, Larry wasn't in...'

'You know, I thought I saw him staggering down the street

after you arrived, but I thought I had to be mistaken. Who let you in then?'

Alice's jaw clenched at the memory.

'Sandra.'

'No! She's still with him?'

Alice nodded. 'She is. And, Val, what a state she's in.' She went on to recount the whole story, and with every detail, Val's jaw set firmer, and her knuckles got tighter on the steering wheel.

'He's a horrible bastard, he truly is.'

'He is.'

'And it's a credit to you that you want to help her.'

'I couldn't leave anyone in that position, Val. Problem is, she doesn't want my help. I'm going to give Bernadette a call in the morning and see what she thinks. Maybe the group can do something to help. Meanwhile, I've given Sandra my number and told her to call day or night. She's not ready yet, but hopefully it won't be long.'

Val took it all in. 'I'll see if I can find a way to keep a wee eye on her too.' Val had fingers in every pie of the community and social care, and there weren't many people in their cluster of villages that she didn't know. If there was a way to help, she would find it.

The miles passed way too quickly and they were already approaching the slip road for the airport. Val followed the series of swooping curves round to the entrance to the drop-off zone and zipped right into the space left by a departing minivan.

Zac pulled the cases out of the boot, then gave Val a hug. 'It was a real pleasure to meet you, son. Next time you're in Scotland, come visit me,' she told him, patting his back.

'I sure will. Thanks for everything, Val. We couldn't have done today without you.'

Alice thought yet again what a decent man Morag had raised.

Zac let Val go, and then picked up the cases. 'Alice, I'll just go wait at the entrance and let you say your goodbyes.'

She couldn't even thank him because a rock had just lodged in her throat. Val met her gaze, and Alice saw the same emotion coming right back at her. She took a step forward and wrapped her arms around her diminutive pal, breathing in her heady scent: a mixture of Elnett hairspray, coconut shampoo and a quick squirt of Chanel No5.

After a few moments, she managed to find her voice. 'Val, I'll never be able to thank you enough for what you've done for me. You gave me my life back and I'll always be so grateful. You're the very best person I've ever known.'

There was a large sniff. 'Alice, if I have blue mascara tears down my cheeks, it'll be your fault. You saved your life all by yourself, ma love. I was just there to cheer you on. And this goodbye isn't for long because I'll be down to see you next month.'

'Not the same as drinking tea in my dressing gown with you every morning.'

'True. You'll have to find some other spectacular way to start your day.' Another sniff. Then Val slowly moved back out of Alice's arms. 'Now on you go and don't keep that lad waiting. Give my love to Rory and Sophie and tell them I'll see them soon.'

'I will,' Alice assured her. 'I love you, Val Murray.'

'Right back at you, Alice Brookes. You're going to have a great life.'

Before she could change her mind, and waving all the way, Alice went off to catch up with Zac. By the time she turned around to wave one last time, the bright yellow Jeep was gone.

She was still dabbing her eyes with her hanky when she reached Zac. 'Are you okay?' he asked her.

'I'm fine. Goodbyes are hard. It's taken me a long time to find people in my life that I could count on no matter what. Val is one of those people and I'll miss her every day. I felt that way about your mum too. For what it's worth, Zac – I've been thinking all day about how proud she must have been of you. I just wanted to tell you that.' She felt another wave of emotion coming, so she immediately tried to stem it by snapping into action mode. 'Now, let's go catch these flights before I fall apart, and they don't let me on.'

As soon as they got inside the terminal, they made a beeline for the departures board in the middle of the hall, and both scanned the long list of cancellations and delays at the same time. It struck her that she should have checked the times before she left the house as she normally would, but today had just got away from her.

'My flight is delayed for two hours,' Zac said first.

'Mine is saying an hour, but look at that,' she pointed higher up the board. 'The two earlier flights to Heathrow haven't even taken off yet. Ah well, at least it'll give us time to relax and have a bit of dinner.' She suddenly wondered if that had sounded like she was suggesting that they should eat together, and she immediately clarified, because she didn't want to be an imposition. 'I'll just go check my cases in then. Please keep in touch with me. I'd like to know how you get on. And tell your dad I said hello...' She wasn't sure if that would be welcome or not, given that Cillian had seemingly snubbed her at the funeral, but she meant it anyway.

Before they could say any more, his phone pinged and she saw a puzzled expression cross his brow. 'My dad has sent me a text, saying that he's in the executive lounge. No idea how he got in there. We usually just hang out at the bar upstairs. I'm not a member so I'm not sure how he thinks I can meet him there.'

Alice saw the issue. 'If you want to wait until I've checked my cases in, I can come sign you in. I'm a member, but I promise I'm not saying that to be flash. I travelled a lot with my son in the last six months – making up for lost time – and I racked up the miles, so I just got my lounge pass through. I'll just sign you in, and then I'll leave you and your dad to talk. I'm sure there's a lot you'll want to discuss with him.'

They'd joined the back of the queue now, but they were late-comers, so it wasn't too long. Alice quickly texted Rory and Sophie to let them know about the delay. They wouldn't have left for the airport yet, so hopefully it wouldn't cause them any inconvenience.

Meanwhile, Zac must have thought about what she'd just said, because he broached a different idea. 'Alice, would you come talk to him too? I think maybe it would help if there was someone who loved Mum as much as he did, who knew that she was a good person back then. I know that you lost touch, but I know that you loved her...'

'I did.'

'And I'm sure that my dad will appreciate that too.'

Alice thought that over. It would be nice to meet Cillian again. To chat to someone with a shared history. To talk about Morag and how wonderful she was. 'Okay, but if your dad has any objections, I'll leave, no offence taken. How does that sound?'

Zac pushed her cases forward in the line. 'I think that sounds like an excellent plan.'

Alice just hoped that Cillian felt the same way.

31

ZAC

'Erm, am I seeing things or is that my dad over there with that blonde lady? And does she have her hand on his knee?'

'I think I can confirm both of those things,' Alice replied, her surprise obvious, although he could see that she didn't know what her reaction should be. Neither did he.

'Well, this is a first,' he admitted, scrambling for the appropriate response. He'd only ever seen his dad with his mum and hadn't even contemplated a world in which his dad met someone else. Looked like he should really have thought about that before now.

'Do we stay or go?' Zac asked, floundering.

Alice came in with words of wisdom. 'I think you should stay. He'll have been waiting for you and he'll be glad to see you made it.'

Zac knew that she was probably right, and it only took a few steps for them to reach the bar.

'Dad?'

If he'd been worried about interrupting them, those fears

were now gone. The sheer relief on his dad's face told him everything.

'Son! So glad you made it,' he said, patting Zac's arm like his life depended on it. Cillian wasn't usually one for overly tactile greetings, so Zac sussed that it must be a reaction to the flamboyant woman on his left. Before he could say anything, she beat him to it.

'Ah, you must be Zac! I've heard all about you. I'm Jacinta. I was just keeping your dad company until you got here. Such a lovely man.'

As she slid off her bar stool, she patted his dad's knee again and Zac could see his dad didn't know where to look. Zac struggled to keep a straight face.

'Well, Cillian,' Jacinta purred. Yep, that was the only word for it. 'It was a pleasure to meet you. Don't forget you have my details. It would be smashing to hear from you next time you're in Glasgow.'

'I'll keep that in mind, Jacinta. You have a terrific time in Hawaii.'

'Oh, I will! All the glorious "S" words – sun, sea and...' She paused, threw his dad a provocative pout, and Zac thought his father was about to faint with embarrassment. 'Surfing!' she added with a cheeky wink, before giving them another wave and going off in the direction of the other side of the lounge. The whole place was packed with passengers from the delayed flights, so he soon lost sight of her.

'Making friends, Dad?' Zac asked, finally giving in to laughter.

His dad's flustered expression said it all. 'Son, I was bloody terrified. And my ears are bleeding. I've never met anyone like her. I can't tell you how happy I am that you're...'

Zac saw his dad pause, as his gaze shifted, and he realised for the first time that Zac wasn't alone.

'Hello, Cillian,' Alice greeted him. 'Zac invited me up to join you, but I promise I won't be offended if you'd rather I didn't.'

After a split second of hesitation, when Zac genuinely thought it could go either way, his dad surprised him, by getting up to hug Alice. 'I'd be very happy for you to join us, Alice. It's been too long.'

Relieved, Zac pulled up another bar stool, leaving Alice to take the one that Jacinta had just vacated. Zac was nearest to the bartender, so he took the lead. 'Alice, what can I get you to drink?'

'A gin and tonic please.'

'Dad, another pint?'

'Please, son.'

'So how have you been, Alice? You're looking well...' The two old friends kicked off their own conversation as Zac, with his back to them, waited to catch the bartender's eye. He was grateful for the couple of minutes it gave him to think. He wasn't going to raise anything that had happened today with his dad, he decided. This wasn't the time or the place, and his dad had already had a rough day. A rough year.

To his surprise, though, it was his dad who went straight to the elephant in the room.

'I'm sorry I didn't come over to speak to you at the funeral this morning, Alice. I think emotions were just running too high and all I could think about was Morag. You know, it was one of the biggest regrets of her life that you two lost touch.'

As Zac ordered the drinks, he heard Alice say, 'It was mine too. I was heartbroken. And I don't think I ever understood why. Was there a reason behind it, Cillian?'

In all his life, he'd never once known his dad to lie, so he listened in.

'To be honest, Alice, it was never you. She just couldn't be near that... that... arsehole, McLenn. I can say that now because I read in the papers that you're not with him anymore.'

'No. I managed to leave him about six months ago.'

Zac had been so determined not to intervene, but now his curiosity got the better of him. 'Dad, the reason I went to see Alice today is because Jill found a box of Mum's old letters and photos, and in it was a note from Mum, apologising to Alice. But she never sent it. I know I should have asked you about it, but I didn't want to make your day worse. Do you know what it was about? What was she apologising for?'

'Only if you're comfortable saying, Cillian,' Alice interjected. 'I don't want you to feel that you're breaking confidences.'

His dad gave a rueful shrug. 'I suppose there's no harm in telling you now and you deserve an answer. But Alice, I need to warn you that you might find it upsetting.'

Alice urged him on. 'I'd like to know. I've already got an idea of what it was about, so please don't worry about hurting my feelings. And please don't think that you could ever say anything about Larry that would be worse than what I experienced with him. It's a long story for another time, but I was married to him for almost thirty years and I hated every single day of my life with that man. It took me decades to escape him.'

'I'm sorry, Alice. I wish we'd known that. Morag followed every piece of news about you, and she thought that you were happily married.'

Alice sighed. 'It was all an act because that's what he wanted people to believe. He basically threatened that he would take my child away from me if I left, because he didn't want his political image damaged. People were always very taken in by him, until they saw his true colours.'

Zac handed over everyone's drinks, then sat back, happy to listen to what he knew was going to be the truth.

'That makes what I'm about to say easier,' his dad went on. 'You see, the truth was that Morag was taken in by him too. More than that, if I'm honest. He took an interest in her – I'm sorry, Alice, but it was when you were already together – and she thought for a while that she had feelings for him too. The wrong kind of feelings. He encouraged her, indulged her, and when you were all away on a trip – for her birthday, I think – she said he'd made a play for her every chance he could get. She didn't give into him then though. Her moment of weakness was one night, back in Glasgow, when she went to his bar, and he humiliated her in front of everyone, sent her away and told her she was pathetic. He'd just been playing with her all along, manipulating her for fun.'

Zac felt a rage deep in his ribs and wanted to go right back to that scumbag's house.

'From that moment, it was like the blinkers came off and she saw who he was,' his dad was saying now. 'She was so ashamed. She hated him and she couldn't face what she'd almost done to you. That's why she left. I don't think she ever forgave herself. I hope you can forgive her.'

He noticed the tears pooling in Alice's eyes as she spoke. 'I already have, because I fell for Larry's lies too. I just wish I'd been able to tell her that when she was alive.'

'Me too,' his dad said, with a sad smile. 'The only good thing to come out of it was that I met her the night she'd had the run-in with him. I'd only been in Glasgow a couple of days, and I was walking to my digs when I saw her sobbing in the street. She ended up staying with me that week, because she couldn't even face her family and I fell hard and fast for her in no time. After that, I didn't see her for a few weeks, though – she just needed time to get her thoughts straightened out – then one day out of the blue she called me. Asked if we could start again.'

Zac saw his chance to ask the other question that had consumed him since he found the photos that morning. 'When was that, Dad?'

His dad thought about it. 'That must have been the March, before we came back to Ireland and got married.'

'So hang on, you also had a fling in January?'

'Yeah. Probably too much information, but that was actually when you were conceived. Not that we knew it at the time. But we never actually properly went anywhere until we got together again, so your mum always said our first proper date was in March. We went to the cinema and then up to a wee restaurant called Gino's in Merchant City for dinner. Best night of my life. Apart from when you were born.'

The relief was both instant and overwhelming. Zac wanted to punch the air. To hug his father. To kiss Alice, who met his eyes now, and he didn't know which of them was smiling the widest. Before his dad even noticed their reaction, all their attention was taken by the bing-bong of a service announcement.

'Good evening, ladies and gentlemen, would all passengers on the following flights please contact the airline customer services desk in the departures lounge.'

The three of them listened as the announcer read off a bunch of flight numbers and destinations.

'That's us,' Zac said, as the Dublin flight was called.

Alice's London one was next. 'And that's me too,' she added.

The three of them polished off some more of their drinks, before getting up to join the mass of people heading to the door.

'Doesn't look like we're going anywhere tonight,' Zac said. 'This has happened to me before.'

With that, he took a step back to let Alice go before him. If he hadn't, he wouldn't have seen the red-haired woman in the furthest corner of the lounge.

The one with a face that he'd thought about countless times over the years.

'Erm, can I catch up with you? I've just seen someone I know and I'd really like to speak to her.'

10 P.M. – MIDNIGHT

32

KARA

Drea was on the warpath. In the last hour, she'd been up and down so many times, people were starting to think she worked here. This time, she came thundering back to the table like a woman on a mission.

'Right, folks, we weren't on the scrubbed list that just got called, and the flight board says we've to go to gate 22. I just spoke to one of the stressed-out folks in the high-vis yellow jackets, and he says that now the fog's lifted, they've only got enough slots to get a few planes out before the curfew that stops them disturbing the city's beauty sleep. Our flight to Heathrow is going, but the later Heathrow flights have been cancelled. So let's move it move it move it before they change their minds.'

Kara quickly glanced at Ollie to see his reaction, but his face was inscrutable. One of the downsides of having an interaction with a guy who was a brilliant actor.

She could honestly say that tonight he'd surprised her more than any other time in their lives. And that included the time he'd told her he'd meet her in a park for her birthday picnic and then he'd parachuted down from the skies and almost landed on

a wee old lady's shopping trolley. Or the time he'd put live frogs
in her lunch box in primary seven.

His words had replayed over and over again in her mind, and
still she couldn't make sense of them.

'We'll be in Hawaii for a few days together. Maybe we can... I don't
know. Start slow. Maybe see whether it's something that could be a
possibility for us. You're always going on about the romcoms. Isn't it
always the good-looking best friend they end up with?'

What was he saying? Actually, she got the gist of what he was
saying, but why the hell was he saying it? They had gone through
their entire lives together. They had spent days on end alone
together. They had talked constantly, sometimes until they were
hoarse. When it was just the two of them, their favourite thing to
do was eat pizza and watch movies in bed, so they had slept
under the same duvet on countless occasions and not once, *not a
single time*, had anything even remotely romantic happened.

And then he drops a bomb like this?

The worst thing was, she hadn't even been able to discuss it
with him because Drea had come back to the table, and then a
while later her mum had reappeared from the bar through in the
other area of the lounge and proceeded to loudly announce to
the lady at the next table that she was with her nephew, Ollie
Chiles. Yes, *That* Ollie Chiles. And oh, wasn't he brilliant in *The
Clansman*. Those legs in that kilt!

Her mum had then launched into a twenty-minute rant to
Ollie about the Sienna video and the breakdown of his marriage,
hugging him dramatically, and offering to fly to LA after the
wedding and set Sienna straight about in-flight decorum. Apparently, she and Moira had spoken about it, and they were both on
the same page of outrage.

The whole time that her mum was ranting, Ollie was giving
Kara questioning looks that she didn't know how to answer. Her

heart was aching for him because he looked so miserable and all she wanted to do was hug him, but there were way too many phones with cameras in the immediate vicinity.

'Kara! In the name of the hurry-the-fuck-up, what is wrong with you? You're like a fart in a trance. Let's go. Let's move. Let's show some enthusiasm for the fact that we are actually getting out of this goddamn airport.'

Now slightly terrified that her sister was spiralling into hysteria, she pulled on her jacket, threw her bag over her shoulder and began to walk. They were in the furthest corner of the lounge, so it meant that they were behind everyone else who had now been called, either to their gate or to the customer services desk.

'Jesus, you'd think this was death row. Would you two HURRY UP,' Drea was shouting over her shoulder.

Ollie was in line with her, but he was facing forward, making no eye contact, and she couldn't bear the silence or the slump of the shoulders that cost him £500 dollars an hour with a martial arts trainer.

Checking that everyone ahead of them was facing the front, and happy that they were mostly concealed by jackets and bags, she slipped her hand through his and then watched as he smiled for the first time since their conversation took a sharp left.

They were almost at the door, and she was still staring at her friend's face beside her, when she heard the voice.

'Kara?'

Her. Heart. Stopped.

Stopped.

Right in front of her, blocking the way, so that everyone going in the opposite direction had to walk around him, was...

'Zac.'

Now her heart had started again, and it was thudding like a drum.

'Hey,' he said, smiling.

'Hey,' she replied, staring back. And staring. Until she saw his gaze go to Ollie and then down from their shoulders to the hands that were intertwined between them.

The realisation snapped her out of her daze. 'Sorry! Zac, this is Ollie. I know I told you all about him.'

Zac nodded, but she couldn't read his face. 'You did.'

'Ollie, this is Zac. You know...' She didn't want to finish the sentence, so of course, Ollie gazed at her quizzically.

'I don't think I do know,' he said, and she couldn't miss the familiar grin that told her he was playing with her. Putting her on the spot. As freaking usual.

'Zac is the guy I was telling you about earlier,' she said through gritted teeth. 'We were both on cancelled flights and got put up in a hotel.'

'Aaaaah, *that* Zac,' Ollie said, with just a touch of amusement and drama. Kara wanted the ground to open up and swallow her. Preferably whole so that the end came quicker.

Ollie stuck out his free hand. 'Pleased to meet you, Zac.'

'And you.' Zac returned the handshake.

'So... going somewhere nice?' Ollie asked breezily, as if this was a mate he'd just bumped into in the frozen food aisle at Asda.

'Actually, not going anywhere at all. Our flight's been cancelled so we've been called to the customer service desk. I think lightning's about to strike twice.'

'Lightning?' Ollie repeated, staring at her again, somehow reverted to the twelve-year-old kid who would find out who she fancied and then send them a note with her signature asking to meet. She kicked him on the ankle, and she would never apologise for it.

'What about you two?' Zac asked. He was speaking to them in plural, but staring only at Kara.

She had to clear her throat before it would work. 'Hawaii. Actually, we're flying to London now, staying there overnight and then flying out to Hawaii tomorrow.' *Do not overshare. Do not overshare. Do not...* 'We're going for my sister's wedding.'

'We're so looking forward to it, aren't we?' Ollie chimed in, hamming up the cuteness. Kara had another jab at his ankle.

They were the only people left in the lounge now, until a blonde head popped back in the door. 'Kara, would you two hurry up! Your sister is about to have a dose of the vapours if you don't get to this gate.'

Kara saw Zac's expression change to puzzlement.

'Oh, hello again,' her mother chirped over to him.

'You've met my mother?' Kara asked, confused.

'Yeah, when I got here, she was chatting to my dad. I think they met on the way in.'

This was beginning to feel like a parallel universe. 'Your dad is Cillian? My mum introduced us earlier.'

Zac nodded, still smiling, as if this made him strangely happy. Or maybe his face was just frozen in that expression because he was so uncomfortable his whole body was shutting down.

'What are the chances?' he asked, still staring.

'What are the chances,' she repeated.

Another pause, then another, 'Kara!' from the door. Clearly fearing for his life if he got on the wrong side of Drea, Ollie took over.

'Well, it's been great to meet you, but we need to run. Sorry about your flight. Hope you manage to get home tomorrow.'

With that, he gave Zac his best movie star smile, and then, still holding Kara's hand, swept her along with him as they hurried to catch up with the others. All Kara managed was a quick 'Bye' over her shoulder.

'Hurry, hurry, hurry!' Jacinta rushed them, until they broke into a sprint – a completely wasted effort because when they got to the gate, they found everyone sitting down. Kara's heart was still racing, her legs were still shaking and her head was about to explode at any second.

Zac. She'd wanted to speak to him for longer, ask him so many more questions, but had been rushed away before she could even get his number. It didn't feel illicit now that she was no longer with Josh.

'Where have you been?' Drea was indeed murderous. 'They're starting boarding in ten minutes.'

Ten minutes and then they'd be out of here.

It was too late to go back and speak to Zac.

But it wasn't too late to sort things out with the guy who was still holding her hand. Ollie. The man she'd loved her whole life.

'Come with me,' she said, turning on her heel and pulling his hand behind her.

'Kara... Kara! Where are you going?' That was Drea again, but Kara knew her sister was like animals and children – if Kara showed fear, she'd be toast.

Instead, she went for a fake breezy, 'Just over there – Ollie and I are going to have a quick chat.'

As soon as she reached the far wall and was sure no one around them could hear, she spun around to face him.

'Ollie Chiles, we need to talk.'

33

OLLIE

'Okay, what's going on? You're acting weird and you're saying strange things and if you're on drugs, it's not too late to get you into rehab,' Kara said.

'So it's a "no" on the relationship thing then?' he asked her, deflecting the question, because it was easier than delving into what was going on in his mind. Why had he only just realised today that he could have those kind of feelings for her? Jealousy had been eating him up when she'd been talking about spending those nights in a hotel with that Zac bloke and then he'd bloody turned up! And now she was looking at him with those huge green eyes and he honestly had no idea where she was going to go with this.

'Ollie, you don't want that,' she told him, her voice oozing concern and confusion.

Ah. That's where she was going with it.

He ran his fingers through his hair as he took a couple of steps, turned, then paced back the other way. 'But maybe I do. I mean, have you ever thought about it?'

'No!' she said emphatically, as if it was the most ridiculous question in the world. She followed the denial straight up with, 'Tell me the truth, Ollie – have you ever thought about it before tonight?'

He opened his mouth to answer in the affirmative, then immediately realised that it would be a lie. 'Well, no, but—'

'And let me ask you another question,' she demanded, and he recognised that this was why she'd been captain of the debate team in school. 'Have you – and answer me honestly – ever had a burning desire to rip my clothes off and do the naked stuff? With me, for the avoidance of doubt.'

He could see where this was leading. 'No, but—'

'And have you ever thought I'd be the perfect person to impregnate and then watch a child emerge from my nethers?'

'Actually, not specifically, but I have thought that we'd have great kids. I just didn't dig into the details.'

She slumped back against the wall. 'Ollie, you don't want me,' she said. The captain of the debate team had hung up her hat and now his best mate was back and talking to him with her whole heart. 'You're just having a really shit day and you're feeling a bit blindsided and untethered. And I'm your tether. Just like you're mine. You don't want me, because you already have me. I think what you want is a place that you feel is home.'

'You think?' The truth was, he didn't even need to ask because he immediately recognised that she was right.

'I know for sure,' she said, with firm, but gentle conviction. 'Now I'm going to go into those loos there, and you're going to stop Drea barging in and dragging me out by the hair. And then we're going to go to Hawaii and we're going to have a great time because I love you and we deserve this because both our lives have tanked. Okay?'

The relief that this felt normal, and just the way it always had, felt so much better than whatever was happening in his head an hour ago. He was going to put that down to a temporary, Sienna-induced, cerebral blip.

'And are we going to have any conversation whatsoever about the encounter we just had with your sleepover buddy back there?'

He watched as a flash of something he didn't recognise went right across her face.

She shook her head. 'No, we're never going to speak of it again.'

'Understood.' Wow. That came from the woman who needed to talk about everything, who over-shared even the smallest details, who'd never kept a secret from him and Drea in her entire life until it involved this guy.

'Now guard the door, and don't let Drea shout at me.'

With that, she swerved into the toilets, and he took her place, leaning against the wall, his mind flipping back through everything she'd just said. She was right. It wasn't a person he wanted. It was something stable. Somewhere to belong. Somewhere that he didn't arrive and then leave again two days later. He had the house he shared with Sienna in LA, and that would no longer be home. They'd also had the flat they rented in New York, that they'd given up now that she was no longer working there. Then there were the temporary homes in Vancouver and Croatia when they were filming. The only house he truly felt a connection with was the one in Glasgow, but even then, it still didn't feel like home because he'd only spent about twelve days there in the last year. Time for changes. Time to find something that gave him a real sense of purpose.

He pulled out his phone and rang the person who was offering him at least some of that.

Calvin answered on the first ring. 'Hello lovely. Are you okay?

You haven't called me at this time of night since you were waiting to hear about that part in *Taggart*. I think you were fourteen.'

The memory of that made him laugh. This was what he missed. People who'd known him for a lifetime. 'I never did get the part either,' he said, remembering.

'You wouldn't have wanted it. You were dead by the second scene. So tell me… do you need me to help with something?'

Ollie got straight to the point. 'No. I just wanted to say I'm in on the church. The theatre school. I'll provide the funding for the building, and I'll help you to raise more, and I'll put my name to it and support you all the way. It's a great project, Calvin. I'm really proud of you for taking it on.'

As Calvin cheered, Ollie relished the feeling that this was right. Every word of that was true. He'd be proud to be part of it. The other people who were already committing their names and their time were people in the industry that he had real respect for. Or at least, most of them were…

'But I have two conditions.'

'Pierre, put the cork back in that champagne,' Calvin shouted, before resuming his telephone voice to Ollie. 'I'm really sorry, Ollie, but I was joking about the hall pass. I'm not sleeping with you. At least not more than once.'

'Good to know,' Ollie chuckled, 'but that wasn't one of the conditions.'

'Dammit. Okay, go for it.'

'Was Corbin Jacobs part of this project?'

'Yes. Although I just heard he got bumped from *The Clydeside* today, so there's something going on there.'

Ollie didn't elaborate. 'I'll match whatever he was contributing, but I want him to have nothing to do with it. He's not using the school to get a single line of positive press. And while you're at it, I want you to spread the word that I mentioned I'll never work with the prick. No specifics. Just that. Spread it far and wide. I want a stink attached to his name that he won't be able to wash off.'

'Okay, I'm not going to ask why, but you're the second person who's said that to me today.'

Ollie got it immediately. 'I'm thinking the first one was Casey Lowden, and I'm on her side all the way with this.'

'I hear you.' Calvin had been in the business long enough to give an educated guess as to what was going on, and he was discreet enough never to share it.

'What's the second condition?'

'I'd like some part of the school to be dedicated to my mum and my gran. They both have the same name, so that makes it easier. The Moira Chiles Recording Studio. Or maybe the auditorium. I don't care what it is. I just want them both to be part of it, so people will know that they're special women.'

'I could not love you more,' Calvin said softly.

'Right back at you.'

He spotted Drea waving at him from the gate. 'Calvin, I need to go catch a flight – I'll call you tomorrow to get everything organised. See ya, pal. Go drink that champagne.'

He'd just hung up when Kara came out of the loos. 'Just in time, she's about to come hunting for you,' he said, nodding to Drea.

'Okay, let's do this,' she said, with a sigh that didn't correlate with how most people would be acting when they were setting off for Hawaii.

He stopped, put his hand on her arm. 'You okay?' he asked, searching her face for clues.

'Yeah. I think it's just hit me that I'm supposed to be going to my wedding, and now I'm not. I've spent almost three days being so bloody angry that it's kind of numbed me to the bits that hurt. Josh keeps calling and I'm ignoring him, and—'

With perfect timing, the phone rang again and there was that photo of Josh, on the beach, when she loved him...

'Answer it,' he suggested. 'One way or another, just hear him out. It'll either hurt or help.'

'You're really rubbish at this, you know that?'

'I do.'

But still, she answered, and then she pulled him close so that he could listen. 'Are you still going?' were the first words out of Josh's mouth.

'I am,' she replied.

'With Ollie?'

'And everyone else in my family,' she retorted. Maybe it was her tone, but he suddenly flipped to a different energy.

'I was going to come to the airport to see you, but since Drea cancelled my ticket, I knew I wouldn't get past security.'

Ollie decided the first thing he was going to do in Hawaii was buy Drea a pina colada for protecting her sister. When Kara didn't respond to that little nugget of information, Josh kept on going.

'Kara, please don't go. Please just come back. I'm so sorry. I know I fucked up, and I should have had your back from the start, but I fixed it...'

'I know. Casey Lowden said you helped. I'm glad you did that. It was the right thing to do.'

'I should have done it from the outset.'

'Yes.'

'But that's the thing, Kara. You always know what the right thing to do is. It just takes some of us a heartbeat longer to get there.'

There was a click and Kara pulled the phone away from

between their ears and checked the screen. 'Shit, my phone died. Aaargh! He sounded really upset, Ollie.' She was now standing still, as if frozen to the spot, just a few yards away from the gate. 'What should I do?'

Ollie shrugged, genuinely at a loss as to what to advise her, in case it was the wrong thing, which, let's face it, was likely to be the case.

'I don't know, Kara. But what did Josh say? *You always know what the right thing to do is.* Just decide what that is and do it.'

34

ALICE

'Okay, sweetheart, well, I'm glad you still hadn't left the house. I know, but it can't be helped. I'll call you in the morning and let you know what time I'll be arriving. Love to Sophie and to you.'

'Your son?' Cillian asked, his words almost drowned out by the loud horn that went off to signify that the luggage carousel was about to start moving.

'Yes. Rory. He's the same age as Zac. They actually remind me a bit of each other.'

She didn't say that this morning she'd been convinced that there were physical similarities too. Especially as now she was face to face with Cillian Corlan, she was looking at a real-life reminder that Larry McLenn didn't have a monopoly on pale blue eyes.

Their conversation was interrupted again by the noise of the conveyor belt starting up and beginning its slow trundle around the baggage reclaim hall.

The process at the customer services desk had been remarkably swift. The weary, exhausted ground staff had simply informed them that due to the weather and the resulting backlog, combined with the non-negotiable curfew for planes taking off and landing at night, their flights had been cancelled until morning. Now that the snow had stopped falling and the fog had lifted, they were managing to get a select few out before the curfew – the flights that had been delayed longest – but there simply wasn't time to get them all away. As a result, rooms were being made available to them at a nearby hotel. Anyone with luggage was advised to wait behind, but those who only had hand luggage were free to go.

She'd briefly considered going back to Val's house for the night, but she didn't want to trouble Val yet again, by getting her out of her bed. And then there would be the taxis there and back too. No, this made much more sense. Besides, this was likely to be the only time that she was in the company of her old friend's husband, and she was enjoying hearing about Morag's life and reminiscing about their past.

Decision made, she'd gone along with the instructions from the airline staff.

'Son, is that the hotel you stayed in before?' she'd heard Cillian ask Zac. He'd mentioned that he'd had to stay overnight at the airport hotel on a previous occasion – or was it two occasions? – but Alice hadn't got the details yet. She presumed it would be down to the weather, because he'd mentioned that both times it was in January.

Zac had nodded. 'It is.'

The lad looked shattered now and no wonder. It had been quite a day for him. In the last hour or so he'd got quieter and quieter, and she was worried that the emotional impact of the day was still hitting him. No matter what, she knew he'd be fine though. He'd got the answer to his question about his father, and it was the best result that he could have hoped for. It was so obvious that the two men had a brilliant relationship and that

Cillian adored his son. Every bit of her wished that Rory had a father like that too.

'Why don't you run over then and get the rooms sorted? I'll wait with Alice and get the luggage,' Cillian had suggested.

'Dad, I'm not having you lugging cases all the way over there. I'll wait here for them, and you two go on over.'

'Nonsense. I'm perfectly capable of handling a few cases.' Alice didn't doubt that for a second. If she remembered correctly, Cillian was only a couple of years older than her, so he wasn't even in his sixties yet. And he'd already told her that working with his construction company, on top of three gym sessions a week, kept him fit. 'I'd much rather do that than stand in queues at reception and fill out all that paperwork. Alice and I can chat away while we're waiting. Is that okay with you, Alice? I'll put all the cases on a trolley, so you'll not be having to cart them yourself.'

'That sounds like the ideal plan, as long as you don't mind, Zac?'

'If you're sure...' Zac had checked, to which Alice had nodded gratefully.

She knew that she would have handled this on her own, with no issues at all – she'd coped with so much more than a minor travel blip in recent years – but she had to admit, it was good to be dealing with this alongside friends.

'I think that's my cases there,' she said, pointing to the two purple suitcases that had been going away gifts from Val and all the women in their gang, the friends that she hadn't even met a year ago, but who would now be part of her life forever.

Cillian loaded them both on to the trolley, along with his own and Zac's, and they made their way out of the terminal building and across the signposted path that led directly to the hotel. Someone had cleared the path so that trolleys didn't have to be pushed through the snow, but still the cold had hit them as soon as the doors had opened. Although, it felt strangely refreshing to have the bite of frost in the air.

When they reached reception, Zac was already standing there with their keys.

'Here you go. Dad, you're in 201, I'm next door in 203, and Alice, you're in 205.'

A young man came over from the concierge desk with a brass luggage trolley. 'Would you like me to take your luggage up to your rooms?'

'Yes please,' Cillian nodded, helping to transfer the cases onto the hotel trolley, before giving him the relevant room numbers.

'No problem at all,' the bellboy told them. 'The bar is still open, if you'd like a drink.'

Cillian didn't need much persuasion. 'I think I could definitely do with a pint after all that. Alice? Zac? I'm not trying to lead you astray, but would you like to join me?'

Zac shook his head. 'Sorry, Dad, but I'm knackered. I'm just going to go on upstairs.' He reached over and gave his dad a hug, and then made Alice smile, by hugging her too. 'I'll see you in the morning. And, Alice, thank you so much for everything today. I would have been lost without you, and I'm so grateful. I'm glad we got everything sorted out.'

An unspoken agreement passed between them when he didn't use specifics.

Neither of them would ever discuss Larry McLenn again. It was over. Done. As far as they were both concerned, it had never happened. Which was how she viewed her time with Larry too. Done.

'I am too, and I'm so glad that our paths crossed. You know that divine intervention we were talking about? I can't help thinking that your mum planned that for a reason. Goodnight, Zac.'

He went off in the direction of the lifts, leaving her with Cillian in the lobby.

'Drink then?' Cillian said. The fact that she was still there probably gave her decision away. She might not have made it to her new life with Rory and Sophie tonight, but that didn't mean she should delay her new attitude, new optimism and new determination to enjoy every second of the rest of her life.

'You know what, Cillian, I think I'd like that.'

They made their way into the bar and found a corner table, over by the fire on the far wall. A waiter took their order of a pint and a gin and tonic straight away.

'You're smiling,' Cillian said.

Alice nodded. 'I guess I am. I was thinking about Morag. I hope she heard everything we talked about tonight. I hope she knows how much we'd love her to be here. In a way, I feel like she is. Is that weird?'

Cillian shook his head. 'I was thinking the same thing when we were at the bar in the airport. You know, I'm not embarrassed to say it's been a tough year. Morag and I were married for near on thirty years, and we were happy. We had a good life. I just never thought that I would lose her while we still had lots of it to live and it floored me. But so many times I've felt her around me...' He paused, then smiled. 'She wasn't one for moping or feeling sorry for herself, so when I hear her in my head, she's usually telling me to get my act together and get out and enjoy myself. Maybe it's time I started listening to her.'

The waiter arrived with their drinks, and as soon as he'd left them, Alice held hers up. 'To Morag,' she said softly.

Cillian raised his glass to meet hers. 'To Morag. And to the rest of our lives.'

They'd just taken their first sips and put their glasses down on the table when they were distracted by the sight of a young woman rushing into the bar.

Alice was surprised when Cillian raised his hand and waved, a gesture that brought the red-haired girl tearing over their way.

'Hi. We met earlier,' she said to Cillian, her cheeks flushed and her words breathless.

His tone was welcoming and kind as he acknowledged that he remembered her. 'Jacinta's lass.'

'Yes. Only at the time, I didn't realise that you were Zac's dad. Crazy coincidence, but he's an...' she paused, as if she didn't know quite what to say next, then settled on, 'He's an old friend of mine and I just need to ask him something. Would you happen to know where he is right now?'

Cillian gave her a beaming smile. 'I certainly do. Room 203.'

35

ZAC

As soon as he got to the room, Zac stripped off and went into the shower. It was one of those huge ones, with sandstone tiling and jets that came out of both the ceiling and the walls. Right now, he needed all of them and he wanted them to hit his body hard enough to distract him from everything that had happened today, both good and bad. The sadness of saying goodbye to Audrey and the reminders that brought of losing his mum. The confusion of the things he'd found among his mum's mementoes. The kindness of Alice and Val. The devastating suspicion that Larry could be his father, and the utter horror of meeting him. And then the biggest joy of all – learning that his father was the person he'd always believed him to be.

He'd thought nothing else could add to the emotional tornado that had spun right through the last twenty-four hours, but then there she was at the airport.

But she wasn't alone.

Hands against the wall, he raised his head to let the jets hit his face, then lifted the shampoo and ran it through his hair, barely aware of what he was doing, his actions on autopilot because his mind was elsewhere.

Kara. And Ollie Chiles. The first time they'd met, she'd mentioned her friend, the struggling actor. By the second time, he was a big name. But at that point she'd told Zac that she was engaged to someone else. Tonight, it was absolutely obvious that Ollie and Kara were a couple – the way they were holding hands, the way Ollie looked at her and the way he spoke about them looking forward to their trip to Hawaii. She must have split up with her fiancé and then got together with Ollie.

He didn't understand the timeline of any of this. All he did understand was that if there had been a gap between Kara's relationships, then he'd missed an opportunity to be something more than the guy she'd bumped into a couple of times at an airport.

He'd been so determined to be respectful, not to encroach on her life or her relationship by calling her or keeping in touch, that he'd let a chance to make it into something more slip through his fingers. What. An. Idiot.

Now she would never know that every single year, apart from this year, because he'd been delayed by the funeral, he'd flown in and out of Glasgow on the same date, at the same time, in the hope that he'd find her. Or that he searched every crowd in the hope that he'd see her there. He'd been ecstatic when he'd spotted her tonight, and then... crash. Burn. Over. Idiot.

He rinsed the shampoo off his hair, then switched off the jets, before grabbing a towel from the rack and drying himself off. He wrapped it around his waist and went out into the bedroom, deciding he deserved a beer from the minibar. Even that reminded him of her. He'd just closed it when there was a bang at the door. Probably his dad, up to say goodnight.

He checked in the spyhole and...

Not his dad.

The woman who'd been holding her boyfriend's hand only an hour or so ago.

What kind of fresh, fricking torture was this?

He opened the door, expecting some kind of exchange, but no, she marched straight in, not even looking in his direction until she was past him, turned back and then took in the sight in front of her.

'Aw bollocks, you're killing me,' she groaned.

'Sorry. I'll go put something on,' he offered, suddenly aware that he was half-naked.

'No,' she said, with finality. 'I'll learn to cope. I might just not look at you while I'm speaking. Right, here goes. I need to ask you a couple of things and I need you to be 100 per cent honest, because I just risked my life to be here. If you knew my sister, you'd understand.'

Still keeping her eyes averted, she was now making a beeline for the minibar.

'Okay, so I want to ask you if there's a world, any world at all, where you would think of me as more than just a woman you occasionally bump into at airports?' Question asked, she delved into the small fridge.

He had no idea what was going on right now but he was going with it, mostly because it was impossible to stop the grin that had crossed his face just because she was here.

'Do you want me to go into depth about it or is this a yes or no situation?'

Standing up, eyes now on him, she broke a square off a bar of Dairy Milk and popped it in her mouth. 'Yes or no.'

'Yes.'

Now she was the one who was grinning. 'Really?'

'Still yes or no?' he checked.

'Yes.'

'Then definitely yes.'

'Okay, before I get carried away, I need to provide more information. Would it change your answer if I told you that I only broke off my engagement three days ago?'

So he must have got the wrong idea about Ollie earlier. Huge relief. 'No.'

'Or that I lost my job on the same day?'

'No.'

'Currently without a fixed address?'

'No.'

'Have to leave tomorrow morning on the 6 a.m. flight to London to join my family on the connecting flight to Hawaii or my sister will murder me in cold blood?'

'No.'

'And if I stayed here tonight... would I need to go book a connecting room?'

'No.' That one was the easiest answer of them all.

'Zac, is this crazy? I swear I'm normally pretty sane and rational but this... You know I look for you everywhere. I've come to this airport every year, just because I hoped I'd see you and I was over the moon when I found you last year. And that's so wrong because I was engaged, and yet...' She stopped, running out of words, so he took over.

'I'm normally pretty sane and rational,' he copied her words, incredulous that they'd both been searching for each other all these years. 'But I look for you everywhere too. Every time I come through this airport, I go to every bar, every lounge, every coffee shop, hoping I'll see you too. When I found you last year, it felt like my heart stopped. Tonight, it felt like it finally started again. And I'm not a mushy guy who usually says stuff like that.'

'I'm not a mushy woman who usually likes it,' was her perfect reply.

'So Ollie and you?'

'My best friend.'

'And me?'

She stepped forward, raised her face to his, then kissed him. 'Let's start with being the guy I meet in airport hotels and see where we are by morning.'

EPILOGUE

SIX MONTHS LATER

It was a gorgeous July morning, and a small crowd was already starting to form outside the old church on Newart Street, on the South Side of Glasgow. Most of the bystanders were local residents or fans, desperate to get a glimpse of Ollie Chiles, who was holding a press conference that morning to announce what was happening with the timeworn, neglected building. The banner outside was a bit of a giveaway, right enough – The Moira Chiles Academy of Music and Drama. As far as the neighbourhood was concerned, the place hadn't even opened yet, but already it was making a difference. The crowd of lads who always hung around the end of this street drinking and getting up to no good had been given jobs working on the site, on the condition that they turned up on time every morning and put in a solid day's work. Not one of them had missed a shift yet.

Amidst the chaos of the building site inside, preparations were underway to introduce some of the key members of staff to the media that was congregating in what would have been the vestibule of the old church. Ollie and Calvin were on their third cups of coffee, as they finished preparing what they were going to announce.

'You know, every time something goes wrong with the construction, I think I could be spending my retirement on a sun lounger in Marbella… but I wouldn't swap this chaos for the world,' Calvin said. 'I mean look at me. I have dust on this Tom Ford suit, and I'm not freaking out. I'm like a different man.'

Ollie's million-dollar grin was as wide as ever. In fact, his grin had been a pretty permanent feature lately. Filming had wrapped on the latest season of *The Clansman* at the beginning of May, and he'd spent every moment since in Glasgow, working here full time with Calvin and the rest of the team, and sleeping in his own bed every night. This morning, when he'd woken up, he'd realised that he'd never been happier. Although part of that might have something to do with the woman who had been lying next to him.

As Calvin went off to greet the press, Casey Lowden came into the room, her dark hair swept back in a ponytail, no make-up on, paint stains on her dungarees. He thought he'd never seen a more gorgeous sight in his life. 'Ollie Chiles, you really need to stop looking at me like that or we'll never get any work done,' she said, slipping her arms around his neck and going up on to her tiptoes so that she could kiss him.

'That would be fine with me,' he said, grinning as his lips met hers.

This was the way it had been since they'd got together in January. He'd returned to LA from Drea's incredibly beautiful, romantic wedding and cleared out all his stuff from the home he'd shared with Sienna, into a small but stunning apartment just off Sunset Boulevard. Thankfully, Sienna had been out of town that weekend – footage on social media showed her dancing in a Vegas club with Van and an entourage of people he didn't even recognise – so there had been no awkward reunions or recriminations. In fact, they'd only spoken through lawyers since then, and their quickie divorce was already done and dusted. Her insistence on a pre-nup when they got married, and the fact that they'd never integrated their finances, meant that they both walked away with their own earnings, their own assets, and for him, a large dose of relief.

Anyway, he'd been organising his new crash pad when Casey had called him to say she was in town for meetings. They'd met at the Mondrian for drinks, and she hadn't left his side until she had to come back to shoot her next scenes on *The Clydeside*. After that, they'd made the long-distance thing work, but it had been bliss to wake up next to her every morning since he got back to Glasgow. This was his base now, and he would travel when he was working on location, but other than that, this was where he was going to be.

'Right, Ollie Chiles, put that woman down. I brought you up better than that.' As always, Moira liked to make an entrance.

'Don't worry, Moira, it was me leading him astray,' Casey joked back. Casey's relationship with his mum was like night and day compared to the one his mum had had with Sienna. The two of them had hit it off straight away and that hadn't changed as they'd got to know each other better. Casey gave him a quick peck on the lips. 'I need to go get ready for the press conference. I'll see you there.'

Calvin had amassed an awesome group of talent to spearhead the academy, but Casey was Ollie's favourite member of the board. The deal was that this was a free academy, open to the young people of Glasgow for both full-time and part-time courses and lessons. The other big acting names would run workshops, fund raise and keep the profile of the centre high, but Ollie and Calvin were the main investors.

'You know, son, I'm not sure whether I love her or you more,' his mother teased him, with a cheeky wink, before plonking herself down on the chair Calvin had vacated. 'In case I haven't said this in the last twenty-four hours, I couldn't be prouder of you, Ollie. Or more grateful to be back on dry land.'

One of the first appointments they'd made at the academy was a powerhouse singing talent, who had forty years of experience in the business. And Moira couldn't wait to pass everything she knew on to the next generation. Neither could her best mate, one of the actresses who would be volunteering to teach drama, and who was currently wafting in, kaftan trailing behind her.

'Darling, why are you sitting down?' she asked Moira. 'We have press to greet and people to charm. Let's go.' Jacinta McIntyre, ever the consummate professional, wafted right back out again, taking Moira, before pausing to greet two new arrivals in the doorway.

Kara gave both her mum and Moira quick hugs, as she passed them, feeling yet another huge wave of nostalgia at seeing the two women together again. They'd been inseparable since Moira had come home and moved into Jacinta's spare room and Kara was pretty convinced that they were out most nights living their best lives. As they definitely should. They'd even been polite and friendly to the man standing next to her.

'Ollie, Josh is here and he just wants to run through the key points of his speech.'

Ollie immediately got up to shake Josh's hand and Kara appreciated that Ollie was making an effort too. It helped that Josh had redeemed himself for the lack of judgement that had caused her to call off their wedding, by offering to run the PR for the academy free of charge. Of course, it was great profile for his company, and there were already lots of overlaps with his existing client base. He still represented the Clydeside Studio, but he had dropped Corbin Jacobs, who had last been seen doing an advert for washing up liquid, as people in the industry had strangely become reluctant to work with him. Kara tried not to relish his downfall, but it wasn't easy.

'I'll leave you two to get organised – the construction manager has a couple of questions for me about the wardrobe department.'

'Dinner later?' Josh asked her.

Kara had managed to repair her friendship with her ex-fiancé, and their working relationship too. When she got back from Hawaii, they'd both sat down and talked honestly for the first time in way too long. When all the high tension and drama had been taken out of the equation, they'd both agreed that they'd been coasting for the last couple of years of their relationship and that the blowout, while painful, had actually been a sign that it wasn't right. They'd run their course as a couple, but they'd both committed to the friends part. The fact that both their lives had got so much better since then was a definite sign that they'd done the right thing.

'Dinner sounds good. Is Issy joining us?' Issy. Josh's lovely, funny, beautiful girlfriend of the last few months.

'She is,' he replied.

'Great – see you then.' With a cheery smile, she left the two of them to talk and made her way back through the stone corridors to the area of the academy that had been designated for the wardrobe department. Here they planned to teach design and every aspect of the creation of the costumes that would be worn in acting classes and academy shows. Kara had never been more excited or felt more creative in her work. It was a long way from the everyday street wardrobe that she'd managed in her job at *The Clydeside*.

That seemed like such a long time ago, it was hard to believe it was only six months since she'd left. By the time she'd returned from a glorious week in Hawaii, her new contract was waiting for her. They'd offered her job back with a sizeable increase in salary, and a sincere apology for the incident that had occurred on Hogmanay. Abigail Dunlop had personally met with her to talk the offer through, but in the end, Kara had declined. Like everything that had happened at that time, it felt like she was being somehow nudged onto a new path. She'd decided that it was time to find a role that would inspire her to work to the very edges of her creativity, and she'd found that in the most unexpected place. While she'd been contemplating returning to *The Clydeside*, she'd taken a week-long trip to visit a friend, and while she was there, she'd heard that a new production in that city was looking for someone to head up their costume department. It was a historical spectacle to rival *Downton Abbey* and *The Gilded Age*, and it was set in eighteenth-century Dublin society.

'Have I told you how fricking gorgeous you are when you grin like that?' The Irish accent still got her every time. As did the bloke who was sitting patiently in the corner of the room, looking over the latest batch of contracts and agreements that Calvin had dumped on his lap the minute he got here. Zac Corlan was of course offering his legal advice free of charge as a favour to his girlfriend's best mate and his business partner.

Zac meant every word of what he'd just said and he still chose to believe that everything that had happened in the last six months was a result of his mum and Aunt Audrey, sitting on that cloud somewhere, rustling up a bit of divine intervention.

Kara getting the job in Dublin had been incredible, although they'd decided to take it slow and make sure that they got to know each other properly before jumping in to anything serious – a plan that had lasted about a month, before they both fessed up to being utterly in love with each other. She'd moved into his

Dublin flat and every night since then had felt like the 2nd of January. Their jaunts to Glasgow every couple of weekends were brilliant too – Kara helped with getting the academy's wardrobe department set up, he gave free legal advice, and it gave them a chance to spend time with his cousins, Jill and Hamish, and their families. Of course, they all loved her. As did…

'Right, Kara, where do you want the lights in this room?' His dad had a pencil behind his ear, a set of blueprints in his hand, and a twinkle in his eye that had been missing for the longest time after Mum died.

He'd stepped in to help Ollie and Calvin after Kara had told him they were struggling to get a top-tier project manager that could oversee the construction and deliver the academy renovation on time and in budget. Cillian had been running his own construction company for three decades, and he had a brilliant team back in Ireland, so he had been able to split his time between there and here for the last few months, working with local tradesmen to get this place into shape. As Zac watched his dad and Kara pore over the plans and mark out the locations for the lights, Zac could see he was loving every moment of the new challenge. He was also absolutely sure that his dad's new work environment wasn't the only reason that he had a renewed zest for life.

'Found you! Oh my goodness, this place is like a maze.' Alice gasped, as she came through the door. 'It feels like we've walked for miles, but I think we might have been going in circles.'

'I haven't been able to feel ma feet for the last ten minutes,' Val chirped in, and Alice wasn't surprised. These stone floors were not made for furry mules.

Alice still felt a flush of bashfulness as Cillian greeted her with a hug and a kiss in front of everyone. The first time he'd kissed her had been in the bar that night at the airport. It had just been a brief but lovely exchange, probably fuelled by the courage of a few pints on his part, and a few gin and tonics on hers, but it had been enough to spark the start of something quite wonderful. Since then, she'd come up to Glasgow on some of the weekends that he was here and gone to Dublin for weekends there too. He'd also come to Reading a few times and he'd been a big hit with Rory and Sophie, who were absolutely delighted for them. As was the woman in the mules who was now taking her turn to hug Cillian.

'All right, you big handsome devil. You know, I'd love you even if you weren't a lovely big sod, because you give my pal an excuse to visit me.'

Alice greeted Kara with a kiss, but as she turned to Zac, she spotted a change in his expression as he realised that there was a third person with them. Alice immediately stepped in with the introductions.

'Everyone, we want you to meet Sandra. She's going to be working here one day a week, helping with admin, and maybe more than that once the academy is up and running properly.'

Sandra had finally called her from the Emergency Department of Glasgow Central hospital about a month after their January meeting at Larry's house. Larry had put her there with a broken wrist and it had been one time too many. 'I can get there tonight, Sandra,' Alice had promised. It was the weekend, so she had two days off from her new job cleaning the local school. Enough time to get up to Glasgow and back if she caught the last flight that night. 'But in the meantime, I'm going to call my friend, Bernadette, that I told you about. Hang tight and don't leave until I get someone to you.'

She'd immediately called Bernadette, who, thankfully, was just about to clock on for her shift at the same hospital. Alice's next call had been to Val, and by the time Alice made it to

Glasgow that night, Sandra was out of hospital and what little belongings she had with her were in Val's spare room. Over the next few weeks, long after Alice had returned down south, they'd all supported Sandra as she'd escaped Larry for good. Alice had helped her to get work cleaning at the council offices – one of the jobs Alice had left when she'd moved to Reading. Val had given her a place to stay and someone to listen. Bernadette had given her loads of encouragement and practical support. And Alice had called her every night to make sure she knew that people were rooting for her. If anyone thought it strange that she was helping the woman who'd been her husband's mistress, Alice just reminded them that once upon a time she'd been trapped by Larry McLenn's bullshit too.

Today was the last step in Sandra's climb back to her old life. When she'd met Larry, she'd been the office manager in a busy taxi office. Now she'd be working here one day a week and hopefully that would lead to a full-time job that she'd love.

'Right, well, Sandra and I will get off to go nab good seats at the press conference,' Val announced.

'We'll come with you,' Kara piped up. 'I promised Ollie we'd sit in the front row ready to cause a diversion if any of the journalists try to go off course and ask questions about Sienna or about him and Casey.'

'I'll be two minutes,' Cillian told them all. 'Alice, why don't you wait with me a second and walk round with me after I mark up these drawings?'

'Of course,' she agreed, not giving it a second thought.

The others left while he was scribbling with his pencil on the drawings, but as soon as they were gone, he stopped what he was doing and came towards her, then wrapped his arms around her waist. It had taken a while for her to get used to physical touch again, but now she welcomed it at every stolen opportunity.

She'd been in an unhappy, cruel, loveless marriage for so long, it still stunned her that she'd found love again at this time in her life.

'So, I've been thinking,' he said between kisses. 'This long-distance stuff, well, it's not really working for me anymore.'

Wait, was he breaking up with her? Had she got this all wrong?

But no, if he was saying goodbye, his hands wouldn't be stroking her back right now.

'So what do you say we do this properly? You move to Dublin or I'll move to Reading, and I'll make whatever changes are needed at work to help that happen.'

She didn't have to think about it.

'I say yes,' she replied. 'To you, to us, to wherever we go, for as long as it takes.'

She meant every word, and as he picked her up and kissed her again. Somehow, she knew that her oldest friend, the much-missed Morag, would approve.

ABOUT THE AUTHOR

Shari Low is the #1, million-copy bestselling author of over 30 novels, including *One Day With You* and *One Moment in Time* and a collection of parenthood memories called *Because Mummy Said So*. She lives near Glasgow.

Sign up to Shari Low's mailing list for news, competitions and updates on future books.

Visit Shari's website: www.sharilow.com

Follow Shari on social media:

facebook.com/sharilowbooks
x.com/sharilow
instagram.com/sharilowbooks
bookbub.com/authors/shari-low

ALSO BY SHARI LOW

My One Month Marriage

One Day In Summer

One Summer Sunrise

The Story of Our Secrets

One Last Day of Summer

One Day With You

One Moment in Time

One Christmas Eve

One Year After You

One Long Weekend

One Midnight With You

One Day and Forever

The Carly Cooper Series

What If?

What Now?

What Next?

The Hollywood Trilogy (with Ross King)

The Rise

The Catch

The Fall

BECOME A MEMBER OF

THE SHELF CARE CLUB

The home of Boldwood's
book club reads.

Find uplifting reads,
sunny escapes, cosy romances,
family dramas and more!

Sign up to the newsletter
https://bit.ly/theshelfcareclub

Boldwood

Boldwood Books is an award-winning fiction publishing company seeking out the best stories from around the world.

Find out more at www.boldwoodbooks.com

Join our reader community for brilliant books, competitions and offers!

Follow us
@BoldwoodBooks
@TheBoldBookClub

Sign up to our weekly deals newsletter

https://bit.ly/BoldwoodBNewsletter